T0277161

THE SERPENT UNDER

Also by Bonnie MacBird

Art in the Blood
Unquiet Spirits
The Devil's Due
The Three Locks
What Child Is This?

The Serpent Under

A SHERLOCK HOLMES ADVENTURE

BONNIE MacBIRD

COLLINS
CRIME
CLUB

This book is a new and original work of fiction featuring Sherlock Holmes, Dr Watson, and other fictional characters that were first introduced to the world in 1887 by Sir Arthur Conan Doyle, all of which are now in the public domain. The characters are used by the author solely for the purpose of story-telling and not as trademarks. This book is independently authored and published and is not sponsored or endorsed by, or associated in any way with, Conan Doyle Estate Ltd. or any other party claiming trademark rights in any of the characters in the Sherlock Holmes canon.

COLLINS CRIME CLUB
An imprint of HarperCollins*Publishers*
1 London Bridge Street
London SE1 9GF

www.harpercollins.co.uk

HarperCollins*Publishers*
Macken House, 39/40 Mayor Street Upper
Dublin 1, D01 C9W8, Ireland

Published by Collins Crime Club 2025

Copyright © Bonnie MacBird 2025
All rights reserved.

Drop Cap illustrations © Mark Mázers 2025

Bonnie MacBird asserts the moral right
to be identified as the author of this work.

A catalogue record for this book is available from the British Library

Hardcover: 978-0-00-838088-5
Trade Paperback: 978-0-00-838089-2

Set in Sabon by Palimpsest Book Production Ltd, Falkirk, Stirlingshire

Printed and bound in the United States of America
24 25 26 27 28 LBC 6 5 4 3 2

For
Ryan Johnson

Contents

PART FOUR – THE SSSS-SIBLINGS

PART FIVE – TANGLED STRANDS

PART SIX – THE SERPENT'S NEST

PART SEVEN – EVEN A DRAGON

NOTE TO THE READER

English Gypsy/Romani characters appear in this story. In Holmes and Watson's time, such travellers were called 'Gypsies' and sometimes 'Rommany', though at present 'Roma' is more common. Even today, vehement disagreement on the correct nomenclature persists, and I could not discover consensus. I hope the readers of this tale will understand that 'Gypsy' used here in Watson's tale reflects the era in which he wrote, and that no slight is intended by him, or by me as I bring this historic tale to light. The reader can trust that Watson, as he always does, writes of *individuals*, not types.

Prologue

History unfurls and has always done so in twisted, meandering strands, looping and weaving and doubling back on itself. It is peace, it is war, it is plague, it is famine; it is drought, flood, earthquake, winter; and then once again it is summer.

In the tumultuous modern times during which this manuscript came to light, I took refuge in a trip back to what many imagine was a simpler era.

The late Victorian age in England conjures up images of golden, gaslit streets in which mist shrouds the details, of silk top hats and kid gloves, bright yellow opera capes and lorgnettes, lace-covered tables laden with fine china and heaped platters of chops and buttery vegetables. Perhaps we imagine elegant gentlemen recounting the adventures of the day at the fireside, over a pipe and a brandy.

Well, in some places it must have been exactly that.

For Sherlock Holmes, it was not simply a golden era. Dastardly crimes abounded in the city and beyond. In this adventure, which Watson called '*The Serpent Under*', their journey took them from Windsor Castle to some unusual and dark corners of London, plunging them into politics and physical peril while challenging the great intellect to solve more deaths in a single case than ever in his career.

Of course, we may expect the detective's path to be fraught with danger and like an undulating jungle river filled with threats from beneath the surface. Treachery loves a hiding spot. As Lady Macbeth said to her husband, '*Look like th' innocent flower, but be the serpent under it.*'

If you have read my other accounts, you will know that what follows is Watson's account verbatim – from a manuscript found in a trove bequeathed to me by a woman from the British Library. All words are his, except for certain areas of this 130-year-old manuscript in which the ink has blurred or a random tear in the paper made parts unreadable. Once again, I beg the reader's forbearance as I attempt to fill in the odd missing sentence or paragraph.

Meanwhile, may the recounting of this tale distract you from current world events, over which one has little say, as it has distracted me.

—Bonnie MacBird
London, December 2024

PART ONE

A TWIST OF FATE

'Love hath made thee a tame snake.'
—William Shakespeare

CHAPTER ONE

Heffie

ondon. March 1891 is marked in my notes as the month in which Sherlock Holmes and I encountered one of the most twisted and diabolical set of cases ever to slither across the threshold of 221B. The tangle of mysteries I call 'The Serpent Under' enmeshed Sherlock Holmes, and me along with him, in a conundrum which propelled us from some very arcane corners of the city to the glittering pinnacle of the British Empire, took more lives than any other single case of our careers, and nearly cost us our own.

It is said that every man has a weakness, every man has an Achilles heel. Equally true, no man is without enemies. Either can be our downfall, and our guard must be up at all times against a serpent which may lie beneath the surface, ready to rob us of our best intentions, our lofty aspirations, our souls. This adventure, which I am about to relate, revealed the serpent below a palace, below a family, and to a lesser but significant degree, below the Great Detective himself.

It was early one morning when it all began, as so many of our cases did, in the cosy confines of our Baker Street sitting room. A fire crackled in the hearth, lazy snowflakes drifted sideways in the grey air outside our window, and the enticing aroma of Mrs Hudson's beef and ale stew wafted its way upstairs. The March weather had been madness, warm one day and snowing the next. Today was winter once more.

Seated on the couch, Hephzibah O'Malley stared up at us through a fringe of wild blonde curls which encircled her face, giving her the look of a small lion ready to spring. This seventeen-year-old hellion known to most as 'Heffie', was a former street urchin of unusual character and intelligence. What she had just related to us had Sherlock Holmes pacing furiously in front of the windows.

'You'll do it, Mr 'olmes?' she said. 'Back me if Inspector Lestrade takes offence?'

I eyed our curious guest. After her very able assistance on one of our cases, Holmes had secured for Heffie a job with the Metropolitan Police, a position created especially for her, which got the young lady off the streets and doing work uniquely suited to her brave and inquisitive nature. She excelled at infiltrating those shadowy groups who inhabited the edges of the criminal classes, as well as some downright street villains, befriending those as needed, often helping to solve complex cases and even, at times, to prevent violence.

Under Holmes's tutelage, her repertoire and reach had expanded into a much wider range of London's denizens. At the moment, she sat alert and still, except for one foot which did a very slow twitch, left, then right. A cat's tail, as its owner waited at the mouse's hole. This was one cat it would be well to not provoke.

'It weren't my fault. 'Twas Constable O'Keefe's.' Resentment frosted her words.

Heffie was the product of unusual parentage, her late father an Irish boxer of renown and her mother a Jewish schoolteacher who fought unsuccessfully against her daughter's assimilation into the largely criminal culture which dominated their impoverished surroundings. Her death when Heffie was only nine had left the girl without a tutor.

Both parents had been the victims of bigotry but had not sat still to take it, and when her father was killed in the ring when the girl was eleven, Heffie O'Malley already possessed the courage, skills and street sense to defend herself against any and all, and the impatient intelligence to need a challenge in her own life. Her moral compass pointed at True North, and she had evolved into a formidable young lady.

I was proud of my friend's championing of her and wished her the best. But it was hard to be kind to Heffie, for she was not the sort of person who accepted friendship easily.

'Fact is,' she continued, 'I wants to take Constable O'Keefe out in the alley and show him what's right,' said she, balling up a fist. Noting Holmes's glare, she continued, 'But, of course, I ain't doing that.'

'*Will not* be doing that,' he corrected. 'And it is just as well for him.' He stopped pacing and peered down at the street below. 'Do you still *have* your position with the police, Heffie? You have not managed to alienate Lestrade, have you?'

'No, not exactly.'

'You must not embarrass him in front of his fellow police officers. It doesn't pay to appear smarter than the police, Heffie.'

I laughed. My colleague was hardly one to give advice on this topic.

'I knows well enough to give him the details in private like, so as not to make him look the fool in front of the others, Mr 'olmes,' said Heffie. ''E just wouldn't believe me!'

'What was the result, Heffie?' I asked. The young woman turned her penetrating gaze to me.

'O'Keefe let the thief get away. And on his next little job, the little rat beat the victim to a bloody pulp. I knows, because I was on the scene.'

'Did you try to stop him?' said Holmes.

'I didn't just try. I *did* stop him. Thief ended up in hospital.' She smiled. 'But 'e's in gaol now. Where 'e should be.'

'My goodness, Heffie. Were you hurt?' I asked.

'Clearly not, Watson, you see her here before us with nothing but bruised knuckles. Let the doctor have a look, Heffie, would you?

'No. It's fine. But I'm 'ere on another matter. There's a little kid who floated up in the Serpentine from the thaw we 'ad two days ago.'

'Yes, I read. Unidentified. Pauper's clothes. Why, Heffie? What of him?'

'I knows him.'

'Go on.'

'Lash Crowley.' She shrugged. 'I tol' the police. They did nuffink . . . *nothing*.' She corrected herself.

Holmes sighed. 'I'm afraid this is a very common state of affairs, Heffie. I make no excuses for them, but they are sorely overtaxed—'

'No, you don't understand. You knows him, too.'

'I don't recognize the name.'

''E were in the Irregulars. Wiggins brought 'im in. And then 'e kicked 'im out.'

'What a shame,' said I. That ragtag bunch of street urchins was one of Holmes's most treasured resources, travelling unnoticed and gathering information where few would venture.

'He must have had a reason to do so,' remarked Holmes.

'I dunno. The boy could find anything, anywhere. You need it, 'e would find it. 'E were a wonder. But 'e's dead and I thought you should know.'

I had a sudden memory of the boy. He had impressed me. I could not at that moment remember why.

'Was there a suspicious cause of death?'

'No one even looked, so far as I knows. Coppers thought 'e was a Gypsy.'

Holmes looked thoughtful. 'I suppose I should follow up. The least I can do for an Irregular, even if he was booted out. Those boys have no one, generally. Heffie, would you look into it, please?'

'S'all I wanted.' She had moved to the window and looked out. 'Uh oh. 'E's comin' to see you! Lestrade, I mean!'

7

Holmes joined her at the window. 'Lestrade!' He smiled. 'He's in a bit of a state. Are you sure you are square with him, Heffie?'

'I figure so, Mr 'olmes,' said she. 'Though he don't . . . *does not* . . . understand me much.'

'You don't need to be understood, dear girl. Only allowed to do what you do best.'

'Well, I best be going,' said the girl, standing up. The doorbell sounded. She looked about uneasily. 'The back window all right?'

Holmes hesitated only a fraction of a second then nodded.

She grinned. 'Don't want to push my luck!' And she was off, onto the landing where I heard the large window being slid open. Holmes had occasionally exited our rooms that way as well, when he did not wish to be seen.

Inspector Gregory Lestrade soon stood before us, a light dusting of snow on the shoulders of his dark wool coat. The wiry little inspector was pale with excitement.

'I've been sent to collect you, Mr Holmes. Urgently. It's important. A carriage will be arriving!' He ran to the window and peered out. 'Ah, here it comes. You'll be in for a long ride. Hurry, please!'

'Going where?' drawled Holmes, refusing to be ignited into haste without information.

'Windsor Castle, Mr Holmes. Summoned from on high, I'm told. Not me, just you and the doctor. There's been a . . . an unusual death.'

'Ah!' Holmes was instantly on his feet and reaching for his hat. Of course he was on fire. *An unusual death!* We had not had one of those in weeks. And Windsor Castle, no less.

I glanced down. I would need to change my boots.

'Never mind your shoes, Watson,' shouted my observant friend, reaching for his scarf hanging near the fire. 'Grab your warmest hat!' He called down the stairs. 'Mrs Hudson! We will miss supper, I'm afraid!' His delight was unseemly, though I will admit I shared it.

As we ran for our outer garments, I felt a twinge of regret about the stew. Perhaps she'd keep some warm for us.

CHAPTER TWO

To the Castle

ome two hours later our carriage pulled up at Windsor Castle. En route, Holmes had questioned the individual who had been sent to accompany us, a morose little man with a pockmarked nose and refined, costly garments intended to offset the effect. This was a Mr Palfrey, a private secretary at the royal residence, who would reveal little of the case except to say that a young lady of good repute had been found 'expired' in unusual circumstances. He would not elucidate any further, nor explain his exact duties.

'When was she found?' demanded Holmes.

'Dawn.'

'It is now after noon.'

'Her family had to be notified. And the coroner, and then a second coroner. And the situation . . . discussed.'

'Has the body been moved?'

The man looked out of the window. Holmes shook his head. Try as he might, he could get nothing more from the resolute Mr Palfrey. We rode in silence for a time. Holmes's knee began to bounce. I recognized frustration.

'I doubt the body has been left *in situ*,' said Holmes. 'People cannot restrain themselves from performing their own examinations at the scenes of violent crimes. Well, those who are not vomiting in the bushes. Or the spittoons.'

'Spittoons, Holmes?' My friend's humour surfaced at the oddest times.

Palfrey's face wrinkled in horror, presumably at the notion of spittoons in the royal residence.

'I jest. In any case, hubris. Well, we shall see what is left for us, won't we, Mr Palfrey?'

Mr Palfrey did not reply.

Soon we arrived at our destination, passing through a gate, up a cobbled hillside and into the main quadrangle. The inner sanctum of the Palace.

Windsor Castle was a fairytale wonder in the glitter of the new snowfall. It struck me as a child's toy in a snow globe, a place of fantasy and romance – for children, at least. I knew better, of course. It was staffed by an army of hardworking servants, toiling long hours in a strict, unbending hierarchy. Between them and their employers stood a layer of civilian positions of honour, ladies-in-waiting, Privy Council and the like, whose exact duties and privileges eluded me. Topped over this elaborate and intricate scaffolding sat the Royal Family itself.

It was to this mysterious middle rank of Palace denizens that our victim belonged. She was a companion to some

Duchess friend of Queen Victoria. Finally I learned from the kitchen staff, as we waited on a bench outside the royal kitchen along with a meat vendor and a florist, that the deceased was a Miss Jane Wandley, twenty-four, daughter of Sir James Wandley, a wealthy industrialist knighted for his charitable works for the blind.

Holmes, irritated at being asked to cool his heels, seethed on the bench beside me. I could sense an impending outburst. I struck up a conversation with the man seated on my other side. A wicker basket at his feet held a great volume of expensive, colourful blossoms, most likely imported or from greenhouses, given the weather.

'Mr Fairweather,' I said, for so he had been introduced to me. 'Can you recommend a long-lasting bouquet to a gentleman wishing to delight a lady in this unseasonable weather?'

The man looked up at me in surprise. 'Roses. Always roses.' He waved his hand dismissively at me. It was bandaged, and protruding from the edge of the dressing I noticed a large black mark on the skin.

'Sir, I am a doctor. Your hand—'

'It is nothing.'

'What happened to you?'

'Snake bite. An adder. In our poppy fields. It is fine.'

'Poppies? In this snow?' asked Holmes. I thought his attention had been elsewhere.

'South of France,' said the florist. 'No snow.'

'Really, where?' asked Holmes. 'It is an area I know well.'

'That is our trade secret, sir,' said the florist crisply.

I supposed that those supplying the Palace must be well

connected. Her Majesty enjoyed not only the fruits of many nations but would naturally be provided with only the best flowers, too.

'That can turn necrotic if you are not careful,' I said. Adders were the only venomous snakes to exist in Britain and France, and although bites were rare I had treated a couple. Typically, they were a minor injury, painful to be sure, but could then fester and cause a great deal of trouble if not tended properly. I was once consulted on such a bite too late, and death had, in fact, followed. 'I would keep an eye on it, sir,' I added.

From a large bouquet of long-stemmed chrysanthemums at his feet the florist plucked out a pink one and handed it to me.

'Er, thank you,' I said.

Holmes sprang to his feet next to me. 'Come, Watson,' said he.

At the doorway to this anteroom stood a tall, elegant man in formal attire, who introduced himself as Jonathan Henderson, the Master of the Household. The man struck me as the epitome of a career servant, former military no doubt, ramrod straight, hair sleek as glass, unctuous and autocratic all at once. Henderson seemed to look through me, then nodded to Holmes. 'This way, Mr Holmes,' he said.

In a room just outside the pantry, we were introduced to Chief Inspector Slade of the Windsor police. I had heard of Slade. He was the highest-ranking officer assigned to the Royal Family. I had never met him, although Holmes and his brother Mycroft had previous dealings with him. Slade was a tall, well-muscled man sporting a large sandy-coloured moustache groomed to perfection, and had a commanding stare that could intimidate all but perhaps my friend.

Slade, Holmes and I were ushered by Henderson into a large, cold room. There we faced a long wooden table under the bright glare of several overhead electric lights. Its proximity to the kitchen led me to believe it was a kind of cold storage pantry. Standing in attendance were two other policemen and, I assumed from their aprons and sombre faces, two coroners. One of the latter looked familiar. Jones, I remembered. He nodded respectfully to Holmes as we entered.

On the table was the covered body of a slender female, recognizable as such even under the draping of a white sheet.

'The body has been moved, then,' said Holmes bitterly. 'You have most certainly destroyed evidence!' Henderson and Inspector Slade exchanged a look.

'Mr Holmes,' intoned Slade, 'we are here by the special invitation of a great lady whose identity you may infer. It is by her grace and pleasure that the doors open to you to assist us in our investigations. There is protocol. Do you understand?'

The Queen herself had asked for Holmes!

'Hmm.' Holmes was now staring at the covered body like a racehorse eyeing the track just before the starting pistol.

'Yes, we understand,' I said.

Holmes stepped forward, but Slade held up a hand.

'Stop! You may look but not touch. You must ask for anything you wish to see or know. Mr Jones, the coroner, and his assistant will uncover the body and take your instructions. You may begin.'

Holmes looked up to face Slade and Henderson. 'Gentlemen, Mr Jones has worked with me before. I cannot examine evidence without touching, as he well knows,' said Holmes coldly. 'If you would like me to assist in this case you must allow me the freedom to conduct my investigation in the way I see fit.'

Slade did not move a muscle, but his eyelid twitched.

'It is that or nothing,' said Holmes, simply. 'My methods are my own and I often observe minute details that have eluded others.'

Another silence.

'See us out, then, would you, Mr Henderson,' said Holmes to the Master of the Household.

I was horrified. But Holmes had called the bluff. He had been asked for by Her Majesty. These people would not defy the Queen. Slade gave in and nodded to Henderson.

The room changed over like a surgical suite between operations. Within a minute, Holmes was put in charge, and the coroner and his assistant stood aside but remained at his beck and call. It did not hurt that Jones was an admirer of Holmes's. Slade and Henderson retreated a few steps from the table, where they stood motionless during the proceedings, their eyes riveted on Holmes's every move.

Slowly he withdrew the sheet.

Holmes inhaled sharply and my eyes watered instantly in reaction to the sight. We had both seen many a shocking death, but what lay before us was the stuff of nightmares. It was the body of a beautiful young woman. Yet . . . strangely altered.

CHAPTER THREE

The Body

 should say *once* beautiful. The poor creature, a young woman under twenty-five, had been mutilated in a most terrifying and unusual way.

A tattoo of particularly intricate and stunning design had been carefully inked across the delicate planes of her lovely features. It depicted the writhing bodies of two snakes, one blue and gold, the other red and green, with scales inked in detailed and delicate black tracery. They seemed to emerge from under the hairline at the top of her forehead, curving down over her eyes and cheeks, encircling them then crossing over the mouth and disappearing back into her hairline at the temples.

The execution and design were masterful – dare I say even beautiful in a ghastly way. Whoever had done this work was a virtuoso of his art.

Holmes stood frozen at the sight, as did we all. Even those in the room who had already seen the girl's face were cowed in the presence of its terrible effect. As we stood, unmoving in the silence, I could hear water running in the next room and the crunch of horses' hooves in the snow outside the window.

The work had been recently executed. The skin around the tattoos was red and shiny, more so on the left side of the face, which was slightly swollen, and several drops of dried blood were in evidence.

'This will have taken some time, Holmes. Days, I would imagine,' I said. Had this young woman been conscious through this ordeal? It would have been excruciating.

'She was missing for four days,' said Slade.

'Her name, again? Occupation here?'

'Jane Wandley. Companion to the Duchess of Ormond.'

'Married?'

'No.'

Holmes nodded, frowning in thought. 'Has this been photographed?' he asked.

This. Not *she* or *Miss Wandley*. Holmes often objectified the victims in the first moments of his investigation. His scientific mind was processing the evidence. The practical details. The how, the what. The who and why would come later.

'Yes.'

'I will need copies of these photographs before I leave. The artist is a rare one and I will find him.'

'Copies are being prepared for you.'

Of course, the Palace would have its own darkroom. It was a veritable city state, I had been told.

17

'Something is missing here. Where are the heads of the snakes?' said Holmes.

The coroner shrugged. 'They left those out, I suppose. We looked.'

'Help me lift her head,' said Holmes. 'I want to see the back of her neck.'

'They are not there.'

Nevertheless, one of the coroners stepped in and helped lift up the corpse's head, as Holmes peered under it and along the neck on both sides. Nothing.

'Fine then,' said Holmes as the man set her head down gently. 'The hair. Is this as you found it?'

The poor victim's voluminous auburn hair was arranged in an elaborate chignon, piled atop her head in the style favoured by so many young ladies of my acquaintance, with a few stray curls framing the face. They now lay limp and flattened.

'Well, yes,' said Slade. 'We had no reason to – *stop that!*'

But Holmes had raised the beautiful but disfigured head himself and was loosening the pins that held her hair in place. 'It is necessary. Help me, Watson.'

I approached that end of the table and helped support her head. As the hair tumbled down we were shocked at what we found. A six-inch circle at the crown of her head had been shaved and there, tattooed in the same exquisite detail as on her face, were the heads of the two brightly coloured snakes, the bodies intertwined one last time, and *with the tail of each snake being swallowed by its own head.*

'My God!' I exclaimed. 'What on earth . . . ?'

'It is an ouroboros,' said Holmes. 'Two, in fact.'

'What is an oro . . . whatever you said?' asked Slade.

'A snake consuming itself. An ancient alchemical symbol. It stands for "infinity". As in mathematics.' Holmes frowned. 'And there are other meanings as well.'

'But why . . . ?' I wondered.

'That is only one of many mysteries here, Watson. I have made a study of tattoos. While the rendering of the scales and the colours are Japanese, the symbol is universal.' That he was an expert on tattoos should have come as no surprise, I suppose. That a technical response would be his first was equally typical.

I gently laid the poor girl's head back on the table.

'Watson, let us confirm the cause of death. Start at her feet.'

'She committed suicide,' said Slade. 'The girl slashed her wrists.'

Holmes leaned in with his magnifying glass to look at the beautiful, ruined face. 'Watson! Look at her left temple. Is that a bruise I see?'

I took the glass and looked. Indeed there was a dark bruise, very difficult to see because of the inking around and over it.

'It is. A blow to the head,' I said.

'Could it be the cause of death?'

'Technically yes,' I said. 'Or might at least have rendered her unconscious.'

'Carry on, Watson. Examine her closely . . . look for signs of struggling, more bruising, injection points, restraints, or what you will.'

I nodded and got to work. I took out my own magnifying glass and began to inspect the body quite closely, starting with her feet, looking for anything that would tell us more of the story.

'We examined her thoroughly,' said the coroner.

'Except for her head,' said Holmes.

'Well, only missing that. She slit her own wrists, as I said,' Slade remarked. 'I might have done so, myself, discovering that all over my face!'

'Where, then, is all the blood?' Holmes could not keep the sarcasm from his voice.

No reply.

'Where was the body found?' asked Holmes.

'In her private bath, this morning, by the maid,' said Henderson.

I presumed the Master of the Household had his eye on all.

'More detail please,' said Holmes.

'She was fully clothed but submerged to the neck in her own bathtub. The, er, water was . . . was all red . . .'

'She bled out in the bath, then,' I said.

'Obviously, Watson.' This from Holmes.

'Yes. The maid fainted.'

'So you removed the body, removed her clothing, cleaned her and brought her here?' said Holmes.

The coroner and the Master of the Household both nodded.

'And in so doing you destroyed valuable evidence.'

Henderson was aghast. 'Well, we could not just leave her there. That bath is shared with three other ladies, and—'

Holmes hissed in frustration. 'What was she wearing?'

'We have disposed of the clothing—'

Holmes grimaced.

'But it was identified as the same dress she was wearing when she vanished a few days ago,' said Henderson. 'Are you finished here?'

'You are sure it was the same dress?' asked Holmes.

The Master of the Household was not used to being challenged. 'The friend who shares rooms with her identified it,' he said, ice in his voice.

'Get her for me. And I'll need to speak with the girl's family. You have no doubt called them. Watson, what do you see?'

Henderson paused, then departed in a cold fury.

Chief Inspector Slade stepped closer to Holmes. 'Mr Holmes, you have much to learn of protocol in the royal residence.'

Holmes looked up at him dreamily. 'Have I? Do you suppose Her Majesty has called me in because of my manners? No, I rather think Her Majesty would like a solution to a murder which took place here. Carry on, Watson.'

I turned my attention to the girl's feet, looking for traces of needle marks between the toes. There were none. The ankles bore faint traces of binding. I indicated this to Holmes. He shook his head ruefully.

'We have not seen all, I am sure. What then? How and why was the body disrobed and moved here to the pantry?' asked Holmes.

Slade informed us that the Palace doctor had been summoned, confirmed death by exsanguination, and a cursory examination was done in place. It was he who had ordered the clothes removed and the body cleaned. She was then transported to the room in which we now stood, and examined fully by the coroner, Jones, in the presence of Henderson and Slade.

I could sense Holmes's mounting fury. Much evidence would have been lost by these actions.

'Watson, the wrists?'

'Look,' said I, raising her arm to display the inner right wrist. A deep slash crossed it, clearly severing the radial artery.

'Poor thing,' said Inspector Slade. 'Must have caught a look at herself in the glass and then took her own life in despair.'

Holmes stared at the man incredulously. 'You think she noticed her tattoos, then filled the bath, stepped into it fully clothed, and did the deed?'

I raised up the left arm. 'And the left, Holmes. Look.'

Holmes stepped closer and picked up each wrist in turn, examining it with his pocket magnifier. 'So I see.' He put down the second wrist and confronted the inspector. '*Not* self-inflicted. This was no suicide.'

'Agreed,' said I.

'How do you read that?' said the policeman.

'The slash is *in the same direction on both wrists*,' said Holmes.

'Also,' I added, 'the radial artery has been cut. On both. It is deliberate – note the depth of the incision.'

'Incision? You make it sound like a surgical procedure.'

'Very much so,' I said. 'It is actually difficult to commit suicide in this way. Most veins and arteries in the wrist are fairly superficial and will not suffice. Except this one.'

I held up the delicate arm again.

'Whoever cut these wrists knew exactly what they were doing. She would have died of exsanguination in less than ten minutes,' I added. What a terrifying ten minutes. I briefly wondered if perhaps she might have done the one wrist, then been helped along with the other.

Holmes took out his pocket magnifier and inspected the wounds more closely. 'It appears to be the same type of blade. Watson, do you concur?'

I looked closer and agreed. That confirmed murder.

'One question is the precise time of death,' said Holmes. 'Clearly her head was not submerged?'

'No.'

'When she was brought here, was any further bleeding noted?'

'None,' said the coroner.

Holmes stood silent. No one made a move.

'Take me to this room with the bath.'

'It has been cleaned,' said the Master of the Household, who had returned to the room.

'Why?' exclaimed Holmes in disgust. 'You hamper me exceedingly!'

'We wished to avoid panic. Word spreads quickly in the Palace.'

'Ridiculous. Everyone knows already,' said Holmes.

Jones, the coroner, nodded almost imperceptibly. Of course they did.

The two guards posted at the door exchanged quick looks of embarrassment, further confirming Holmes's theory.

At last Holmes straightened and nodded for me to cover the body. I did so, as he stood back from the table, thinking.

He did not move for over a minute. It was as though the Difference Engine, that steam-driven computational wonder invented by Charles Babbage, was at work inside his head. If the human brain were not made of gelatinous and mysterious stuff, I was sure that I would have heard the faint hissing and clanks of wheels and gears spinning at utmost capacity.

At last he turned to Chief Inspector Slade. 'All right,' said he, 'I am ready to hear the rest. And then I shall inspect the bath.'

CHAPTER FOUR

The Palace Investigation

he 'rest' was little enough. We spent the next three hours learning of the timeline and further details of the gruesome discovery and interviewing Palace staff.

Miss Wandley's body had been discovered just before dawn, and while Palace security and the Metropolitan Police initiated their preliminary investigation, so destroying critical evidence, word came down from the Queen herself that she wished them to call in Sherlock Holmes.

Before this could happen, family members were notified. The father of the deceased, Sir James Wandley, had been summoned. But Wandley instead sent his man, a Peter Oliver, who was visibly saddened by the sight of the girl and left once he confirmed the identification. Both her siblings were called and further confirmed the identity of the body, her brother Clarence fainting in the process.

Arriving only moments after these was poor Jane Wandley's betrothed, Count Charles Harold Augustus Friedrich. This gentleman arrived and was violently sick upon seeing his dear lady's face and could not depart the Palace soon enough, it was reported.

The account of these reactions piqued Holmes's curiosity, and he declared his intention to interview both the family and the fiancé in all haste.

'Much appreciated, Mr Holmes,' said Slade. Now that murder *under the Palace roof* was in the picture, the policeman seemed eager to hand the reins to my friend.

He nodded towards Henderson, who said, 'A royal carriage will be provided for your conveyance. It is yours for the day and through the night, if needed. We will assist your investigation in any way possible.'

'Excellent. Have it at the ready. But first I must interview several people here at the Palace.' After a brief consultation with Henderson, Holmes had produced a shortlist.

Ten minutes later, Lady Elizabeth Barnstable, twenty-two, arranged her silk skirts daintily as she sat perched on the edge of a chair in the tiny sitting room of the small Palace apartment she had shared with poor Jane Wandley. Her eyes were red from crying, and as she related the following to us, the tears continued to flow.

'Simply one of the sweetest women at the Palace,' she said. 'Jane . . . er, Miss Wandley, was a true friend to me, and to many. That this happened to her, of all people—'

'A friend to many, you say? Would this be a universal appraisal? She had no enemies?' asked Holmes.

'None of whom I was aware. Jane was popular,' said

Lady Elizabeth. 'She recently helped patch up a squabble between two ladies-in-waiting. It was a misunderstanding, and now all three are – were – good friends. That was typical of Jane.'

'What of jealousy?'

'I would say not, sir. To be blunt, Jane was not high up in the hierarchy here. The Duchess of Ormond, to whom she was attached, was once a close confidante of Her Majesty but has grown cantankerous and something of a problem. Jane was hired to soothe the savage beast, so to speak, and to distract the Duchess from her some-what destructive inclinations. It took a great deal to manage this difficult lady, and several before her had failed. Jane, however, managed admirably. No one envied Jane's position, not for a moment.'

Holmes nodded. He next made a careful assessment of poor Jane Wandley's bedroom and private sitting area, finding nothing of note, then asked to see the adjacent bath, where the body had been discovered.

There, the latest in indoor plumbing had been luxuriously supplied, even for companions and ladies-in-waiting, and a full-size cast-iron tub with gleaming brass fittings filled the space. Holmes bent down to inspect it.

'It has been scoured!' he exclaimed in disgust. He then proceeded to spend the next ten minutes circulating through the small, tiled room, magnifying glass in hand, examin-ing the walls, the corners, the towel racks and the floor, like some giant spider weaving a web through the space.

'As I feared,' he said, pocketing his lens. 'We will learn no more here. It is likely she was unconscious when brought here, and the body then placed in the bathtub where the murderer, perhaps thwarted in some larger plan, slit her wrists and left her to her fate. There are no signs of a struggle, nor droplets of blood anywhere in the room.'

'But thoroughly cleaned,' I reminded him. 'As was the bathtub.'

'Do you doubt me? Traces would remain and I would have seen them!'

'Of course, Holmes. But . . . this is diabolical. She was brought here . . . and placed in this bath? It all seems so odd.'

'Your talent at understatement can always be relied upon. You noticed the faint marks of bindings on both ankles. My initial thought was they were from a restraint during her torture, but they would have been deeper, and she would have had other marks on the body if so. There were none. Likely this was to ease transporting her. I think her wrists were cut here, without a struggle. There must have been a great deal of blood.'

'Hence the blood we found under her fingernails.'

'Yes. He was remarkably cold-blooded about all of this.'

'For it must be a he?'

'Unknown, although statistically it is likely. This clearly was an extremely personal crime. The villain, whoever he was, wanted her found here at the Palace.'

'Why, I wonder?'

'Undoubtedly for maximum effect. Publicity. Shame in front of those whom she no doubt wished to impress. Perhaps even a kind of retribution for having taken this position.'

'Or jealousy? Perhaps Lady Elizabeth was wrong.'

'The motive is unclear, many are possible. And now to the "savage beast".'

After being made to wait some twenty minutes to interview this character, we found ourselves in the sitting room of the elderly Duchess of Ormond, Georgina de la Tour. Lamp-post thin and clad in expensive layers of a bilious yellow-green, this spectral creature raised an elaborate lorgnette which sparkled with jewels and peered at Holmes and me with a malevolent eye. She waved us to take a seat.

'Not there!' she barked, as I started to sit on a green velvet chair. Holmes had taken the only other seat, so I stood awkwardly throughout the following.

The Duchess turned her attention to my friend.

'I have heard of you,' she said. 'You are famous. You see *things*.'

Holmes smiled, and it seemed most genuine. 'Your Grace, I am delighted to make your acquaintance. You are, I believe, the patron of one of the finest art galleries in London.'

How he knew this was a mystery.

She did not seem to melt but leaned back in her chair and lowered her lorgnette. Her face twisted slightly in what perhaps was a smile. 'Jane. You wish to hear of Jane,' said she in a voice which quavered most irritably.

'I am deeply sorry for your loss,' said Holmes. 'I hope to solve the mystery surrounding her death.'

The Duchess sniffed. 'Jane was the best friend a woman like myself could have, Mr Holmes. Some call me "difficult". You would be so yourself had you led the life I have had.' She dabbed at a rheumy eye with a lace handkerchief.

'I am sure that is so, ma'am,' said Holmes without a trace of sarcasm. 'In what way was Miss Wandley helpful to you?'

'Patience. She put up with my, shall we say, wants and needs.'

'Like a servant, then?'

'Not at all. I have several servants. No, Jane was more of a friend, really. A professional friend, as she was assigned to me in the wake of . . .' The old woman turned to stare out of the window.

'In the wake of what, ma'am?' asked Holmes. He smiled at her and I wondered at his ability to turn on the charm in the face of such a disagreeable woman.

'In the wake of the departure of two predecessors. I do not take kindly to being managed, you see.'

'No one does,' said Holmes with a smile.

'And yet I do need it. My patience is not what it once was. You! Don't tread on those draperies!' Her voice cut like a knife.

I backed away from the window, to where I had gravitated. 'Sorry, ma'am.'

She turned back to Holmes. 'Miss Wandley was a kind young woman, and she "handled" me, as the Palace likes to say, with humour and the art of gentle distraction,' said the Duchess. 'I shall not see her like again, I am afraid. What a terrible, terrible loss. Now leave me, please, you two. It is time for my nap.'

Over the next two hours, Holmes spoke to one Palace denizen after another, the indelible picture of an extremely well-liked young lady emerged. Even under probing questions and careful observation Holmes could find no strong evidence – not even a hint – that this heinous crime originated within the castle walls.

By the time we left Windsor, he and I were convinced that despite the cauldron of intrigue that is any royal enclave, the perpetrator of Miss Jane Wandley's crime was much more likely to have come from the outside world.

But why, Holmes wondered, would her body have been transferred to the Palace? Was it a message? And if so, designed for whom?

CHAPTER FIVE

The Family Seat

he family seat of Sir James Wandley and the late Lady Wandley was north-east of Windsor Castle, a two-hour drive over rustic roads. We departed a little after four from Windsor and proceeded there in haste. A Palace carriage and four fast horses were provided once again, and I was grateful for the cushioned ride. We soon found ourselves rolling up a winding driveway, past poplar trees with persistent snow lingering in pale blueish mounds beneath them. This led to a stone courtyard and the entrance to a grand edifice, designed to emulate a medieval castle with towers and ramparts. This was, no doubt, some wealthy nobleman's conceit of the last century.

Inside, a butler escorted us into a large parlour. Masculine in decor, the room featured hunting trophies along one stone wall, low bookcases filled with richly bound books, their gilt decorations glimmering in the firelight cast from an enormous fireplace flanked by marble caryatids, whose sombre faces contradicted their elegant, draped forms. A table with glittering crystal glasses and decanters of port, whisky and wines sat in one corner.

I wondered about Jane Wandley's father. He had received word of his daughter's death early that morning, along with a description of her condition. Yet Sir James had refused to travel to Windsor but had instead sent someone in his place, a man named Peter Oliver. This deputy had represented the family and formally confirmed the identity of Jane Wandley's body.

That curious fact had propelled Holmes here. He had insisted on this interview and that it take place at once.

We stood for a minute or two, alone in the room. In one corner a longcase clock ticked loudly. Holmes moved to a table near the window, where he boldly inspected a collection of small daguerreotypes in ornate silver frames, all tarnished.

I joined him and peered over his shoulder. Prominent among them was a portrait of a proud woman of perhaps thirty-five, handsome in an intimidating way. Her expression was softened by a faint smile, Mona Lisa-like in its ambiguity.

'The late mother,' said Holmes. 'Honora Wandley.'

'What do we know of her?' I wondered.

'Nothing,' said he.

'A wonderful woman,' said a voice behind us. 'Much missed.'

We turned to see that a handsome, fair-haired young man of our own age, early thirties perhaps, had entered the room. He had a thick shock of curly blond hair rising in profusion from his forehead and curling unfashionably around his ears. 'You must be Mr Sherlock Holmes. My name is Peter Oliver.' He smiled warmly at us and approached, extending his hand. His movements were graceful, and he was clothed in an expensive but worn Norfolk jacket, soft moleskin trousers and old but good quality riding boots, polished to a sheen. Country wealth. I wondered at his role here. Perhaps a cousin.

He turned to me. 'And you are?'

'Dr John Watson. My colleague in my investigations,' said Holmes. 'We are here to speak to Sir James in the matter of his daughter's death.'

'The Palace sent word you were coming. I am afraid that Sir James is indisposed. This news has hit him very hard, as you might imagine.'

'He did not travel to the Palace this morning,' said Holmes. 'I am told he sent you instead. Why?'

Oliver looked away in discomfort. 'He had been told of her . . . her state. And he simply could not . . . could not bring himself to see Jane like that.'

'He is of a delicate constitution, then?' asked Holmes. 'I would speak with him anyway.'

'He and his daughter are . . . were very close. But he took a strong sedative only an hour ago. He will be unapproachable until the morning at the very earliest. In the meantime, I may be able to answer many of your questions.'

'Even with word of our imminent arrival, he took a sedative?' asked Holmes.

'I could not dissuade him, sir. But I doubt he would have been able to be of help. The poor man was not himself. Allow me to be of assistance, if I may. Can I offer you a refreshment?'

'No, thank you. Are you a member of the family, Mr Oliver?' asked Holmes.

'Not precisely. But intimately familiar. I shall explain. Do sit down, gentlemen.'

He indicated a group of chairs near the fireplace. Holmes ignored him and took a seat somewhat apart, with its back to the window, rendering him in silhouette. I joined him there.

Peter Oliver stood facing us, a curious smile frozen on his handsome face.

'What is your "intimately familiar" role here, Mr Oliver?' asked Holmes.

'Forgive me! I have been unnecessarily mysterious.' Oliver smiled and moved towards the drinks table. 'Some call me Sir James's factotum. "Estate manager" might be more accurate, perhaps. I joined the staff here right out of Cambridge, some thirteen years ago, and I now run the businesses connected with the estate. And, since Jane's departure, I run the household as well.'

Jane. Not *Miss Wandley*. He referred to the dead girl rather informally, I thought.

'And what are the businesses, precisely?' asked Holmes.

'Sherry? Port? Are you quite sure you would not like a refreshment? Sir James keeps only the best.'

'This is not a social call,' said Holmes coldly.

Oliver smiled good naturedly. 'Yes, of course. I am just trying to make the best of a very dark moment. Here, let me join you.'

35

Oliver pulled up a chair to sit closer to us. The last of the sun slanted in, highlighting his handsome, chiselled features in a distinct chiaroscuro.

'We have several businesses, Mr Holmes. My employer owns a factory that produces aniline fabric dyes of the latest hues. I began here as chief chemist and have been responsible for certain innovations. We also run a foundry that services several nearby villages. And third, more of a hobby really, we make a remarkable elderflower cordial.'

'Why so many businesses?' asked Holmes. 'Sir James, I am told, inherited a vast fortune.'

'No man wishes to be bored.'

'I see. Tell us of Jane, then, if you would, Mr Oliver,' said Holmes. 'She is, or was, twenty-four, correct?'

'Yes. Jane was the eldest of three children, and her father's favourite.' Oliver's face softened as he described her. 'A singularly beautiful girl, she also is . . . was – how do I put this? – the eye in the centre of the storm. Her siblings were of a more excitable temperament. And when her mother died suddenly, Jane stepped in—'

'Died suddenly?' interrupted Holmes. 'How and when?'

'Long ago. I don't see how that is relevant,' said Oliver.

'I will determine that. Please answer the question.'

'Lady Wandley died of a heart attack some twelve years ago.'

'Miss Jane would have been twelve. And you had recently joined the staff? Quite young yourself, then?'

'Yes. I took my degree at nineteen and upon the recommendation of my professors I obtained a post in Sir James's factory post-haste. I am something of an expert in the field of chemistry, you see. My particular knowledge of benzene derivatives—'

'We will come back to you, Mr Oliver. Lady Wandley's death. Details, please,' said Holmes.

'It was quite sudden. She was but thirty-five and in apparent good health.'

Holmes nodded at me.

'She kept in good form?' I asked. 'No congenital illness? Weakness of the lungs? Brain fever? Recent cough?'

'No indications of ill health whatsoever,' replied Oliver. 'Although I was not living in the main house at the time. Her death came as a deep shock to the family.'

Holmes stood and began to pace. 'Did anything precipitate this heart attack? Some tragedy or conflict of some sort?'

'No. On the contrary, she was in a celebratory mood.'

'Why?' asked Holmes.

'Lady Wandley was delighted that some trespassers had finally vacated the north fields where they had been camping – to her extreme irritation.'

Holmes paused in his pacing. 'Trespassers?'

'Some Gypsies. They had been seen in the countryside round here every spring for many years. This land is apparently on some kind of route of theirs. That particular winter they had camped at the far end of our north fields.'

'Camped. Do you mean a caravan? Wagons? Visible from the house?'

'Yes, wagons, but not visible. A bit remote, in fact.'

'Interrupting the planting, perhaps?'

'Those fields were unused.'

'What was the issue, then?'

'Lady Wandley was superstitious. She felt Gypsies were a dark omen. And a possible danger to the family and employees. Or, if not a danger, then perhaps a bad influence.'

'You were there. Did you agree?'

Oliver smiled. 'I was a lowly new man then, barely twenty. It was not my place to voice an opinion.'

'And yet you seem singularly observant about the household.'

'I was friends with the cook. Certain benefits in that.' He smiled, patting his abdomen. It was flat as a board. He was clearly quite fit. 'I did not personally sense any danger from them.'

'Can you tell me more of Lady Wandley's death and its effect on the family?' said Holmes, adopting a gentler tone.

'It had deep reverberations. Perhaps this is why Jane's sudden death has so affected his Lordship. After his wife's passing, Sir James began to lean on his eldest daughter to run the household.'

'A twelve-year-old?'

Oliver seemed to struggle with his grief and briefly closed his eyes. 'I . . . ah . . . sorry. Jane is, or rather was, an unusual girl. As brilliant as she was pretty. Very advanced for her age. Even as a child she began helping her father at once with planning the meals and overseeing the laundress with her father's very particular clothing needs. Within a year, Jane was quite literally managing the household. And, I dare say, more efficiently than her mother had done!'

'What particular clothing needs?' asked Holmes.

'Oh, trivial really. Something about how he liked his collars and cuffs pressed.'

'And you, over time, became more involved with running the house?' Holmes had picked up a photo once again from the nearby table and indicated the tarnished frame. Oliver smiled thinly. 'What of Jane's siblings?'

'Two, both younger. Jane took over their care.' Oliver paused. 'I hate to disparage family members, but to be honest there was little love lost between Jane and the other two.'

'Few children like to be managed by a sibling,' said Holmes crisply.

Mycroft Holmes floated into my mind.

'Their names and ages?' asked Holmes, withdrawing a small notebook and a silver pen from his pocket.

'Kate, two years younger, and Clarence, three years younger.'

'Ten and nine, then, at the time of their mother's death. That would make them twenty-two and twenty-one. And where are these siblings, now?'

'Both are in London.'

'Doing what?'

Oliver shrugged. 'Living independent lives. Once Jane took her position at the Palace, Sir James had hoped that her sister would step in to run the household, but Kate, er, the younger Miss Wandley, would have nothing of it. She was not of the same temperament, to be sure. A headstrong young lady. Sir James might have made a mistake in sending her to Girton College earlier, as she wanted, as this perhaps indulgent exposure to higher education has produced a radical. Kate currently lives in London where she is active with some questionable woman in some kind of political movement.'

I thought I detected the smallest of smiles from Holmes. 'What "questionable woman"?'

'Lady something-or-other . . . Ferndale, I believe. Yes, Emily Ferndale. Activist, rabble rouser. Upset her father to hear of it.'

'And the brother?'

'Clarence is a great disappointment to Sir James. He is an . . . an artist.'

'Amateur? Professional?'

'Oh, he is employed. Successful, in fact. He designs for the Christie Atelier.'

'That is a renowned design firm,' said Holmes. 'Highly respected, and in fact rival to the William Morris company, if I remember correctly. Why should this be a disappointment to his father?'

'Sir James is a remarkable businessman, who has turned his factories and scientific research into extremely profitable entities, at the same time benefiting the surrounding countryside. His charitable endeavours include a school for the blind, a university and a hospital.' Oliver stood and approached Holmes. He politely took the photograph from my friend's hand and replaced it back on the table. 'He is much respected here and had rather hoped Clarence would follow in his footsteps. He views Clarence's art as . . . frivolous.'

'I see. I sense disapproval from yourself as well, Mr Oliver.'

'You misread me, sir. I am neutral on the subject.'

I doubted that Holmes had misread anything.

'What interaction, if any, do you have with the Wandley offspring?'

Oliver sighed. 'Sir James underwrites his children's living expenses. While he does not approve of their lifestyles, either one of them, he supports them generously with monthly stipends.'

'Contingent upon anything?'

'No.' Even I detected some emotion under this answer.

'Very kind of him. Keeping up appearances, then. Again, your role in this?' Holmes asked.

'I travel to London monthly to deliver their stipends by hand. Sir James does not trust the banks. But a secondary purpose, of course, is to check on their well-being and to report back. Although his Lordship may not approve of his children's lives, he supports them in style and cares that they are thriving. He is a generous man.'

'And *are* Kate and Clarence thriving?'

'In a manner of speaking.'

'More details, if you would.'

'Both are healthy. Comfortable. They have . . . friends. Occupations. They do not seem to miss living here.'

'Let us return to the relationship of Jane to her siblings,' said Holmes, picking up a framed photograph. 'These are the three in question, I presume. Was this recently taken?' He handed the framed image to me. There were three good-looking young people in their early twenties. In the centre, I recognized the late Jane Wandley – tall, proud, and elegantly attired. She had been a striking beauty before her disfigurement. Jane was flanked by a shorter, younger woman, dark-haired and also quite pretty, carelessly yet fashionably dressed, and a slender young man, who resembled the younger sister, and who had adopted a self-consciously 'poetic' look in a cape and jaunty hat. Both of the younger siblings stared sulkily at the camera, with Jane's serene smile a stark contrast.

'Yes. This was taken a few months ago,' said Oliver.

'At the front of the house, I see. Did they gather here often?'

'No. It was the occasion of their father's birthday. Frankly, it was difficult to get them to assemble at all.'

'Tell me more of the siblings' relationships, please,' said Holmes.

Oliver hesitated. 'Well, I . . .'

'Or perhaps I should query Sir James closely on the matter?'

'The two younger siblings never got on with their elder sister. As I said, Jane took on maternal responsibilities quite young. She was perhaps a bit bossy.'

'That is understandable. Jane was made to shoulder a heavy load at a very early age,' I said.

Holmes set down the photograph and returned to his chair. 'Tell me more, Mr Oliver.'

'The two younger ones made it their mission to under-mine and harass her. They played pranks. Continuously. Most annoying.'

'What kind of pranks?'

'Oh!' Oliver seemed surprised at the question. 'Let's see . . . Poured salt into the stew. Put a frog in her bed. They splattered India ink on her favourite day dress.'

'Trivial, yes, and yet cruel,' remarked Holmes. 'Any others you can recall?'

Oliver shifted uncomfortably. 'Well, they hid the recipe box their mother had lovingly compiled from her own childhood in France. I found it, later. Most of the recipes were missing. Family treasures, as the mother was quite the epicurean. The mother, and later Jane, had been training the cook to replicate these, and Jane personally treasured that box.'

Holmes continued to stare. Oliver hesitated. Holmes had noticed something. 'I think you have not told me the worst,' said he.

'They, er, kidnapped her much-loved cat. I don't know what became of it.'

'Don't you?' said Holmes.

Oliver did not reply. The silence lay heavily. This last was far beyond a childish prank, I thought. The poor girl. Her short life had been an unhappy one, first at her childhood home, and then . . .

'I take it that when Jane was offered the position of an official companion at the Palace, she was happy to escape?' said Holmes.

Oliver nodded. 'Yes. It is complicated. At nineteen, Jane begged for a formal education and her father indulged her by sending her briefly to Newnham, but it was not a match, and she returned to run the house after only a month. This was just as well, as it had been a disaster under her younger sister. Kate then demanded an education and was sent off to Girton. She thrived there, but it was a mistake, I fear. It put strange ideas into her head.'

Holmes smiled.

'Two years ago, Jane was invited to the Palace as a companion to the Duchess of Ormond. It was a great loss to her father. To us all. Everyone had hoped she might return one day. But no one would ever have predicted that she . . . that this . . . would . . .' He struggled to hold back tears.

'And when Jane left, who took her place here?'

'Kate was called home from Girton, but it did not work out. I, er, stepped in to help.'

'Elaborate please.'

'I attempted to assist her in organizing, but she simply had no interest in running the estate and convinced her father to set her up in London as an independent woman.'

'Doing what?'

'I don't know. I think she intended to write.'

'I understand you were sent to identify Miss Wandley's body on behalf of the family early this morning?' asked Holmes rather abruptly.

Oliver's composure crumbled. 'Yes, at Sir James's request. Those . . . those tattoos. How could anyone . . . ? The horror. It is no wonder that Jane took her life.' Tears were visible, as he put a hand to his face.

'She did not,' said Holmes simply.

'But they told me—'

'They were mistaken.'

'Do you mean, in addition to the . . . the snakes, someone . . . ?' Once more Oliver's voice failed him.

'Yes.'

A sob escaped the young man and he covered his face. I was on the verge of offering comfort, but Holmes stopped me with a sharp look.

Oliver regained his voice. 'Forgive me. Would you care to stay the night? Perhaps you may talk to Sir James in the morning. I can have rooms prepared for you.'

Holmes stood, seemingly unaffected by Oliver's distress. 'I think not, but thank you. We shall be off to see Count Friedrich, her betrothed. I understand his estate is not far from here?'

I noted a flicker of distaste from Oliver, gone in an instant. 'The Count Charles Harold Augustus Friedrich lives about thirty minutes due north, via the very fast carriage you came in. But it is now after dark. And without a Palace introduction, he will not see you, I fear. He is a terrible snob.'

'They will have sent word, as they did to your employer. He will see us; I will ensure it. Did Miss Wandley meet her fiancé before or after she moved into the Palace?'

'Right after. They met at a ball.'

'Hmm. What of any previous suitors? She was not courted while living here, then? Such an attractive young woman?'

'Sadly, no. Her father kept her far too busy for her to have any kind of social life.'

'Fine. Thank you. If you would have your man summon our carriage, please.'

Oliver rose and rang for a servant.

At the door, Holmes hesitated. 'One more thing, Mr Oliver. What was your relationship with the late Miss Wandley?'

'Always cordial. I respected her but kept my professional distance.'

'And yet . . . her competence must have impressed you, not to mention her beauty.'

'I would have been blind not to notice, Mr Holmes, but I value my position and work too much have allowed any impropriety to sully either her or my own reputation. Or to interfere with the functioning of this estate.'

'I see. Write out directions to Friedrich's estate for our driver, if you would.'

Our precipitous leave-taking had me puzzled. I wondered why Holmes did not wish to stay to talk to the father. But he kept his plans to himself and, as we waited on the front steps, he denied my request to stop at a pub for some supper. A footman overheard this interchange and we were kindly supplied with sandwiches and fruit from the kitchen.

We soon departed in a clatter of hooves on cobblestones into the moonlit night.

'Not a bad chap, that Oliver,' I said as we charged through the iron gates at great speed and approached the main road. I unwrapped a sandwich. While I had taken refreshments at Windsor, Holmes had eaten nothing. 'Ham! There is chicken, I think, as well. Which do you prefer?'

Holmes shook his head. 'Neither. Watson, this is an ugly tale. Darkness in every direction. The father who would not come to the Palace and who would not see us. The fiancé who could not bear to linger at Windsor to meet with me, but who turned around and rushed back to his estate, washing his hands of the entire affair. I would like to know why. These are hardly the actions of a loving fiancé. Now, if you don't mind, I need to think before we question the Count.'

Poor Jane Wandley, I thought. The girl deserved better. And for all her terrible suffering, those who loved her could not, somehow, deal with her horrific fate.

PART TWO

ENTANGLEMENTS

'Self-love forever creeps out, like a snake,
to sting anything which happens to stumble upon it.'
—Lord Byron

CHAPTER SIX

What is the Question?

t was eight in the evening when we arrived at Count Friedrich's country estate. A huge, recently constructed building, it was fashioned in some mixture of Tudor style and an alpine retreat, with Germanic looking carvings on the ramparts.

Its newness was evident; every detail pristine and nearly shining with polish. The bright moonlight rendered it a stark black and white and the costly place glistened like a cheap greeting card picture. A nearby single-storey, elongated building fashioned in a similar style was possibly the stables, and several bright lights glowed from within. As we alighted from our carriage, the high-pitched squeal of a horse and a muffled shout came from the building.

Holmes turned to look in that direction.

At the front door of the main house, a page answered the door but was smoothly replaced by a tall, liveried manservant with gold buttons so shiny and a countenance so imperious that he might well frighten royalty.

'I am Albrecht,' said he. 'The butler. State your name and purpose in coming here.'

'My name is Sherlock Holmes, and this is my colleague Dr John Watson. We have urgent business with the Count.'

Albrecht's eyes raked over us both, clearly assessing our status and finding it somehow lacking. 'You are expected?'

'Do not play games with me. Windsor sent word to you. It is regarding the matter of Miss Jane Wandley's death.'

The butler's face tightened. 'There is nothing here for you, Mr Helms.'

'Holmes. Count Friedrich was betrothed to Miss Wandley. I must speak with him urgently.'

'He is occupied. You may write to the Count for a future audience which he may or may not grant. Good evening.'

'Are you accustomed to declining requests from Her Majesty?' said Holmes pleasantly. He stepped aside, indicating the carriage waiting in the driveway. The royal crest was clearly visible on the door.

Albrecht took this in. He still would not give way.

'As you seem to be from the Palace, sir, you know that the lady took her own life. In any case, with her passing there is no longer any connection to the Count. Please convey our condolences, if that may serve your purpose.'

'Albrecht, you are out of line. I would speak with your master at once.'

I wondered if this buffoon had *carte blanche* in guarding the gates.

The man drew himself up, offended.

'Have you some kind of warrant? A letter of introduction, perhaps?'

'Turn us away now and I'll have the police here within an hour. Foul play has caused the lady's death, and the Count's indifference will be made public without delay.' Holmes turned to me with a rueful smile. 'In fact, Watson, I'm of a mind to return with the police in any case.'

'Good idea, Holmes. Shall we be off?'

The butler paled visibly. 'One moment, please. We were not informed of your visit. I will . . . but the Count is occupied.'

Behind him we heard the echo of female laughter and then a burst of applause. Some kind of party was clearly underway.

'Evidently,' said Holmes. 'It's been a busy day for the Count. The press should hear of the deep grief expressed by the victim's betrothed.'

Albrecht's voice dropped to a near whisper. 'Sir, the lady took her own life. The Count, you see, has washed his hands of the matter. His reputation—'

'Washed his hands, you say?' said Holmes. I could feel his anger rising. It was rare for Holmes to become riled. 'Miss Wandley met a terrible end. A heinous act has been committed and the victim was engaged to be married to the Count. Break into that party and deliver him to us at once.'

Albrecht's face froze in repressed fury. 'He is in the stables, Mr Holmes. There is an emergency with one of his prize mares. You may wait inside. I shall inform him.'

Another horse scream pierced the air.

'Trouble foaling, perhaps?' said Holmes. 'Watson is a medical man. Perhaps we can be of assistance. Come, Watson!' Holmes turned and departed in a run in the direction of the stables.

What was he thinking? I had never helped in an equine birth. Nor, frankly, a human one.

'No! Sir, you may not—!' shouted the butler.

But he was drowned out by another anguished equine squeal from the stables. I ran after Holmes.

We entered the low building and found a small group gathered in an open stall at the far end. Many lanterns lit up the scene to near daylight.

Laying on the straw, her head cradled and supported by a groom, was a glossy, spectacular mare, her belly swollen. She snorted and moaned, thrashing in agony. Kneeling at the other end of the mare, with his arm disappearing up to the shoulder into her womb, a swarthy middle-aged man, sweating and blood spattered, frowned in concentration. The veterinarian, no doubt.

One groom kept a strong grip on the terrified mare's halter, gently stroking her head as a second helped steady her. The horse's eyes rolled wildly. She gave another cry.

'Keep her still,' said the veterinarian.

Standing off to the left, and well back from this, was a tall, angular and supremely handsome man of forty, a mane of blond hair sweeping back from a high forehead. He might have walked off the pages of a society magazine in his perfectly tailored morning coat, white shirt and embroidered waistcoat. He surveyed the chaos before him with detached interest.

Count Friedrich.

'Come on, Swann, pull it out!' he barked at the veterinarian. 'You have already cost me a fine dinner party. Now you wish to ruin my entire evening.'

'Breech,' muttered Swann, sweat pouring down from his forehead. He shook it from his eyes.

'Well, obviously,' said the Count. 'Save the mother. Damnation, I paid a king's ransom for this one.'

To my great surprise, Holmes had removed his jacket, hung it on a post and was rolling up his sleeves. He bent down to kneel beside the vet. 'What are you holding?' he asked.

'Left rear leg. Right one anterior. I fear the umbilical is tangled,' replied the veterinarian.

'Watson?' said Holmes.

'No idea, Holmes,' I said. Equine births were notoriously tricky. The baby's hooves posed a threat to the dam. Any variation from the normal presentation was fraught with danger. I knew no more than that.

'Let me help you,' said Holmes.

The horse screamed again and struggled, her movements twisting the veterinarian's arm and flinging him from his knees sideways onto the straw.

'Unfortunate. Push in and it may unfold,' said Holmes. How on earth did he know this?

'Yes! I am trying,' said Swann, righting himself and adjusting his arm.

'Let me help you calm her,' said Holmes.

To my utter surprise, my friend moved to the mare's head and, taking over for the groom there, bent to whisper to her and stroke her neck. 'Rub her back, down the spine, vigorously,' he instructed the groom. Somehow this managed to calm the thrashing mare. She continued to moan but went still.

Soon Holmes moved back to assist the veterinarian.

In twenty minutes, a tiny, delicate foal struggled to his feet before us – wet and on shaky legs. Swann and two stable hands dealt with the afterbirth and clean-up, while Holmes attempted to wipe the blood from his arm.

'It's a colt, sir,' said Swann to the Count. He turned to Holmes. 'And thanks to the timely help from this gentleman here, the foal and its dam will live.'

In a few more moments, once the umbilical cord was dealt with, they carefully allowed the mare to take her feet. She began nuzzling and licking her baby, while nickering softly to him. The little colt's ears swivelled in her direction.

'They learn their mother's voice first,' said Holmes, 'as she memorizes their smell.'

Holmes washed his hands in a large bucket of water brought by a groom as Swann did the same in a second bucket. The veterinarian eyed the foal with admiration. 'By God, that little one is a beauty.' He looked up at the Count. 'You are blessed, sir.'

But the Count's face was a mask of indifference. He approached the newborn and grasping its head, roughly turned its face to him. Across the shiny brown face was a crooked slash of white colour, in a jagged stripe down the nose and around to one side, over the ear.

My stomach lurched as the distinctive marking made me recall the tattoos we had seen that morning on the unfortunate young woman. Holmes and I exchanged a look of surprise at this bizarre coincidence.

Examining the face, the Count sighed. He released the baby's head and the colt nearly fell, but Holmes reached down to steady the little one.

'Careful!' said Swann to the Count. He moved in and took over handling the fragile newborn.

'Colt's got that cursed white question mark,' snarled Friedrich. With one finger, he traced down his own face a crooked imaginary line round one eye and up to the ear. 'His grandsire's legacy! They assured me that trait was recessive and would not show in him. Damnation. I cannot use him.'

'*That Is The Question* is his grandsire?' asked the veterinarian. 'I did not know. *Question* was a champion! This is a fine little fellow, sir.'

'Yes, yes, perfectly formed. But that marking. I do not like the look,' said the Count. He waved contemptuously at the stall. 'They do not help me with my breed plans. Destroy them both.'

'Sir!' cried the veterinarian. 'It would be a terrible waste! I can easily find you a buyer.'

'I will not propagate this line. Nor will I allow anyone else.'

'I'll buy the mare and the foal from you,' said Holmes quietly, drying his hands. 'On behalf of Her Majesty. The Palace will not breed, and I will sign a document on Her Majesty's behalf saying so.'

The Count turned to him as if seeing him for the first time.

'Who the devil are you? I thought you were with Swann here.' He took in our city attire and frowned.

The veterinarian shook his head. 'No. But lucky they were here, sir.'

The Count continued to stare at Holmes.

'I am Sherlock Holmes sent by Her Majesty the Queen,' said my friend. 'Her Majesty, as you no doubt know, loves horses. This colt will make a fine riding mount.'

I well knew that Holmes had hidden talents, but this combination of equine expertise and boldness delighted me.

The Count hesitated and I could see him struggling whether to accept this new information. I became aware that Albrecht and two burly footmen were standing just outside the ring of lantern light. How long they had been there, I could not say.

'Albrecht, did you let these two in? They say they are from the Palace.'

Albrecht stepped into the light. 'I could not stop them, sir. But they are, indeed, from Windsor. The royal carriage . . .'

The Count considered this and smiled. 'Very well.' He turned to Holmes. 'How much will you give me for them?'

'Five hundred pounds,' said Holmes.

'Done. A bargain at that price,' said the Count. 'Meet me in the house and we shall draw up papers.' He turned on his heel and departed.

Albrecht eyed us fiercely. He then turned to the two footmen. 'Kyle and Arthur, see that Mr Hemmes and Doctor Willie find their way to the house.' Then he, too, followed his employer.

Despicable fellow. *Hemmes and Willie!* It sounded like a vaudeville act. Holmes laughed.

'Mr, er, Hemmes?' ventured the veterinarian.

'Holmes,' said I.

'Sir, I must thank you,' said Swann. 'A breech in that position is usually fatal.'

'I know,' said Holmes. 'Mr Swann, I will ask you to remain for the night in this inhospitable place. Attend to the foal and his dam. I'll send transport for them in the morning. Tomorrow, please travel with them to Windsor and ensure their welcome and care there. Fifty pounds for your trouble.'

The man nodded. Holmes turned to me. 'Have you the cash, Willie?' he asked with a wink.

I laughed and reached into my jacket for my wallet. I knew from experience that carrying cash with me on my travels with *Hemmes* was frequently useful.

CHAPTER SEVEN

Count Him Out

n five minutes, we were inside the main
house and standing in a kind of recep-
tion room, gaudy to an extreme degree
with too many statues, too many paintings and rows of matching books which
looked untouched. We faced the hand-
some, arrogant Count in front of an unlit, black marble
fireplace. Albrecht loomed in the doorway, ready for a
call to action. I would be hard pressed to say whether
this house or poor Jane Wandley's family seat was the
more inhospitable.

From a nearby room the sounds of female laughter
continued to drift out. I shuddered. The man's betrothed
lay murdered at Windsor and the fellow was enjoying
himself with friends, having casually ordered a prize horse
destroyed over a white marking.

'What is your business from the Palace, precisely,

Mr Holmes? I have already put in my appearance there.' The Count put on a more friendly mien, as if this were a social call.

'Another of your breeding projects.'

'To what breeding project do you refer? My greyhounds?'

'A young lady, whose appearance has perhaps led you to disdain her as you do this foal. And so you left the body of your betrothed – the late Miss Jane Wandley – unattended and uncollected this morning at Windsor.'

'Gentlemen! I came when called, I confirmed the identity, and I released the body to their care,' said Count Friedrich with a smile. 'The girl was a suicide. There was nothing I could do to help her.' He shook his head. 'A sad story, to be sure.'

'Your compassion overwhelms me. But the death was no suicide, Count Friedrich. Your betrothed was murdered.'

The man swallowed. 'All the more reason to leave this to the experts.'

'I am charged with finding the culprit,' said Holmes. 'And I require your full cooperation.'

'And how do you think I can help you?'

'We shall begin with the facts,' said Holmes. 'I would like you to tell me exactly your whereabouts for the last four days.'

'This is outrageous! Do you consider that I am to blame for disfiguring the woman to whom I was betrothed? Why would I do such a thing?'

'Perhaps she broke off the engagement and you didn't want others to obtain "breeding rights" – as you have just demonstrated in the stable.'

'That is ridiculous.'

'It could certainly motivate a man of your temperament.'

'She did not break off the engagement.'

'Perhaps *you* did.'

'I would never have done so. It was a felicitous match for me.'

'Felicitous?'

'I had much to gain. Jane did not know it, but a condition of our betrothal was my being named in her father's will. I was to inherit his entire estate. Her two siblings were omitted from that will. Why would I wish to give all that up? So, you see, I do not have a motive to kidnap and disfigure Jane. On the contrary! The whole thing is a terrible disappointment to me.'

'A disappointment.' Holmes stared at the man closely.

'Well, much more than that, of course.'

My impression of the Count grew worse by the minute. 'Did you love the young lady?' I asked.

The man could not bring himself to meet my eyes. 'In my way. Yes, I suppose so.'

'And I suppose you find it just as well that she did not survive with her disfigurement?' said Holmes.

That fact was evident even to me.

'It is sadly better this way. Had *I* awakened from such an ordeal to discover my face ruined in that manner, I think I might have taken my own life.'

'Count Friedrich, you will provide the information I have asked. We may do this here, or at the police station. Quite publicly. Make your choice.'

The man capitulated. 'Of course, I will help you. That is an easy matter. I was here. Enjoying the company of several friends who await me now at the dinner table. They and my servants will vouch for my uninterrupted presence, and for every moment of the last four days – except for a few choice hours which took place behind closed doors. But even there I have an alibi. If you insist.' He winked at Holmes, attempting to imply a sudden camaraderie. This worked about as well as one might imagine.

'Sir?' It was Albrecht, standing in the doorway.

From behind him peeked a diminutive blonde woman, beautiful in a childlike way, who could be no more than twenty. She wore a bright, rose-coloured dress with a deep décolletage, and sported a flurry of blonde curls.

'Augie!' she chirped. 'You finish now mit de horsies?' Her accent was German.

Only then did she note our presence and seemed surprised. 'Oh, my apologies! Darling, de chef for you has saved a plate. We begin at cards. Shall we keep for you a place at whist?'

'This is Erna,' said the Count. 'A dear friend. She and her two companions have been my guests here for the past week.'

Holmes and I exchanged a glance. Poor Jane Wandley. Her betrothed had scarcely missed her throughout her ordeal.

Over the next hour, as he interviewed both the guests and servants, Holmes confirmed beyond a doubt that the despicable Count truly had not ventured from his estate for over a week. There he had been glued, awaiting the birth of the much-anticipated foal and enjoying the company and favours of his lady friends.

It was after two a.m. before Holmes was ready to leave this sordid house, and with a final check on Swann, the mare and her foal, we departed in the royal carriage for London.

While our investigations of the last twenty-four hours had effectively eliminated her betrothed and provided needed background on her family, the mystery of the who and the why of this heinous crime had only deepened.

The road under our wheels widened to the larger thoroughfare leading to the capital, and our carriage picked up speed. The gentle rocking of our luxurious conveyance was soporific in the extreme. But just before Morpheus seized me, I ventured a question to my friend that had been burning for the last two hours.

'Holmes, where on earth did you learn to attend an equine breech birth?' I asked. 'Is there nothing out of reach to you?'

'Oh, a great deal, Watson, as you often list for your readers. But you forget, my friend, that my family were country squires. I have attended several foaling mares in my time.'

'Really?' I exclaimed. 'I thought you were not so fond of country life.'

'You are correct. That is because I suffered it. There is much about me you do not know.'

'Ha! What lies beneath your city demeanour?'

'Very far beneath, Watson. I am a confirmed Londoner now. Ask me no more, I need to rest.' He closed his eyes and with that preternatural ability he had of being able to go to sleep like a cat, he was under in thirty seconds. I soon followed.

CHAPTER EIGHT

Lash

he next morning, I awoke and stepped downstairs to discover Holmes poring over books and papers crowding the dining table. My friend had busied himself with a dive into *Debrett's*, his own voluminous filing system and the day's papers, and would not be drawn into conversation. I knew that the Palace tragedy weighed heavily upon him and that he had been frustrated by yesterday's preliminary investigation.

'Ah, Watson! At last!'

'At last? Holmes, it is barely seven in the morning.'

'Watson, there is something I would like you to do for me.'

'Can it wait 'til after breakfast?'

'No. I have here a note from Heffie regarding the boy fished from the Serpentine.'

'It's early days.'

'You know our girl. She confirms the boy was Lash – who we knew as Crowley – but here's something. While she was there, they told her another young person also came to claim the body, but swore the dead boy's name was Burton, not Crowley. They wouldn't release the body to him, either. Apparently they suspected both this boy and Heffie of working for some medical school. Heavens, Watson, I thought that all finished with Burke and Hare!' said Holmes.

'It is less overt, but still a lucrative profession, I am afraid.'

'Watson, Heffie said there are some personal effects awaiting collection at the police station. They would not release them to her.'

'What now, Holmes?'

'Go to the coroner's and tell them you are Lash Crowley's employer. Collect his belongings, if you will.'

'Why would they think I am legitimate?'

'There is not a man alive more universally legitimate looking than you, Watson. Think of something.'

'Surely I can be of more help on our primary mission, Holmes?'

Holmes smiled. 'Soon, my friend. What I need to progress in the Palace case is *quiet*. I am thinking.'

Stifling my annoyance, I wondered what disturbance I had been in the past while Holmes was *thinking*? However, I complied, and after a brisk cab journey I found myself in the coroner's office. In a matter of moments, a brusque young man with a sallow face and a surly demeanour accepted me as the owner of a printing company and the employer of one Lash Crowley, drowned boy.

'We still have his possessions, but the body's been sent off. Name was Burton, I think. Gypsy by the looks of him.' The man indicated his ear, suggesting a piercing.

'May I have the items, please? They are likely company property.'

The man hesitated only a moment as he stared at me, then nodded, and in a moment handed me a damp paper bag.

'Is there a coroner's report?' I asked.

His face twisted into a sour grimace, and he left the desk briefly to return with a card. 'Here is all there is. Police report,' he said, handing it to me. 'Be quick.'

It required no more than a glance.

'Male, ident. by itinerant as 'Lash ~~Crowley~~ Burton',
Gypsy, 10–12 years. Contusion above L eye. Drowned.'

Time and date of death were unrecorded. Clearly they were not entirely sure even of his name. But that contusion was as Heffie had said.

Clipped to this was a grotesque photograph. A young, drowned face, blurred by poor lighting and submersion in freezing water. Despite the distortion and water damage, I could make out a deep cut on the forehead. The boy had been struck before entering the water. Had I the chance to examine the body, I could have determined more. But that chance was gone.

Sadly, I recognized the lad. He'd been at Baker Street once. I remember being struck by the intelligence in that young face, the eagerness.

'There is clearly a wound, here,' I said. 'No investigation was done? Or notation of the name of the person who identified him?'

The clerk took back the card and glanced at it. 'Gypsy,' he sneered. 'But no proof, so we didn't release the body. The police are busy. *We* are busy. Sir, I can spend no more time on this. Next!'

He waved me away and I turned to see a line of people waiting. London was nothing if not replete with corpses. Vast interment fields had been set up outside the city limits to handle the steady stream as city cemeteries were packed and pushing their boundaries. And along with these corpses there were scores of grieving relatives and friends.

I paused at the exit to the building to open the bag. In it was a cheap metal ring and a waterlogged business card, still damp and beginning to mould. I turned it over. It was Holmes's card! They might have followed up on this, if anyone had cared. Heffie had been right. I took a closer look at the ring. Crude, made of iron, the details largely missing. I tossed it and Holmes's card into my pocket.

My cab home became snarled in traffic due to an accident on Oxford Street. I disembarked to walk the rest of the way. The recent thaw and balmy temperatures had reverted and a brisk, cold wind made me regret I had left my muffler.

As I walked north, I passed a newspaper stand and was stopped by a headline I spotted. It read: 'Angry Women's Mob Batters Police!'

In no rush to return to the irritable Holmes, I purchased the paper and paused on the pavement to read:

'Constable Robert Billwood, 24, was sent to hospital with concussion after he was hit by a rock as a crowd of over fifty – mostly young women – demonstrated in front of the Liberal Club. Miss Emily Ferndale, the erstwhile organizer of this noisy melee is none other than the daughter of the highly respected MP, Lord . . .'

Miss Emily Ferndale! That was the 'questionable woman' whose movement the younger Wandley sister had joined. I felt compelled to let Holmes know at once. I tucked the paper under my arm and proceeded in haste north on Baker Street, excited about the news.

CHAPTER NINE

The Dissident

 arrived at 221B to find the rolling black-board that Holmes had once used to solve the mystery of the dancing men cypher had been reinstalled in our sitting room. Holmes stood motionless before it, chalk in hand. On it was written:

Ouroboros – meaning
Serpents – history/genus/venom
Kate Wandley – Ferndale – activist
Emily Ferndale – activist
Clarence Wandley – artist?
Clarence's friend?
Sir James – industries, inheritance?
Peter Oliver
~~Count Friedrich~~
Palace intrigue – not likely

Tattooist – style, name?
Gypsies – ?
Lash Crowley/Serpentine?

He hated interruptions but I felt my news was too urgent to hide.

'Holmes?'

He ignored me.

'Holmes, I have just this moment read—'

He turned to me with a dramatic wave of his arm. 'Watson. Not now!'

'But I have news, Holmes! Remember that "questionable woman" that Peter Oliver said the younger sister was involved with? I just read—'

'Later, Watson. I sent you to follow up on that young Irregular who drowned.' He turned to me, frowning.

I stifled my irritation. 'I could not examine the body. It had been removed for burial. But the report, *brief* as it was, mentioned a wound on the forehead, as did a photograph.'

Holmes looked up, interested.

'Foul play, do you think?' said he.

'I suppose it could have been an accident. But . . .'

'But what?'

'Position of the wound – more like someone struck him.' I indicated the top of my forehead. 'Possibly his name was Burton, not Crowley. A Gypsy identified him as such. Oh, and there was this.' I removed Holmes's card from my pocket. He glanced at it and tossed it away.

'Heffie was probably right, then. An Irregular, if only briefly.'

'Yes. I am pretty sure I had met him once. If so, he was a bright lad. Impressed me. And there was this.' I pulled the worn ring from my pocket.

'Give it to me,' commanded Holmes. He squinted at it, grabbed his magnifying glass and inspected it closely. Holmes's eyebrows shot up. 'Hah! Now this is something!'

'What?'

'To begin with, it is very worn, inexpensive but . . . did you not notice?'

'Notice what?'

'Dear Watson, what have I said so many times about seeing and observing?'

I was inches from shouting but managed to speak in a normal tone. 'Spit it out, Holmes. What do you observe?'

'This ring, Watson. Look again!' He handed me the ring and his lens.

I held the thing up to the light. With the magnification, I could just make out the shape. Crude, and the details were quite worn down. But it was inarguably . . . a snake!

'Surely a coincidence?' I said. 'At least it is not an ouroboros.'

'You know how I feel about coincidences, Watson. But we shall keep this in mind.' He pocketed the ring. 'Anything else?'

'Not about the boy. But—'

'Well, Heffie is right then, it is likely the unlucky Lash Crowley. Or Burton. And now, let me work.'

'But there is something else, Holmes. I just—'

'Later, Watson.' He turned back to the blackboard. 'There are so many threads here, so much to understand. The motive and sequence of events, for one. Why would someone do this? What could they hope to achieve? Was the kidnapper the same as the murderer? How and where was the tattooing done? How was she kept still? What is the significance of the ouroboros? Is it a message *to* someone other than the victim herself? And to whom? But the largest question is the obvious one. It is a devious, complicated crime with a great deal of thought put into it. Why on earth go to all this trouble?'

'It is truly a conundrum, Holmes.'

'Now, follow along. It helps me to speak this aloud. I am nearly certain the villain is not a rival at court, nor her betrothed, that unsavoury Count. His alibi is solid and his motive distinctly lacking.'

I capitulated. 'Yes, I suppose. But might she have rejected Count Friedrich and he sought revenge? Hired it out, perhaps?' I asked. 'For all we know, he is penniless. He was eager to sell you his horse,' I said.

'No. His reaction upon seeing her and his own personal tastes argue against. And there are those alibis. By her death, he stands to lose too much. No, much as I despise the fellow, I do not think the Count was the perpetrator.'

'But what of the little foal and the dam, Holmes? Shall I wire the Palace to make sure that they arrived safely?'

'Already done, Watson. I was up early this morning. I have a contact at the stables there, and all went smoothly. The foal and his mother arrived there hours ago. Swann knew to get them away safely from their despicable owner.' He paused and found his pipe on a side table and looked about for his tamper.

'It's over there, on the floor,' I said. He fetched the tamper and busied himself with his pipe. 'Now, Holmes, what I should like to tell you is that I just read—'

'My thoughts run counter to a Palace intrigue. Not only was she well-liked, she was not envied at all. No one coveted her role. I think that the outré elements and the very complexity of the crime reek of some long-seated emotions. No, this was a deeply personal action. It has meaning. I would reckon it had great meaning to the girl herself.'

'Unfortunately, she cannot tell us,' I said.

'No. But I don't think the murder was an intentional part of the plan.'

'Why not?'

'Think, Watson! Too much care was taken in the planning. The artist is formidable. Expensive, if he was complicit, and paid. Finding him . . . or more likely his remains . . . will be the next step. And where the tattooing took place. It must have taken days.'

'Yes, and with some kind of anaesthetic, I think.'

'Precisely, Watson! This entire plan was not the work of one person. And it was done to have some kind of effect. More than just the visual horror of it.'

'But Holmes, this still does not make a lot of sense to me. Why, after all that, did the killer slash her wrists?'

'The answer is obvious, Watson. The tattooing did not have the result the villain wanted.'

'But what was that, I wonder?'

Holmes shook his head. 'And there the mystery lies. To shame her? To punish her? To ruin her chances at life in the royal household? Vengeance, perhaps. Those do seem the obvious, Watson. And still . . . there are the siblings. We need to know more of this family.'

'Fine. Now listen to this, Holmes, I have been trying to tell you—'

He flung down the chalk. 'All right, what is it?'

I held up the morning's newspaper. 'Miss Emily Ferndale? Lady Summers. The "questionable'" lady with whom the younger sister Kate Wandley is involved? In this morning's papers it says—'

'Trouble with the police. Following on from an even more violent altercation last week. She struck a copper with her umbrella!' He smiled mischievously. 'I read about it in the late edition after you went to bed.'

Did the man never sleep? Holmes seemed to have completed two days' worth of investigations while I had learned precious little of interest.

'Holmes, I was thinking that perhaps if we approached this Miss Ferndale—'

'No need, Watson.'

'Why not?'

Below us the doorbell sounded.

'It would be much better if the lady comes to us.' As he said this, he turned the blackboard over so that its written contents faced the wall.

I laughed. 'Wishful thinking!' Sharp female voices were heard from the floor below. 'How on earth would you manage that?'

Just then Mrs Hudson presented herself at our door.

'Mr Holmes. A young lady to see you,' said she. 'She will not give me her name. I told her you were quite busy.'

I stared at Holmes in surprise. No, he could not have . . .

'That is true, Mrs Hudson. Did you send her away?' Holmes glanced over at me. Was that a wink?

'Not Miss Ferndale?' I whispered.

'I cannot send her away, Mr Holmes,' said Mrs Hudson, aggrieved.

'Why not?' said Holmes.

A tall young woman in an overcoat and enormous hat abruptly loomed behind Mrs Hudson. 'Because I will not take no for an answer, Mr Holmes,' said the lady.

Holmes took in this formidable figure and rose to greet her. 'Ah, Lady Summers. Although I know you prefer Miss Emily Ferndale. I have been expecting you. It is all right, Mrs Hudson. Please have Billy summon a cab in fifteen minutes if you would? Thank you.'

'Fifteen minutes? But you have not heard why I am here,' said our visitor.

With a frown of disapproval, Mrs Hudson melted away. How the devil had Holmes enticed this lady to Baker Street?

'I already know why you are here,' said Holmes. My brother Mycroft had a word with your father late last night. My brother – and your father – both think that I might be able to help you.'

Of course! Mycroft Holmes, his long fingers into every corner of London, had furnished the link. But while I had heard her father's name, Lord Summers, I could not remember anything about him specifically.

'Yes. And while I do not always listen to my father, he was quite compelling. Is it true? Can you help me?'

'That depends. I am pressed for time but may briefly hear you out.'

The lady turned to look at me, suspicion clouding her features.

'Dr Watson is my friend and colleague. You may be assured of his discretion. Pray take a seat, Miss Ferndale.'

It was all I could do to hide my astonishment.

CHAPTER TEN

The Fomenter

oments later, Emily Ferndale, minus her coat and hat, sat stiffly before us next to the fire. Her mouth was pressed into a thin line of determination, her posture rigid, her voice strident. She was a handsome young woman in her late twenties, with dark hair simply styled in a chignon and dressed in a navy-coloured dress of conservative lines and a flattering cut. She took out a gold watch from a pocket in her skirts and consulted it.

'Fifteen minutes is all, then, Mr Holmes?' she said.

'I am glad you have been released from gaol swiftly, Miss Ferndale,' said Holmes pleasantly.

'You know the reason, then, for my visit?' said the lady, crisply.

'Your father is the Right Honourable Lord Summers,' said Holmes. 'You are aware, of course, that your status will only protect you for so long.'

His name came to me then. Summers was a renowned member of Parliament, known for his progressive ideas on education. Hence the Mycroft connection.

She stiffened. 'Of course I know that. While my father may have interceded on my behalf with the police this time, I will not ask for his help ever again.'

'Perhaps, then, you should refrain from throwing rocks at policemen.'

'I did not. If you will hear me out, please.'

'Miss Ferndale, I am quite occupied at present.'

'Are you not at least curious, perhaps, to hear from the harridan who has the police quaking in their boots?' Her quick glance caught me before I could hide my smile. She frowned and turned back to Holmes. 'First of all, I threw no rocks. But I have come with a purpose, and I should like to at least consult you, if for no other reason than to ask your advice. I can pay.'

'Very well. Please be brief,' said my friend.

She eyed her watch. 'Fourteen minutes. When you recognized me, you had a negative reaction, Mr Holmes. I presume that is because of what you have read of the events yesterday outside the Liberal Club.'

'Miss Ferndale, you clearly endanger both yourself and your followers. I understand you have attracted a group of worthy, like-minded females. Perhaps you should reconsider your violent tactics.'

'Mr Holmes, know this. I do *not* foment violence. I believe very strongly in the rights of women, in our inherent value to society, in our equal reserves of intelligence, resolve, strength, and courage, and our right to have the vote.'

'You and many others,' I said, intending encouragement.

'You patronize me,' she said.

'Not at all, Miss Ferndale,' I said, 'I support these ideas myself.'

'Many men do in theory, yet they do nothing.' She turned back to my friend. 'Yes, Mr Holmes, it is a growing movement. And, yes, I have followers. Women of all ages. And a few men, too. But I do not condone violence.'

'Rocks were thrown yesterday,' said Holmes. 'A young policeman suffered a concussion and is still, I believe, in hospital.'

'Not by me, nor from any of the women who were with me.'

'That is not what the police say.'

'I know. That is why I am here. I am being undermined from within. There is a snake in the grass, and this person is perhaps connected to the police.'

Silence blanketed the room. She stood up and began to pace.

'Mr Holmes. Do you believe in the emancipation of women?'

'Is this how you wish to use your remaining twelve minutes?'

'Yes.'

'That is an ill-defined question.'

'But in general? Social? Political?'

'I cannot answer in general,' said Holmes. 'I believe that women should have more say in the direction of their lives. Access to higher education, of course—'

'And to be able to matriculate at university? Receive equal pay for equal work?'

'I will not argue. But . . .' Here Holmes paused.

'Go on.'

'I have given nowhere near the amount of study as you have to the larger question, Miss Ferndale. I do, in fact, support many of the ideas I have read from you and your female colleagues. But frankly, I abhor the violent tactics a number of you have brought to bear in your protests. I abhor the thought of young women adopting the worst traits they see in men in order to make their point. I abhor—'

'Oh, stop abhorring and listen. The line is very clear in my mind. I do intend to educate and, if I must, to disrupt, embarrass and, yes, even inconvenience. But violence? Never. That is where I draw the line. I tell you, there is treachery at work here. There has been violence at our demonstrations, but not by one of us. The who and why are not clear. I need to get to the bottom of it. I am told you are a very successful detective and may be of help. Is that true?'

Holmes remained silent. I sensed he was intrigued by the lady, even while resisting.

She clearly sensed it, too.

'Someone in my organization is leaking the when and the where of our every demonstration. Then, when our crowd appears, so do the police, and then this traitor, or someone hired by them, incites violence to discredit the movement.'

'It is a known tactic,' said Holmes. 'And, incidentally, the claim of every dissident movement, isn't it, Miss Ferndale?'

'I don't care about other movements. And we are not "dissident". We are the movement *for* equality, the movement *for* your mother, your sister and your daughter, so that they may all live free of tyranny and oppression, and so that they may all achieve their potential. Just as you and Dr Watson have been allowed to do.'

She looked around herself. 'Of course, you sit in a home devoid of any female influence, yourself an avowed bachelor. Yes, I have read about you. Perhaps women are anathema to you? Or seem to be a species apart?'

Here, I thought, she was treading on dangerous territory, and yet she was not entirely in error. I believed Holmes to be conflicted in his views of women on a deeply personal level. Verbally, and in private, I had heard him decry their emotional nature, puzzle over their apparent illogic, and occasionally speak dismissively. And yet his actions on behalf of many female clients belied these occasional disparagements.

'Miss Ferndale. I am not unaware of your good intentions. It is your *methods* to which I object. Yesterday was not the first incidence of violence. I refer to the infamous umbrella incident from the week before.'

Of course! I recalled a photograph in *The Times* that Holmes and I had – I am embarrassed to admit – laughed over only last week. It was of the very same young lady who now sat before us! In it, she brandished a closed umbrella high over her head, about to strike a policeman standing before her.

He had raised his hand to defend himself. Their expressions were almost comical: the man, utterly surprised, the lady tight with unflappable determination.

'That photograph!' she cried. 'That is . . . oh, the harm that photographer did to me! Context, sir! A lack of context! Do you realize what I was doing? I was raising my umbrella, which had been a birthday present from my mother, as it was in danger of being wrenched from my hand and trodden into the mud as I had seen several of those of my friends thus destroyed. I was holding it back, away from his grasping hands, and it only looked like—'

'The report stated that you hit the man on the head,' said Holmes.

'Well, yes.' She looked skyward. 'Yes, I did. But not just then.'

Holmes raised an eyebrow.

'He tried to steal the umbrella, then, just after this photo was taken. He brutally yanked my arm and tore my dress, then *spat at me*.'

'My goodness, Miss Ferndale!' I said.

'And only *then* did I hit him.' She paused and I could see tears in her eyes, as well as fury. 'Either of you would have done the same, I warrant. I was frightened. And hurt. Look.' She rolled back her sleeve to reveal a dark purple bruise on her forearm.

There was a pause as we took this in.

'I am sorry this happened to you, Miss Ferndale,' said Holmes gently. 'And I believe you. I have been subject to such smears by the press personally. A photograph can most certainly give the wrong impression. The photographer's name, if you have it?'

'Pettifer. The scoundrel!'

Holmes made a note. 'Good. There is no excuse for the policeman's violence. But perhaps taking your argument to the streets is not the best approach. Consider that there are other ways to make your voice heard.'

'Mr Holmes, please,' said she. 'I write. Give lectures. Distribute pamphlets. Petition members of Parliament.' Her words grew heated. She stood and began pacing. 'I have tried all peaceful means. Repeatedly, and to no effect! I believe that *only by raising public awareness* will we ever achieve anything of lasting value.' Her voice rose to a shout. 'No, sir, you will not convince me otherwise. But I do hope to convey to you that I have not now, nor have I *ever* been, a violent person!'

There was a pause. Suddenly realizing that her loss of composure belied her very words, she sat back down and lowered her voice to a normal level. 'Forgive me.'

Holmes shook his head. 'All right, Miss Ferndale. Let us consider who within your group might compromise these peaceful demonstrations, conspiring in some ways to have them turn violent. Have you any close confidants to whom you reveal your plans in advance?'

Miss Ferndale stiffened, shaking her head. 'Only two, but neither is the traitor, I am sure. One I have known for many years – Laura Benson, whose mother is close to mine. The other is a new woman, whom I believe to be the best addition to the group by far. I trust her completely.'

'Name?'

'Kate Wandley.'

Holmes nodded. I admired his composure; he gave nothing away.

'Thank you, Miss Ferndale. I will take your case. When is your next planned demonstration?'

Emily Ferndale hesitated and a flicker of worry crossed her brow. 'I will gratefully accept your offer. I suggest that you come to a planning meeting tomorrow where that will be determined.'

'And where I would be a clear interloper and tip your hand? Oh, come, Miss Ferndale. If there is a ringer in your group as you suspect, one who tips your peaceful demonstrations into violence, the streets are where I will spot them. If such a person exists. But I will send a young woman who works for me. Her name is Hephzibah O'Malley. She goes by "Heffie". She is remarkably subtle and intelligent, and she will fit in with your younger, working-class compatriots.'

'I would prefer that you—'

'You must trust me, Miss Ferndale. I cannot show my face near your group, as it will alert your traitor. But if at all possible, I will attend your next demonstration. If I cannot be there personally, another of my associates will assist.'

I hoped he did not mean me. I sincerely doubted my suitability for this job.

'Now let me know of your next demonstration as soon as it is planned.'

Miss Ferndale's face radiated hope. It was like the sun coming out after our recent blustery days. 'Oh, Mr Holmes, I will, and thank you. About payment . . . ?'

'Thank me when I have a result, and pay me then, if so. If you are correct in your suspicions, we may find this serpent and at least remove some risk to you. Tell none of your friends, not even Miss Wandley or Miss Benson, of my involvement. Keep me informed of your activities via Heffie O'Malley. But be warned – I will not help you if you resort to violence in your protests. Good day, Miss Ferndale.'

The moment the lady had left the room, Holmes crossed to his desk and scribbled a lengthy note. Summoning the page, he directed it be delivered to Heffie at her last known address. 'This should be a relatively simple matter for Heffie to handle.'

'Will you not at least go to a meeting to find Miss Kate Wandley?'

'No. Best to meet her in isolation. But something else must come first.' He ran into the hall for his coat and hat. 'Come, Watson! We have an appointment on Jermyn Street.'

'Your tailor?' I asked. 'Why now?'

'Not my tailor! James Featherington,' he shouted, half-way down the stairs.

I fumbled to take up my coat and hat. 'Who is James Featherington?' I shouted back.

Holmes paused on the landing below and looked back up at me. 'Tattooist, Watson. Hurry!'

How strange! A tattooist in Jermyn Street? These were more likely to be found in Limehouse or similar environs.

'Tattooist to the Royal Family!' Holmes's voice echoed up from the floor below.

How could it be? My imagination immediately created the bizarre image of Her Majesty with an anchor and rose on her bicep. I laughed at the thought. And yet, I was soon to be schooled . . .

PART THREE

OUROBOROS

'The serpent if it wants to become the dragon
must eat itself.'

—Francis Bacon

CHAPTER ELEVEN

The Royal Inkmaster

ur hansom cab had barely left 221B before we became snarled in traffic on Baker Street. Holmes tapped impatiently on the armrest.

'You say members of the Royal Family are tattooed?' I asked. 'Who, for example?'

'All of the Alberts, Watson. The father some years ago, the two sons following in his footsteps more recently. Although they were done in Jerusalem. It is a fashion.'

'What sorts of tattoos?'

'All three had the same. A grouping of Jerusalem crosses and crowns.'

I had seen this type of tattoo many times. 'How do you know this?' I asked.

'Come, come, Watson. How do I know anything?'

Of course, Holmes read widely, including the gossip rags. And he had many sources, high and low, threaded through

London and elsewhere. But the wonder was not only that he gathered all of this data, but that he remembered *everything*.

'It seems so out of character,' I said.

'Does it? The family are untouchable and they can do as they please. I would wager it began a vogue. There are undoubtedly others, and among the general aristocracy as well. Featherington has decorated several minor royals. He is the best in London, it is said.'

'You don't think that he is the artist of this heinous disfigurement?'

'No.'

'Then why are we—?'

'Whoever did the tattoos on our poor victim was a tattooist of the first order. Featherington may recognize the style, perhaps even the artist.'

Our hansom continued to make slow progress southward. Holmes tapped his foot in impatience.

'Tattoos,' I mused. 'One thinks of military service or prison, generally. Not Windsor, to be sure.'

'I am surprised you do not have one yourself, Watson.'

'How do you know that I don't?'

Holmes smiled. 'Why, I have seen you, my friend.'

'You have not!'

'You are forgetting that moment of drunken indiscretion in Marseilles last year?'

'Oh, that!' I laughed. I had gone out with friends and indeed had far too much pastis. Upon my return to our hotel, Holmes apparently had stopped me from going out again to post a letter in what he later described as 'the altogether'. Or so he had recounted.

'All right. No tattoos. But I very nearly got one in Afghanistan. A cherub, I think. On the left shoulder. My memory is hazy. But in the end, no.'

'Well you may again get the chance!'

'Or you. You seem unafraid of the needle, Holmes.'

He laughed. 'That was a low blow, Watson.'

We arrived at Featherington's studio. A doorway on Jermyn Street had a discreet brass plaque that read 'James Featherington, artist'. We rang a bell and a page escorted us upstairs into an elegant anteroom where a beautiful female clerk sat behind an impressive desk bearing a name-plate reading 'Miss Pickert'. The lady was dressed in an elegant, deep purple lace ensemble, in the height of fashion, with an unusual feature. The long sleeves of her dress were split at the bicep and draped open down her forearm, reconnecting at the wrist, and in the opening were revealed two glorious tattoos of climbing flowers: a rose on one forearm, a clematis on the other. A delicate colouring had been applied into the design.

The work was surprisingly beautiful. It was not as vivid as the snakes we had seen yesterday on the unfortunate Jane Wandley, but nevertheless quite effective.

I had seen a tattooed woman at the circus as a child, but the images had been crude black marks including anchors, crosses, eagles, dogs, cats, hearts, flags and names, seemingly placed on her body without rhyme or reason and in a variety of styles. By contrast, this woman's tattoos were true art, designed to enhance her beauty and become an integral part of her.

After introductions, Holmes took the lady's hand and

regarded the forearm festooned with roses. 'Excellent work, Miss Pickert, and most flattering,' said he.

'Why thank you, Mr Holmes! These were done by Mr Featherington, of course,' said the woman. 'Perhaps you have a lady friend who might be interested?'

'One never knows,' said Holmes, releasing her hand with a smile.

I barely stifled a chuckle. The receptionist turned to consider me with a mischievous smile. 'Or perhaps you, doctor? Someone as dashing as you are, sir, must have many lady friends. Perhaps an adventurous one among them?'

'Oh, well, er, no. I—'

'He does indeed attract the ladies,' said Holmes. 'But we are not here as clients. If you would kindly inform Mr Featherington that Sherlock Holmes is here to consult him on a Palace matter.'

Within a minute or two we stood facing James Featherington in an airy back room with a window overlooking a well-kept mews, within which potted small trees lined the elegant space. Inside, the room was bright white and almost surgically clean. In the centre was an expensive barber's chair, gleaming and pristine in hand-carved wood and polished maroon leather. Standing next to it was our man.

Featherington was a small, compact fellow, muscular, with black marble eyes, black hair cropped very short, and a coiled energy about him. He wore a crisp white shirt, sleeves rolled up, under an expensively tailored waistcoat. On a table next to him were the tools of his trade: needles, pots of ink, unguents, a bottle of alcohol and bandages.

Introductions made, Holmes told, in a roundabout way, of the curious tattoo on a certain beautiful young woman, and the need, of course, for discretion. He did not, however, mention the lady's position, name, or that she was deceased, only that the Palace, and the Queen in particular, wanted the name of the artist. While he said nothing, I could see the question set Featherington on edge. I wondered why.

'The tattoo was of the highest quality, Mr Featherington' said Holmes. 'Very artistically placed across the lady's face.'

He gestured across his own face to convey the curves of the tattoo on Jane Wandley.

The man gasped. 'On her *face*, you say? At the Palace?' Featherington seemed both horrified and intrigued.

'The work was complex and detailed. I know for a fact that you are the artist to members of the Royal Family, including the Prince of Wales.'

'I will neither confirm nor deny that, sir,' said the fellow, with a smile. 'But I would never tattoo the face of a young woman, not for any amount of money. Even if she demanded it.'

'What young lady would demand such a thing?' I asked.

'A performer, no doubt. There are several notorious tattooed women. They make a great deal of money. But that is not my trade.'

'Understood,' said Holmes. 'But perhaps you may help us to identify the style, the technique, and even the artist, if you can, of this very singular and very strange tattoo. The Palace would like a name. Watson?'

I pulled the photograph from my pocket and handed it to the artist.

Featherington did not move but stood staring at the picture with great interest. 'Remarkable. The style is Japanese. It looks to be done in colours. Was it?'

'Yes. This snake is red and gold, this one here is blue and gold,' said Holmes.

'Were the hues vibrant or delicate, as in Angela's?'

'Vibrant. Much darker and more vivid than your work on Miss Pickert.'

'Of course. But . . . where are the ends of the dragons?'

'Snakes. They meet up in the crown of the head, shaved to accommodate them. But hidden by her hairstyle. Show him, Watson.'

I pulled from my pocket two photographs, the first of the scalp, the second of the face.

'And each snake is eating its tail,' said Holmes.

Featherington regarded the two photographs intently. 'Most unusual! The images are of an ouroboros. Or rather, two. What is unusual, besides the execution, though, is the placement. I have tattooed very few heads in my time. It is extremely painful, the skull bone being so close to the surface. Brave girl, to make that choice. Let me have a better look.' He picked up a magnifying glass from the table adjacent and peered more closely at the photograph.

'Is the ouroboros a common subject for tattoos?' asked Holmes.

'Not common, but I occasionally get requests. Some are attracted to the arcane quality, the connection with ancient alchemy.'

Holmes nodded. 'I suppose. Infinity. Rebirth . . .'

'I have no idea. I never ask.' He looked up at us with a conspiratorial wink. 'Though I've done one notorious one.'

'Who?'

'Lady Jenny Churchill has a small ouroboros on her wrist. Mine, of course, and her specific request. But much simpler than these. Don't look so shocked! I'm not being indiscreet, she keeps it quite on view to all.' He studied the photo again. 'Why don't you ask this lovely filly who did her face?'

Holmes did not reply.

Featherington looked up from the photograph, the truth dawning. 'Is the woman in the picture . . . asleep?'

'She is dead. And she is, or was, Miss Jane Wandley, companion to the Duchess of Ormond.'

Featherington swallowed. 'Dear God. Apologies for my disrespect! I assumed a performer. But surely she did not die from this? Why would this girl choose this elaborate—?'

'It was not her choice. This was done to her. She was later killed. Now, what else can you tell us of this tattoo? Do you recognize the artist?'

The man grew pale and looked about, as if for an escape.

'Mr Featherington!'

He cleared his throat and willed his attention back to the matter at hand. 'Apologies. It is just so deeply shocking. The image itself is singular. Note the very fine lines, the detail, the design itself as it delicately weaves across the hills and valleys of the anatomy. This is the work of a master. The colour confirms the style. It would have taken many hours. Over several days. She must have been drugged to tolerate it. I know of only one man in the world capable of such delicate, such perfect work. An artist in Kyoto. And, as far as I know, he is no criminal, although—'

'The name,' said Holmes.

'He . . . it is rumoured that he has done some very secret work on high level Yakuza. They are the—'

'I know who they are. What is the man's name, please?' Holmes was growing impatient.

Featherington frowned at the photograph. 'Wait!' He inspected more closely and gasped. 'Oh, my! This is interesting.'

'Mr Featherington, kindly be forthcoming,' said Holmes.

'There are two, no, three flaws here. Four! See how these scales don't match the rest? This man I was thinking of never makes errors like that. I understand he has tattooed royalty throughout the Orient, though not in Japan, and several crowned heads of Europe.'

There seemed to be two reasons for his reticence to give the name: a potentially dangerous underworld connection, or perhaps competition for the royal clients.

Holmes looked through the lens. 'Could this work be done by another, then? Or by more than one person?' he asked.

'No. It is the work of one person. I am certain it is he. But . . . what is the story here?'

'The girl was kidnapped,' said Holmes. 'It is very likely that this was done under duress.'

'I cannot imagine this. I cannot imagine an artist of this calibre agreeing to . . .' He paused, frowning. 'I will not even tattoo any drunks!'

'I warrant you'd ink your own mother if a knife was held to your throat. Let us presume he was coerced. This might well explain the errors you note. And now, Mr Featherington, the *name*. Give it to me or I'll have the police bring you in for questioning!' Holmes was at the end of his patience. 'Out with it, man. I'm not after a tattoo, I am after a murderer.'

The man's face tightened. 'Shojiro Yamamoto.'

'Have you an address?'

'He lives in Kyoto, as I said. But I have heard . . . recently he . . . well, er, I believe he may be in London presently. Some kind of festival. Oh . . . of course! The Japanese Town, I think it is called.'

'Ah!' said Holmes, leaping to his feet. 'Do you mean the Japanese Village? He is there as a visiting artisan, then?'

The Japanese Village! It had been widely featured in the papers. It was some kind of temporary tourist installation recreating Japanese culture with artisans in traditional costume, posed in recreations of Japanese studios, shops and homes. It was extremely popular. 'It is in Kensington,' I said. 'I have read of it. I believe it is just opposite the park, very near the Albert Gate.'

'Yes,' said Featherington. 'That is the place! The newspaper article mentioned a Japanese artist but did not give his name. However, now that I think of it, a colleague said . . .'

But Holmes was out of the door like a shot.

CHAPTER TWELVE

The Japanese Village

ur visit to the tattooist's concluded, we soon made good time in a hansom toward Albert Gate in Hyde Park. Our cab-driver knew exactly where the Japanese Village was, for he had taken many visitors there. A holiday tourist attraction was the last place I had expected to be that day.

En route, Holmes was a bundle of nerves. He exhorted the cabbie to make haste. 'Driver! Time is of the essence!'

'What is the rush, Holmes?'

As our hansom cab raced through the streets, I noted my friend sat silent, stiff and grim. But traffic snarled and our hansom slowed to a stop. He rapped on the ceiling with his walking stick. 'Go around!' he shouted up at the driver. Then, to me, 'I fear we will be too late.'

'Surely not, Holmes?'

'Until we spoke to Featherington, I had envisioned it

must be some underworld Yakuza tattooist in on the plan, presumably for some rich reward.'

'Yakuza are some kind of criminal organization in Japan, correct? I have read of them.'

'Yes. Ubiquitous, powerful and very feared. At the head is a veritable Japanese Moriarty.'

'Why did they come to mind?'

'The vicious criminal aspect of the crime. The clearly Japanese style of the tattoo. And the fact that tattooing is an integral part of Yakuza culture. Many members sport full-body tattoos, very elaborate. A mark of belonging. But never mind that. If the very public and highly respected Yamamoto is our tattooist, this was not an underworld commission. The situation grows darker – and far more urgent.'

'How so?'

'Think, Watson, think! The work was completed within the last thirty-six hours, the state of poor Miss Wandley's skin told us that. If he were complicit, taken on for a presumably large sum, then Yamamoto would know that his special style would be recognized, and he would have flown the country without delay. We would be lucky to catch him now. But I don't think he was a willing participant.'

'Perhaps if the payment were large enough?'

'No. You heard Featherington. There is a code of honour. A legitimate artist would not tattoo a young woman's face, a drugged prisoner, in this fashion.'

'But . . . then how would someone coerce such a man to do such detailed and fine work – and over several days?'

'How indeed? You cannot physically torture an artist to

create at that level, but you can threaten him. Something was used for leverage. We must find out who or what.'

'Or talk to Yamamoto himself,' I said.

'Dear God, man, the tattooist has either fled or he is dead.'

'Then what do you hope to find here?'

'The trail, Watson, the trail!'

Our cab had pulled up to our destination and, without another word, Holmes leaped from the cab. I followed.

Across the street was the Albert Gate to Hyde Park. A wind had come up and the trees whipped back and forth along Rotten Row. We turned to face an imposing edifice attached to the Albert Gate Mansions. The sight was familiar to me. On a rare visit to London as a child I had been taken roller skating here. But now, the name *Humphrey's Hall* was emblazoned on the façade and it had been repurposed to be the entrance and a part of the Japanese Village. A temporary banner which hung over the door proclaimed this.

'The Japanese Village' was the proud presentation of someone with the improbable name of Tannaker Buhicrosan, who had 'recreated' the idea of a Japanese village for the edification and entertainment of Londoners. The man was evidently some kind of adventurous entrepreneur who had decided to import artisans and concoct a kind of ongoing exposition. Despite the mundane moniker of the place, it had consistently attracted crowds.

Humphrey's Hall faced a courtyard and, as we entered, I was surprised by how elaborate this recreation was. An entire Japanese village, charming and somewhat theatrical, had been created, with shopfronts opening to a central courtyard and painted backdrops recreating Japanese scenery, including the iconic Mount Fuji. It was through this central courtyard we strode, Holmes eagle-eyed and focused. 'Help me look for anything that relates to tattooing, Watson,' he whispered to me. 'Or to Yamamoto.'

I could see nothing that fit. There were displays of pottery and skilled potters working at wheels. Glistening bolts of silks and elegant robes made of them, with traditionally garbed ladies demonstrating how to don a formal kimono. There were shiny little embroidered silk balls called tamari which attracted a crowd of young girls. Three painters demonstrated the contemplative arts of Japanese calligraphy and brush painting. And for sale were tea sets, ivory and chopsticks inlaid with abalone and gold. Several young ladies, resplendent in kimonos, displayed fans, wielding them flirtatiously as several English matrons of dubious grace attempted to emulate them.

The place was filled with eager visitors.

Not only was the effect charming but fascinating as well, I thought. Such a thing could easily have been tawdry or demeaning, and yet that was not my impression. I recalled a scathing commentary of this 'village' in the form of a cartoon that appeared in the weekly satirical magazine *Punch*. It illustrated a role reversal of traditionally clad Japanese onlookers pointing and whispering at 'traditionally costumed' English people in a fictional 'English Village'. Various English types were pictured engaging in a variety of unflattering activities including drinking in pubs, toiling in mines, haughtily attending the opera and puffing on cigars. I smiled at the memory.

By contrast, the Japanese Village was dignified, beautiful, and to my mind remarkable.

There was nothing, however, that either of us saw relating to tattoos. We walked from one end of this courtyard to the other and back to Humphrey's Hall. Holmes's attempt to engage various Japanese participants in conversation was unsuccessful. Their English vocabulary seemed strictly limited to what they were demonstrating.

'A shame, Holmes. I see nothing that relates here.'

'Not surprising, Watson. Most of the population in Japan associate tattooing with criminals. In spite of Mr Yamamoto's international reputation, it is possible they did not wish to advertise his particular talents in this context. I warrant he was brought here to do private commissions.'

We took a second pass up and down the courtyard. Nothing.

'Tea room, Watson!' said Holmes at last, pointing to a small restaurant which had been built near the steps up to Humphrey's Hall. We sat ourselves at a table and I noticed patrons served with small cups of green tea and a platter of delicacies, unrecognizable to me, but charming in their pastel colours and rounded shapes.

An attractive young Japanese lady poured green tea for us. She was clad in full traditional kimono and sandals, her silky black hair arranged in a large pouf and secured with a woven straw hair ornament. A gentle smile seemed to be a permanent fixture on her smooth, impassive face.

'Excuse me, madam, but do you speak English?' asked Holmes politely.

'No, no, no sorry, no Engrish,' said she, then giggled, covering her mouth with her hand.

'Then spiders and cockroaches, please, with a dollop of pond scum,' said Holmes in a friendly tone, gesturing at the menu.

Her eyebrows shot up, betraying her. Holmes smiled and lowered his voice. 'Young lady, I would like to have a word with the man in charge here. I am a detective on a matter for the Royal Family.'

She bowed to him, and as she did, whispered in perfect English, 'Yes, yes. Please wait, I will bring,' and left our table quickly.

Holmes pretended to be further engrossed in the menu but his eyes darted up to track the girl. I followed his gaze to where she spoke hurriedly to a tall, portly man of perhaps forty, dressed in a strange mix of Western and Japanese clothing. His upper body was in the usual jacket, white shirt, waistcoat and tie, his lower half clad in what I later learned was a *hakama*, the long black skirt-like garment worn by Japanese men.

His own nationality was not evident. He had light hair but Asian features. Perhaps he was part Japanese – in addition to his trousers, I thought. He frowned as he looked over at us.

'That is Tannaker Buhicrosan!' said Holmes.

'Odd name.'

'Founded and runs the place. Half Dutch, half Japanese. I recognize him from a newspaper photograph. Watson, excuse me, please, I must have a word. Kindly settle the bill, and then, if you can manage to look behind that little row of false storefronts over there, see if you can find anything – anything at all – that may lead us to something useful. Also, inquire where the artisans are put up when they are not on 'stage'. I mean to interview a few. We must find a lead and find it quickly.'

CHAPTER THIRTEEN

Haruko

did as instructed and soon found myself in what felt very much like backstage at a theatre. The little stores and workshops were indeed constructed like stage sets, and behind them was a warren of storage rooms, dressing rooms and costume and prop repositories. I wandered unimpeded until I came to a locked door. A sign in Kanji meant nothing to me, and so I knocked. An elderly, squat lady in Japanese robes answered.

'Hello,' I began. 'I am looking for Mr Yamamoto.'

She stared blankly at me. 'No English,' said she.

'Mr Yamamoto,' I repeated. I gestured a graceful curve down my forearm, trying to create the image of a tattoo. 'Tattoo,' I said more loudly. 'Mr Yamamoto.'

No sooner had the name escaped my lips the second time, than a child's shriek was heard behind the lady, and she moved to block my view of the room.

'This is the ladies' room. No may come in,' she said in heavily accented English and tried to close the door, but my foot stopped her.

'Please. It is very important. I am investigating on behalf of Her Majesty the Queen.' I did not feel precisely worthy of this, but I supposed it was more or less true.

A tiny girl of perhaps three, wearing what looked like bright cotton pyjamas, appeared around the skirts of the elderly woman. Tears streamed down her small cherubic face, and she shouted, 'Oto-san!' before she was pulled back by a young woman.

'Please,' I pleaded, 'it is very important that I find Mr Yamamoto.'

'He is gone. Gone.' The older woman tried once again to slam the door on my foot.

Holmes appeared suddenly behind me with Buhicrosan in tow.

'Watson, I believe we have our answer. Yamamoto, our celebrity tattooist was indeed here. He is a widower and vanished five days ago along with his three-year-old daughter. Yesterday morning, the little girl was dropped off here alone and blindfolded.'

'She is here. I just saw her!' I exclaimed, gesturing to the room facing us.

Behind Holmes, Tannaker Buhicrosan spoke sharply in Japanese. The lady blocking the door bowed and stood back. We entered the room.

It was apparently a kind of costume and dressing room. Several women lounged about in cotton robes, their expensive and elaborate silk kimonos hanging on racks. Two young women had charge of the tiny girl I had just glimpsed. Clad in red-and-orange pyjamas and looking like an adorable little doll, the child was crying inconsolably. A slender young woman was on her knees, attempting to comfort her.

Tannaker Buhicrosan surveyed the scene with grim determination. He gestured toward the child. 'Yamamoto and his daughter arrived here last week. His absence since has cost me a fortune. He was contracted to demonstrate the highest example of the Japanese tattoo, in private, of course, and had several commissions lined up,' said he. 'I would be much obliged if you would find the damned fellow.'

He looked up at the child and her attendants. He beckoned to one. 'Yoshiko, come,' said the man. Then, to us, 'She can translate for you. She speaks English and knew the Yamamotos in Japan. She has spoken with the child.'

The young woman who was kneeling before the child stood up and approached. She was wearing a sky-blue silk kimono with chrysanthemums embroidered upon it. 'I am Yoshiko,' she said. 'I can translate for you, but I may already have what you need.' Her English was perfect, as was her pronunciation. An educated, aristocratic accent. At my apparent astonishment, she explained. 'I was raised between London and Tokyo. My father is English. I attended Newnham. Do not look so surprised, Mr . . .'

'Doctor Watson,' I said. 'My apologies.'

Behind her, the child's cries subsided into soft moaning.

'Tell us everything you know, please,' said Holmes.

'Five days ago, Haruko and her father were abducted, blindfolded, and taken somewhere at some distance from here,' she said.

'How do you know this? That they were blindfolded, for example?' asked Holmes.

'The little girl. I questioned her closely. She does not understand what happened, but she showed me that her eyes were covered.' Yoshiko gestured, indicating a blindfold. 'She was returned the night before last, alone and blind-folded, left on the steps to Humphrey's Hall. But her father did not return with her. We do not know where he is.'

Holmes pressed on. 'What happened during those four days? Could you learn anything further from her? Any details will be helpful.'

'She could tell me very little. They were taken at night by a man wearing a mask. A knife was at her throat, presumably to make the father compliant. She was lifted, blindfolded, from the carriage and transported inside somewhere. It was raining and then it stopped. When her eyes were uncovered, she was in a dark room with a big bed. The same terrifying masked man was there, but then he left.'

'Tell me more of this room. Did you ask her to describe it?'

'Yes. Dark, as I said, but for one candle. The windows were covered in some way. Besides the bed, there were a few English toys: a ball, and a small stuffed toy, I think, and water. There she remained for the whole of the time. Twice a day, food was brought in and a chamber pot emptied. Strange food, she did not like, she said. She was left utterly alone all day every day except for food being brought in. She cried but no one answered. Every night her father would come to comfort her, and he would sleep with her there in that room until a masked man came and got him in the morning.'

'That is remarkable work, Miss Yoshiki,' I said. 'To get all that from the child.'

'It took some doing,' said she. 'Then Haruko was blindfolded again, bound and brought here. Alone. She was found before dawn yesterday on the steps outside. She does not know where her father is, what he was doing there, or anything else.'

But Holmes was not satisfied. 'I need more,' he said. 'We must find this place.'

Miss Yoshiki turned to Holmes. 'Understood. Today I learned a little more. In the carriage on the way to the secret place, the last part of the journey was bumpy and noisy. I inferred cobblestones. And in the room, there was a sweet smell. A kind of pudding smell. All day long. And there were bells which sounded, at a distance, several times a day.'

Holmes's nodded in admiration. 'Excellent work, Miss Yoshiki. This may help us.'

The young woman nodded and looked over at the child, who was still ignoring her food. 'Haruko is severely shaken by this, Mr Holmes. As one might expect.'

'The poor child!' I said. 'She will require a great deal of care if she is to recover from this.'

'But what of Mr Yamamoto?' the young lady asked. 'We are all so worried about him. Where is he, and why would he not accompany his daughter home?'

Holmes looked at her sadly and shook his head. 'I must speak to you in strictest confidence.'

Yoshiko nodded and he continued, 'A young lady at Windsor Castle was extensively tattooed by Mr Yamamoto.

She was then murdered,' said he. 'I fear your friend will not be seen again.'

'He would never do such a thing! Nor would he ever leave Haruko. I know this family well. It is I who enticed him to come. So soon after his wife's death, and . . . Oh! You say . . .' As the full implication hit her, her eyes moistened but she willed her face to neutral, regaining her composure. She straightened and glanced over at the little girl, sitting motionless in a corner, ignoring the bowl of rice which had been placed before her. 'Oh, but of course. He was coerced with . . . He is dead, isn't he?'

Holmes said nothing but looked at the young woman steadily. It was clear that she now understood the situation.

'I will see to Haruko,' said she, simply. 'If you would kindly inform me when you have made any discoveries. I will then know what to . . . what to arrange.'

Holmes nodded.

'I am sure she will be in good hands,' I said.

'I will do my best,' said the young woman. A tear escaped from her eye and she flicked it away. She now knew, as did we, that Yamamoto had most likely come to no good end.

A cold rain began to splatter down as Holmes and I stood outside Humphrey's Hall, and it took some minutes to obtain a cab. As we moved slowly through the London traffic, Holmes looked defeated.

'This case grows darker by the minute,' he said.

'There must have been someone with medical knowledge involved,' I said.

Holmes looked sharply at me.

'I mean, to keep the girl sedated enough for this work to be completed,' I said. 'That is not a task for an amateur.'

Holmes looked thoughtful. 'Nor is this case, Watson. It is a remarkable puzzle, though. Why go to all this trouble, and then return Jane Wandley, alive, to the castle? What was to be gained there?'

'To shame her, I suppose. In front of her fellow courtiers?' I said.

'A form of punishment, then. But she awoke and saw the villain, I would warrant. A struggle ensued, and he killed her. But Watson, the perpetrator must have had help. A place where the tattooing was carried out. And as you said, someone to keep her quiet. If we could find this place, we may find his accomplices.'

'Well, it could be anywhere,' I said.

As if in concert with the rest of the day, the canopy of our hansom cab leaked. We leaned away from the icy droplets.

'I would place a large sum of money on the premise it was very near the castle,' Holmes replied finally. 'Jane was taken from there and returned there. I think, Watson, that the time for an exploration around Windsor has arrived.'

'I suppose we should get an early start tomorrow,' I said. I hoped we'd find a conveyance without a hole in its canopy.

'No, Watson. The trail is growing cold as we speak!' He rapped on the roof of our carriage. 'Cabbie!' he shouted. 'Turn here. Take us to Windsor next.'

I removed my handkerchief from my pocket and stuffed it into the source of the leak. Where was a royal carriage when we needed one?

CHAPTER FOURTEEN

Cinders at Windsor

t was after eight and dark when we reached Windsor, thoroughly chilled and slightly damp. A groom attending to a carthorse directed us to the police, and we soon stood before the constabulary office a few streets over from the outer perimeter of the castle. This office, we had learned, served the larger Windsor area. Except for the royal residence, Windsor was really something of a sleepy town, and there was but one man on duty.

Blond, corpulent, with red cheeks, he sat behind a desk, his chin upon his chest. The man, who looked to be about twenty, was dozing while sitting up.

'Constable!' said Holmes.

The man awoke with a snort. 'Sir?' He stared at us blearily. 'May I help you? Er, what time is it?'

'It is eight in the evening. I am here on a Palace matter. Snap to it, young man, and give us your full attention.'

His stinging words had their effect and, in minutes, Holmes had recounted, in only the vaguest outlines, the basics of the case. The man, of course, had heard rumours of it but details had been successfully kept within Palace walls. Holmes then proceeded to pull from the fellow a frustrating account of mostly no news at all. No one in the surrounding area had recently gone missing. There were certainly no murders reported. No crimes of violence.

Disappointed, Holmes said to me, 'Perhaps we will have to broaden our gaze, Watson. But I feel quite sure that the work on our poor victim was done near to the castle . . .'

He had a sudden thought.

'Constable, do you know of anyone in the area who has enjoyed sudden good fortune – an influx of cash perhaps?'

'If only I knew . . . Wait! Oh, yes! Well, this is probably not what you are looking for . . . Little shop at the end of Peascod – that's our high street. The Claptons. Dry goods. Mainly fabric, and tailoring. Recently, well . . . they received a big shipment of very costly fabrics and some sewing machines for home use. They engaged my brother – he's a builder – to beautify the front end of their shop. Grand plans, in fact.'

'When?'

'They hired him perhaps two weeks or so ago. Sudden. But he was not to start until next week.'

'Do you know the source of their good fortune?'

'I do not. Inheritance, could be.'

'Take me there, please. I would like to speak to Mr and Mrs Clapton.'

'You're a little late.'

'What do you mean?'

'They're dead.'

'Come, come, man! You said no violence recently,' Holmes thundered.

'I thought you meant foul play. 'Twas an accident. You didn't ask about that.'

'Oh, for God's sake!'

'They was fried to crisps. Their building caught fire and the whole place burnt, sadly with them in it. My brother was sore disappointed, losing the work and all. He had planned—'

'How did this fire happen?' snapped Holmes.

'Bakery next door, they figure. Oven left on.' He shook his head.

'Bakery, you say! Bread or desserts?'

'Specialized in French pastries. My wife was sad for the loss. She loved their—'

'Is this on a street that is cobbled?'

'What does that have to do with—?'

'Never mind that,' said Holmes. 'Is it cobbled? And when did this happen?'

'Cobbled, yes. And, er . . . three days ago.'

'Ah, Watson, the trail warms!' He turned to the constable. 'Take us there, at once, please.'

'There's not much to see. Whole building's a wreck. And I need to mind the station.'

Holmes then played the royal trump card.

After locking up and slapping a note on the door, the man gathered up three lanterns, and hurried to transport us there in the police wagon.

Minutes later we stood near one end of Peascod, a lengthy high street facing the blackened remains of Clapton's Dry Goods shop. There was only one standing building abutting it, containing a barber's shop at the street level. On the other side, what must once have been the bakery was now rubble.

The windows on the upper floors of Clapton's Dry Goods had been blown out by the fire and the burnt-out ground floor had been hastily boarded up. The nearest streetlight some distance away cast an eerie glow on the place.

'I'd wager all we've found our location, Watson. Wait here,' Holmes said, striding toward the boarded front door.

'I wouldn't do that,' said the constable. 'The building's not safe.'

'I'm coming with you,' I said.

'No, gentlemen!'

But nothing would stop Holmes when he was on the scent. The door was only blocked by two boards, and these easily gave way as my friend kicked it open.

The interior of the shop was nearly pitch black, but with our police lanterns we could make out the dim skeletons of display tables, bolts of fabric and a row of sewing machines, black and gleaming in the glow of our torches like large mechanical insects. The place reeked of burnt fabric and a steady drip sounded forlornly.

A fire-damaged staircase led to an upper floor, and Holmes walked directly to it. I was right behind him.

The constable remained in the doorway, frightened to go in. 'Best not go up there!' he said.

Holmes ignored him and paused at the base of the stairs. I could see the damage from where I stood. 'Holmes,' I said, 'he is right. These stairs are not safe.'

'I say, stay off it!' cried the constable. 'One of the fire brigade fell through and was taken to hospital.'

Holmes ignored him and started up the dark stairs, his own lantern lighting the way. I made haste to follow him closely, angling my light to further illuminate the path in front of him.

Slowly we proceeded. The stairs creaked and splintered. Parts were missing, and one entire step was gone. We gingerly stepped over the gaping hole.

On the first floor, the horror of the fire was in full evidence. In the bedroom above the shop, the remains of a large bed betrayed two blackened stains, where evidently the Claptons had perished. But Holmes was only momentarily interested in this.

'Up one more flight,' he said.

In the corridor outside the bedroom, the stairs leading up to the top floor were steep and very narrow. They were also skeletal, having been even more ravaged by the fire.

'Holmes, no!'

But he was already climbing.

I followed.

We went slowly, Holmes first, placing each foot gingerly on the wooden stair, testing by putting part of his weight and then bringing the other to join . . . we finally reached the top floor.

A smoke-blackened door hung partly off its hinges. Our lights illuminated a small room beyond.

'I smell something,' said he. 'An accelerant. Kerosene, perhaps.'

'I don't like it, Holmes.'

'It's not for you to like, Watson. Go back down if you fear it.'

'Of course not.'

He pushed past the door, and naturally I was right behind him. The floorboards creaked. Would they hold?

We shone our lights around. The fire had wreaked havoc in this room far more than in the others. In one corner a gaping hole in the floor led to blackness. The corner of a rug hung down into it.

'Holmes! Mind the floor over there.'

But Holmes was angling his lantern around the room and I followed with mine. The feeble lights revealed a large bed with an iron frame, pushed against one corner. Its mattress had been consumed by fire. The burnt remains of thick drapes had been nailed to the single window nearby.

Holmes moved toward the bed.

'Look, Watson.'

In the beam of his lantern, a flash of silver appeared near the top of the bed. We looked closer. It was a handcuff, attached to the iron headboard.

This was the place that Yamamoto had been held with his little girl. And if we were to doubt it for a moment longer, Holmes swept the beam of his lantern across the room. There in one corner, askew as if flung by an angry child, was the contorted figure of a small, stuffed bear. Next to it was an empty syringe.

'Eureka,' said Holmes bitterly.

'You have found it,' I said.

Just as we took this in there was a loud CRACK and the floor gave way beneath us. I struck something hard on the floor below, knocking me into something even harder. Blackness overtook me.

I awakened in a doctor's office, to the sharp sting of smelling salts in my nostrils.

'You'll be all right,' said a deep, educated voice.

'Holmes?' I murmured.

'Your friend is in the next room. He is a bit worse off than you. But he'll be fine, too.'

The man came into focus. A high arch of curly black hair rose over a heavy-lidded, patrician face. His sardonic smile seemed inappropriate.

'I need to see him. I am a doctor,' I said.

'Well, so am I. Dr Max Vitale. And I tell you to stay put.'

I did not heed him and sat up anyway. I rubbed my head and felt a large knot. Blinking a few times, I saw Holmes looming in the doorway, a white bandage on his head. Blood had leaked through. Dr Vitale turned to face him.

'Ah, now you! What is the matter with you two? Lie down, I say. You are both likely to have concussion!'

'Fix this,' ordered Holmes, pointing to the leaking bandage. 'Patch us up and be quick about it.'

'Hold your horses, man. I don't have a nurse any longer. It's just me attending to the both of you.'

'I can patch myself up,' I said. I held up a mirror. I had a bump with a deep scratch on it. 'Where is the carbolic acid?'

'All right then, doctor.' Vitale handed me a bottle. 'Be my guest.'

'Why do you not have a nurse any longer?' asked Holmes, as Dr Vitale removed the bloody bandage and staunched his cut. A quick glance told me it was not serious, but head wounds do bleed profusely.

'Ran off and married that idiot tailor. She worked in the shop with him.' He moved to attend to Holmes.

Holmes stiffened and pulled away. 'When?'

'Hold still, unless you want to be here all night. A year ago. Made more money with him, or so she said. It was all she cared about.'

'The tailor. You don't mean the man whose house burnt down a few days ago?'

'That's the one. Both went down with it. Girl made a poor choice, wouldn't you say? Though I wouldn't have wished that end on anyone.'

Holmes stared at me and nodded. 'A missing piece of the puzzle,' said he.

'The pain control explained,' I concurred.

'What are you talking about?' asked Vitale.

Holmes was standing and reaching for his coat and hat.

'I am afraid I cannot reveal, sir. It is a Palace matter,' I said.

In minutes, we were in a carriage en route back to London. Today's investigation had uncovered the tattooist, as well as the where and the how of the tattoo. The murderous villain had evidently paid the couple to lend their attic to his plan, even roping in the wife, a former nurse, to keep the girl quiet. He had gone to enormous trouble to cover a beautiful young woman's face with serpents, but the motive for this arcane and complex crime still lurked unseen below the surface of our investigation.

'Beyond poor Jane Wandley, three more deaths are on this man's hands,' I remarked. 'Yamamoto and the Claptons.'

'You have a gift for the obvious, Watson.'

'Why do the deed here, then bring her back to the castle and risk discovery?' I wondered. 'And again, why kill her?'

'We may never learn the "why". But this entire scenario is curious. It is possible our villain had made some acquaintance with the tailor and spotted a vulnerability. Perhaps he was even looking for this. And proximity to the Palace would reduce the risk of discovery while transporting the girl.'

'And that is why you centred your search here?' I said. It seemed precious little to go on to me.

'You are forgetting the bells and the cobblestones, Watson,' said Holmes, with a smile. Some years ago, I spent two days in Windsor on a case and remember those bells. And I nearly turned an ankle on those Peascod cobblestones. They have not been maintained. That and the proximity to the castle . . . call it a hunch.'

'The entire scenario seems filled with unnecessary risk!'

'Somehow the villain did not bring his plan to fruition,' said Holmes. 'She surprised him in some way. I think it likely she regained consciousness early and saw her abductor. She fought – remember the small bruise on her temple? And so he killed her there and then. I warrant that was not his plan.'

'Poor girl. But what *was* his plan, I wonder?'

'That remains a mystery, my dear fellow.'

I was sure that by now Holmes had multiple theories but would only reveal them when ready. I would have to be patient. But where we would go from here, I had no idea.

Holmes, as usual, read my mind.

'You want to know what's next, Watson? All right then. *Snakes.* We need to know more about snakes. Precisely what kind were depicted in the tattoo. There was *meaning* in that choice. Our villain was precise in his planning.'

'If twisted.'

'Yes. And what is the significance of the ouroboros? So unique, and so odd. It may give us insight into the killer and his thinking.'

We rode on in silence for a while. As we rounded a curve, the lights of the great city were dimly visible up ahead of us.

'Holmes, do you think the man will continue to kill?' I asked. 'I mean, the crime was so . . . so singular. It seemed perhaps very personal.'

He cleared his throat. 'Yes, Watson. The crime was personal and specific, which in certain circumstances may indicate the end of it. However . . .'

'What?'

'The man's rage went unfulfilled, I fear,' he said at last. 'My instincts tell me he did not get what he wanted. His reason is still hidden below the surface of these bizarre details. We have much to learn, Watson.'

'You did not answer my question.'

There was a long pause. I became aware of the beat of the horse's hooves, the slight creak of the carriage, the sound of wind that had arisen in the last hour. In the dim light within our carriage, my friend's face was drawn and pale. He turned to me.

'To have gone to such lengths – the casual deaths of this couple, and no doubt that of the Japanese tattooist. All this, and then to have been thwarted. This case takes on new urgency. Because, Watson, I believe he may very well kill again.'

CHAPTER FIFTEEN

The Reptile House

arly the next morning, I ventured to our sitting room and found Holmes up and dressed, standing by the window reading a telegram. His head injury from the previous night bore no dressing, and only the remnants of a small cut were visible. A glimpse of my own cut this morning in the shaving mirror showed similar. I silently congratulated us both on our resilience.

But this morning I also I noticed my friend's posture radiated nervous energy, his foot tapping impatiently.

'At last, Watson! Eat up, we have a long list to pursue. Three days into our case, and what precious little we have found. We shall make up for lost time today!'

'Holmes, we found the tattooist, his daughter, *and* where the deed was done.'

'It is not enough. Hurry, would you? I would like to leave in ten minutes.'

I quickly dished out some porridge and coffee and had barely begun to eat when we were interrupted by the arrival of Heffie, who poked her head into the room unannounced. I had not heard her arrive, and I was embarrassed to be mid-meal and only half awake. But neither Holmes nor Heffie seemed to notice.

'What news have you, Heffie?' said Holmes. 'Any word on when the ladies are holding their next demonstration?'

'Not yet, but the plannin' meetin's this afternoon. I'll be there.'

'Then why are you here now?'

'There's more on my buddy. You know, Lash, the drowned boy. I asked around, tryin' to find more "Crowleys". Wiggins said before he were booted, Lash Crowley tried to bring 'is brother, name of Jez, into the Irregulars, but Wiggins didn't like the look of 'im and said no. Pretty sure 'e was a Gypsy, Wiggins were.'

'Oddly discriminatory,' I remarked, thinking of the other Irregulars I had met. A ragged crowd, to be sure.

'I doubt that was the reason, Watson,' said Holmes. 'So there is a brother hovering about somewhere?'

'Yes. An' Wiggins suspected Crowley weren't their name,' said Heffie. "E checked and it ain't. He thinks it was Burton. So another reason 'e was rejected. 'Twas a shame. That Lash were a funny lad. Always wi' a joke, to make ya smile. And he were resourceful like I said. 'E once found a bank robber's bolt hole in twenty minutes while the coppers ran in circles. Real promise, I thought.' A moment of sadness flickered across her face. 'Liked 'im, I did.' She clearly had a soft spot for Lash, I thought.

'That *is* useful,' said Holmes.

'If those two were Gypsies, I might 'ave something that could help,' said Heffie. 'There's a crowd of Gypsies, whose trade is fairs and carnivals – show people – camped out near Battersea. They're workin' the garden farms jus' now. Maybe they know something.'

'Good work. Any other information?'

'Well, yes.'

'Out with it, dear girl. '

'Somebody 'it Lash in the head. And the coroner did not report it.'

'I saw that in the photo,' I said.

'Wot? You visited the coroner too! You put us both on this, Mr 'olmes?' cried Heffie, offended. And glancing between us, she added, 'Looks like you both got matching head knocks yerselves.'

Holmes sighed. 'Did you get any more details, Heffie?'

I wondered at his pursuit of this at this moment. There was so much else to follow up on our main case.

'Wouldn't let me see the body. But the assistant over there 'as a fondness for toffee. Which I just 'appened to have on me. 'E said there were another blow was to the back o' the 'ead, and 'ard enough to break the skull.'

Holmes frowned at me, and I will admit feeling sheepish. My own investigation had not revealed this. However, I had managed to get hold of Lash's ring and Holmes's business card.

'Keep working on it, Heffie. See if anyone saw anything. If that boy Lash was on the game, they usually work in pairs. Perhaps this brother has information. Find out if this Gypsy enclave is family, in any case.'

'I ain't going to no Gypsy camp alone,' said Heffie.

'Ah, of course not. We shall have to go ourselves, Watson. Belay that order.'

Belay?

'Aye, aye, sir. I'm off. Need to get ready for that plannin' meetin' at Miss Ferndale's this afternoon.'

'Yes, yes, do that, Heffie.' He then thanked the girl and she departed.

Holmes eyed the clock. 'Ah! We are late! Come, Watson, the zoo. We are off to see some serpents!'

The zoo? I could not picture anything useful Holmes might glean from observing a crowd of somnolent, scaly creatures languishing in their glass cases, with no predators and all their needs met. Even if he could determine the precise species of those depicted in the murdered girl's tattoo, of what use would this be?

As usual, Holmes read my reaction in my face.

'All will become clear, Watson. We have an appointment with the leading herpetologist in England.'

The zoo was not far, a short walk through Regent's Park. The day was bright, with a chill wind buffeting enormous white clouds across the sky. Despite the recent snow, daffodils had come up in patches, and the wind whipped their yellow heads in all directions.

We arrived in fifteen minutes at the zoo and found our way to the Reptile House. One of the most popular attractions, it had been very recently expanded and was an impressive structure – a classical design with a large balustrade and four lead cupolas, one at each corner of the building.

Passing through an entry chamber which housed lizards, I noticed that most of the visitors were children. One should never underestimate the attraction of a fearsome snake or lizard to a child! Accordingly, a passel of schoolboys crowded around one large walled enclosure, topped with a thick glass panel at waist level.

Below it, in a pit, an enormous snake at least fifteen feet long had raised its head. Its cold, yellow eyes were fixed at the line of children on the other side of the glass.

One small boy tapped on the glass, hoping for a reaction. The snake responded by flaring its hood. A king cobra!

'No, no, no!' came a voice behind us. I turned to see a rotund little man with round spectacles rushing forward. 'Don't do that!' he called out to the boy.

'Ah, Dr Rupert Flackett,' murmured Holmes. 'That is our man.'

The snake wove briefly and then was still, watching, ready.

The boy tapped again.

'The glass is strong enough, I suppose,' I said.

Flackett rushed in and squeezed in front of the crowd of students. 'I say, young fellow, back away from that glass.' But the words were barely out of his mouth when the snake lunged and, leaping far higher than expected, slammed against the glass. The boys screamed in delight and backed away.

'Blast it!' swore the man. 'Can you not read the signs? Where is your schoolmaster?'

A beleaguered young man ran up to the group. 'Sorry, so sorry, Dr Flackett. I had to – I was relieving, er—'

Flackett stood on the ledge which surrounded the glass and peered into the enclosure. He shooed the children back then spoke in fury to the group. 'Do you not realize the reason for our signs. *Do you not?*'

One boy raised his hand. 'The glass. I suppose over time it could . . . it might break?'

'And it could eat us alive,' said another boy. There was a nervous giggle from the group.

'Not *eat*, you idiot,' cried one boy in glasses. 'This is a *cobra*. You'd die of the venom. You'll need a *python* to be eaten alive. Of course you wouldn't live long, you'd be suffocated as it swallowed you!'

There was one such student in every class. I imagine Holmes might have been the one in his.

Flackett scowled. 'The rules are not only for *your* safety but for the animal's as well. He can harm himself with impact on the glass. Can you not imagine that? This is a living creature.'

'Come, boys,' said the teacher, ushering the group from the display and toward the door. 'It is time for lunch.' They trailed after him. I did not sense they were much chastised.

'Dr Flackett?' said Holmes. 'Sherlock Holmes and Dr Watson. We have an appointment with you.'

The man turned to us, distracted. Flackett bore no resemblance to the subject of his expertise. There was nothing reptilian in his demeanour. Instead, he was a short, red-cheeked, somewhat jolly-looking man, despite his current anger. Worn but well-tailored tweeds and those round glasses gave him the air of a kindly professor.

'Ah – Mr Holmes, yes! Forgive my anger. Foolish children! No number of signs can eliminate that kind of behaviour,' exclaimed Flackett.

'Snakes are easily aroused, I take it,' remarked Holmes.

'At times. But with rather poor eyesight,' said Flackett, 'especially when their skin is moulting. There is an ocular scale which becomes opaque before the snake sheds its skin. But you have other questions, I gather. Please, come to my office.'

Before we could leave, a short, depleted-looking man of at least sixty, wearing a workman's coverall and an eyepatch, approached. He looked like a recent street denizen. 'Sarah's laid,' he intoned gruffly to our host. 'Six eggs.'

'Excellent, Mr Callum. You've taken her away, then?'

Callum nodded. I smiled inwardly at the human name for some slithery beast.

'Keep them humid,' said our host. Callum grunted his agreement and departed.

'I thought snakes' eggs came to term inside the female,' said Holmes.

'Only some. Some lay externally. King cobras are unusual in that they build nests, protected by the female. In captivity, snakes can behave strangely and eat their own eggs. So we remove them. But they must stay humid to survive.' He looked after Callum, disappearing down an aisle of glass enclosures. 'He's a good man, he'll ensure they make it. Now, follow me.'

I wondered that a man with only one eye could look after such dangerous animals.

Flackett occupied a large office upstairs, one floor above the displays. A wide, arched window overlooked the nearby giraffe enclosure. As we sat before his desk, I was distracted for a moment by the heads of these two-storey tall, serene beasts floating by the window. Perhaps feeling my gaze, one giraffe head swivelled toward me. It seemed to be smiling. I smiled back.

'You have a very impressive collection here,' said Holmes. 'I understand a number of them were acquired in the wilds by you personally, at great risk.'

I turned my attention to our host. A snake hunter! I would never have guessed it.

'Over four hundred specimens reside here, and I am personally responsible for a great many of them. For example, look here at the Parson's Chameleon, otherwise known as the *Calumma parsonii*.' Flackett pointed to a glass tank resting on a table near his desk. In it sat a strange creature about twelve inches long, poised on a branch and so still that I wondered if it were alive.

Then, it blinked.

'A miniature dinosaur!' I exclaimed. It did indeed look like one, colourful with blue striations.

'Forgive me, Dr Flackett,' said Holmes. 'But my colleague and I are rather pressed for time, and it is on a very specific mission that I have come to you.'

Flackett's face registered disappointment. I sensed his eagerness to lecture.

'I am afraid I have a rather grotesque photograph to show you, sir.'

'Well, *grotesque* is our stock in trade,' cried the fellow with a hearty laugh. 'Have you ever watched a python swallow a live rabbit? It is extremely popular with the schoolboys.'

I shuddered, despite my usual sangfroid. Flackett caught it. He turned to me with a smile. 'Pythons have been known to eat human beings, too!' he said. 'In the Malay Archipelago, only last year—'

'Although this is most fascinating, it is not why we are here, Dr Flackett. If you please . . .' Holmes withdrew a small leather packet from his pocket. Untying its binding, he removed another of the now familiar photographs, taken very close up, of our poor victim's face.

Despite his penchant for the reptilian grotesque, even this gentleman quailed at the sight of the hideous tattoo on the beautiful girl.

'Dear me!' exclaimed Flackett, going pale. He sat down abruptly. 'What . . . how? Is she . . . ?'

'Dead, yes. But Dr Flackett, can you tell me what kind of snake is shown here?' Holmes asked.

'A fictional one! Those markings are quite beautiful, but they do not exist in nature.'

'An artist's fancy,' I mused.

Holmes next revealed photographs of the scalp. Flackett leaned close, fascinated. 'The triangular shape of the head indicates these are most likely venomous snakes. Of course, this is an ouroboros! A snake consuming itself. Two of them. What a wonderful depiction! It is a very ancient symbol, you see. Not unrelated to the caduceus. You are a medical doctor, Dr Watson?'

I nodded.

'Snakes have been an evocative symbol throughout the ages,' said he, warming to the topic. 'I particularly love the ouroboros! It can be traced as far back as ancient Egypt.'

'But what is the *significance*, Dr Flackett, of the ouroboros?'

Holmes replaced the photographs in his pocket. 'It appears to depict a rather violent form of suicide.'

'In life, yes, it is. Unintentional, of course. But as a symbol, on the contrary, it has positive connotations.'

'Such as?'

'Varied. Some say it is a symbol of rebirth, infinity . . .'

'Yes. Anything else?'

'Let's see. A "return home" is another meaning, I believe.' He paused as Holmes made a note in his ever-present notebook. Then his face brightened. 'Oh, and there is this! I can't imagine you have heard of Kekule's benzene theory? I delight in snake analogies wherever I find them. As a scientist, I find Kekule's triply delicious, being both ssss-scientific, ssss-substantial and ssss-snakeish!'

'Kekule!' exclaimed Holmes. 'The structure of the benzene molecule. Of course! A remarkable chemist, Watson. It came to him in a dream, or so he claims. Ha! Yes, indeed!' Holmes jotted another note.

'What about the benzene molecule?' I wondered, feeling excluded from some kind of inside joke.

'It is circular,' said Flackett.

'I don't follow.'

'It is significant, Watson, as decoding the structure of the benzene ring unlocked a whole volume of organic chemistry. Led to understanding aromatic compounds, with so many uses. And the structure came to him as a vision of an ouroboros, either while dozing on an omnibus or later in a dream. There are two stories – ah, but let us come back to our purpose.'

'I do have a question, sir,' I interrupted. 'You said a snake consuming itself *rarely* happens in life. Which means it does, occasionally? Can you elaborate, please?'

'Rarely, but it happens, and then it is a tragedy. The snake perishes, of course. Chokes to death, generally.'

'Why would a snake do this?' I asked.

'It is a phenomenon that is little understood. Some snakes prey on other snakes and it is said that they may mistake their own tail for another snake.'

'But it must be rather confused to do so, mustn't it?'

'Indeed,' said Flackett. 'We theorize that it is disorientation, worsened perhaps by inhospitable ambient temperature. Snakes are poikilotherms.'

At my puzzled look, Holmes interjected 'A creature that cannot regulate its own temperature and must seek out heat or cool to place itself in a narrow range, Watson. Otherwise its brain does not function well.'

'Well, I knew *that*,' I said. 'Just not the term!'

'Temperature control!' exclaimed Flackett. 'That is one of the main challenges in keeping snakes in captivity.' He turned to me, 'I did, however, once rescue one trying to swallow its tail. A very tricky business.'

'Tricky in what way?' I asked.

'Snakes' fangs angle backward. It secures their prey and makes it extremely hard for their victim to tear free, giving the predator time to fully inject their venom. This same positioning of the fang can make the snake unable to release its own tail. It was such a snake that I managed to save.'

'How?'

'I had to pry open its mouth with great difficulty to disengage the body.'

Herpetology had no room for amateurs, I thought.

'But would it not have already injected its venom into itself?' asked Holmes.

'Yes. But snakes are immune to their own venom – even if it would kill another snake. Or one of us.'

'Was it grateful, do you suppose?' I asked. Holmes and Flackett looked at me in surprise.

'I mean, did it know that you had saved it?'

'I doubt it. Snakes do not show gratitude, affection or friendship in any way,' said our host. At my sombre reaction, he added, 'Although sometimes they learn to recognize a person who feeds them and may hesitate, in that case, to strike.' He smiled. 'But Mr Holmes, what of your case? It seems most peculiar.'

Holmes stood up. 'Sadly, I am afraid I cannot discuss it, Dr Flackett, and I must request your complete silence on the matter. As I mentioned in my note, there would be legal ramifications. As much as I have enjoyed our meeting, we must be off.'

He headed towards the door. Following, I felt our visit might have been a waste of time. While interesting, I could not see that it provided useful insights into the case. Holmes, of course, might disagree. As we neared the door, he stopped before an assembly of framed photographs on the wall.

'Hullo!' he exclaimed.

He stepped in to regard one closely. The photograph showed a man in a turban, seated on the ground cross-legged and playing an instrument. A snake arose from a basket before him. A cobra, I inferred, from the hood. Surrounding him was crowd of what appeared to be Gypsies of all ages, flamboyant in their embroidered, flowing costumes and headscarves.

'A snake charmer!' exclaimed Holmes. 'Did you take this photograph?'

'My wife did,' Flackett said softly. His demeanour had darkened perceptibly.

'Where? When?'

'Just outside of Leeds, fifteen years ago. This family were one of the very few Gypsy practitioners of this ancient art roaming Britain at the time. For this reason, I sought them out.'

'I associate snake charming more with India than Egypt. I saw plenty there,' I said.

'Contrary to popular belief, and their misnomer, Watson, Gypsies originated in India, not Egypt,' said Holmes, harking back to what I presumed was his schoolboy pedantry. 'Or so some anthropologists posit. But no matter.' He turned back to our host. 'Can you tell me more of this . . . family? Their name, perhaps?' asked Holmes.

'I can't recall. Gypsies often take on very common English names. *Smith*, and so on. To blend in, I suppose.'

'Do they still ply this trade? Have you kept up with them?'

'No. I believe they either left or gave up snake charming. To my knowledge, there are no more Gypsy snake charmers in this country. I know because I have tried to locate some. It is too cold much of the year here for this practice.'

Callum, the workman, appeared in the doorway. His one eye expressed alarm.

'What is it, Mr Callum?' asked Flackett.

'Trouble with moulting in cage thirty-four.'

'Well, give our little friend a hand, then. Watch yourself, Callum.'

'Course I will.' The man shuffled off.

'Good man,' remarked Flackett.

'I would imagine it is hard to keep staff here,' I ventured.

Flackett barked out a laugh. 'Indeed!' He looked through the open door after Callum shuffling off down the hall. 'Oh, he seems something of a derelict, doesn't he? But the man knows his snakes. I made sure this time. Our last fellow came to work drunk one day and made a fatal mistake. Bitten and died within minutes. That will not happen again. Callum spent years in India. He even hires out to private collectors. And he does not drink.'

'Hires out?'

'Yes, like a dog walker. For those unusual enough to keep snakes as pets.'

Holmes had turned his attention back the photograph. Several children were close to the serpent, and I wondered at their bravado. One child seemed to reach out toward the snake. Holmes had noticed this as well.

'This little boy, here—' he began.

'Yes. The child in the picture was courting disaster. He was yanked back and schooled. There is little room for error in that trade.'

'How is it that the snakes do not bite the snake charmer?' Holmes asked.

'They are distracted by the "been".'

'The "been"?'

'Yes, that musical instrument you see there. Like a very crude oboe. Snakes are nearly deaf, but both the shape and the movement seem to mesmerize them. But not fully. They hear very little. Only low pitches, badly.'

'Risky – unless, of course, they have de-venomed the snake,' said Holmes.

'They do not. De-venoming is difficult and impractical. They sometimes pull out the fangs, which is useful only until new ones grow in. In any case, the danger adds to the thrill for the audience. The snakes are kept in those baskets. When they emerge, they are quite drowsy and looking only for food, which slightly lessens the risk. An angry or a frightened snake will strike, but the movement of the instrument transfixes them. A stick will do, and those of us who hunt snakes in the wild use a stick to distract and, if needed, to deflect.'

'What of anti-venom medications?' Holmes asked. 'Chemistry is a hobby of mine. And I have read that a man named Calmette –.'

'Yes, working with Louis Pasteur in Saigon. There is a theory afloat that an anti-venom medication may be on the horizon, but if so, it will be species specific. At present we must rely on old-fashioned precautions. We treat these deadly creatures with the respect they deserve.'

'What kind of precautions?' said Holmes.

'Tongs, or other devices. And I always carried a vial of ammonia. Most snakes are repelled by the odour. Even the very deadly ones.'

I had once witnessed a death by snake bite in India. A young porter, only twenty, was bitten on the hand by a serpent hiding in a stack of luggage. Someone beheaded the serpent, then slashed near the wound with a knife and tried to suck out the venom, but I had learned later that this was a false cure that never worked. The poor porter died, writhing in agony that very day.

'Has anyone you know ever been bitten by a venomous snake and survived?' I wondered. 'I mean, without anti-venom?' Holmes gave me a sudden look of warning and I turned to our host. He was staring at me strangely.

'I have,' he said.

There was a silence. He looked at my friend. 'You knew this, didn't you?' Flackett was an observant fellow. I suppose he had to be, in his profession.

'I had read something about the tragedy with your wife, sir,' said Holmes. 'I hesitated to ask. But . . .'

Flackett looked down and a tumult of emotions seemed to play across his face. He steeled himself to continue. 'Caroline was a herpetologist also. And an expert photographer. She was with me in the field. It was ten years ago, now. A cobra, in Africa. We were manoeuvring to get a closer image of a female laying an egg. Naturally, that is a time when a snake is least amenable to distur-bance. But we mistakenly thought it was unaware of our presence. We were being so careful. *So careful.* But a small piece of my equipment fell off near the nest. This distracted me for a split second and the snake reared and lunged at me. Caroline leapt between us and took the bite on her cheek. I pulled her away but the snake pursued. It bit her a second time and then fixed on my leg, and this time it did not release.

'I beheaded it, but Caroline died in my arms, asphyxiated, not long after. The cobra venom, you see, paralyses the diaphragm. Makes it impossible to breathe. She had received a large amount.'

'Dear God,' I said. 'I am so sorry,'

'It is a wonder you did not die as well,' said Holmes.

'Our native guide saw what had happened. He removed the head from my leg. I passed out, still holding my wife. We were far from our camp, and seeing that Caroline was gone, he apparently gave me artificial respiration for some time.'

'Would a native guide know how to do that?' I asked. I thought of the warring theories even in England of reviving a drowned person – face down, face up, etc.

'I do not know. I was not conscious at the time. And the man vanished as soon as Caroline and I had been transferred back to our camp.'

'I presume snakes have a finite amount of venom, is that not true, Dr Flackett? Perhaps it used up all its venom on your unfortunate wife?' asked Holmes.

'Your wife saved your life, then,' I said.

'So the newspapers related. It made a romantic story for them. But the answer is not so simple. Venomous snakes have sufficient venom to make several strikes without depleting their reserves. The Asian king cobra has enough to kill an elephant.'

'Pointless though that is,' said Holmes. When I looked at him in surprise, he added. 'They can't eat an elephant, Watson.'

'No, indeed,' said Flackett. 'In answer to your question, doctor, there is no way to tell. Sometimes venomous snakes may give what's called a "dry bite", injecting nothing.

Or, at least, any amount from a very little to less than a lethal dose. My dear wife was unlucky, may she rest in peace. I, on the other hand, was lucky, I suppose.'

'What about the ammonia, sir?' asked Holmes.

'It happened too fast for me to try that,' said Flackett. 'You may wonder why I have come to dedicate my life to these creatures. We knew the danger of our profession, but we loved our subject with a passion. We vowed to each other to carry on if one of us . . . if either . . .' He broke off, then added quietly, 'I promised her to teach the world about snakes.' Breaking the mood abruptly, Flackett pulled out his watch. 'Well! Gentleman, do you have what you need? I must go downstairs soon for feeding.'

As we turned to leave, Dr Flackett called out. 'Oh, Mr Holmes! I have just remembered about the Gypsies. Their last name. It was Burton!'

Holmes paused at the head of the stairs and smiled. My mind reeled.

'Burton?' I whispered.

'Shh.'

Once outside, I could wait no longer. 'Lash *Burton*! Possibly the real name of your former Irregular who drowned in the Serpentine? A coincidence, do you think?'

This time he did not deign to answer.

PART FOUR

THE SSSS-SIBLINGS

'Those serpents! There's no pleasing them.'
—Lewis Carroll

CHAPTER SIXTEEN

Kate Wandley

t was still before noon, and Holmes secured us a cab in Regent's Park, directing it to an address near the British Museum. There, he told me, we would make the acquaintance of Kate Wandley, Jane's younger sister.

'Is she expecting us?' I asked.

'I have requested an interview twice, with no response. Strange, isn't it, Watson? But let us take the chance that she is at home.'

Arriving at an address in Little Russell Street, where modest Georgian houses faced more modern brick mansion flats, we rang at a rather pretentious doorway of one of the latter, with carvings of lion faces bracketing the door. A surly housekeeper reluctantly showed us into the young woman's modest salon on the first floor. It was furnished in well-worn mahogany and sombre colours.

Kate Wandley sat writing before a bow window looking down on the narrow street, steam rising from the cup of coffee next to her on a small table. She did not acknowledge us. I knew she was twenty-two, but I might have guessed a little older. She was dressed conservatively in a dark maroon wool dress, softened by a rose silk scarf crossed high around the neck and tucked into the bodice. A matching pink silk flower was pinned onto the collar. It was a severe look but with a touch of style, rather like a schoolteacher inspired by a sojourn in Paris.

We stood for several moments. I could not help but admire her. Hers was a delicate face, with sharp cheekbones, piercing blue eyes which slanted up slightly at the corners, and a slight pout to her generous lips. Her hair was nearly black, unlike her sister's, and stylishly worn away from her face with a hint of careful curls around the hairline. France must have been on my mind at the time, as even her physiognomy drew me to thoughts of Paris.

She did not look up. Perhaps she was still in shock, as anyone might be, considering the recent and terrible fate of her sister.

Ignoring our cool reception, Holmes removed his hat and placed on a table by the door. 'Miss Wandley,' said Holmes with a smile, 'thank you for seeing us.' He then introduced us both, adding, 'We are here, charged by Her Majesty, to investigate the matter of your sister's death.'

But there came neither a reaction, nor an invitation to sit. Kate Wandley looked briefly out of the window as if for inspiration, then turned back to writing her letter.

Holmes glanced at me. We waited for perhaps another

half a minute. Suddenly he took up a large vase on a nearby table and dashed it to the floor where it splintered into a hundred pieces. The girl leaped from her chair in alarm. 'My God! What do you want?' she cried.

'Your attention, Miss Wandley,' said Holmes. 'Whatever it takes.'

'That was a very costly vase!'

'I beg to differ. I have seen it on Tottenham Court Road for half a guinea. Here is a guinea for its replacement, and the trouble.' He placed a coin on the table. 'Now, your sister's death. You were called in, I believe, to view the body. What was your reaction to her transformed state?'

Miss Wandley gave in, but not gracefully.

'I was appalled!' she said. 'What other reaction could one have? It was a travesty. Disgusting. It is probably best she did not live with that desecration.' She sat down abruptly and fixed her eyes upon Holmes with purpose. 'All right then, sit down.' It was less an invitation than a command.

'Perhaps it was for the best,' said he, still standing. 'But your sister, from all descriptions, was a strong young woman. I am told that when your mother died – what was it, eleven years ago—?'

'Twelve.'

'Twelve years ago, that Jane became like a mother to you and your younger brother.'

'You have interviewed Clarence, then,' she said with a trace of derisive amusement. 'I said sit down. Please.'

'I have not yet met your brother.'

'Then where did you hear this?' she asked.

'Mr Oliver told us when we went to your family home.'

'You've been busy. Peter Oliver misled you.' Something like a smirk passed across her lovely features. 'You have not got the full story. Jane was a clever one, she was. Remarkably so. And she did take over for our mother. I say, what are you looking at?' she demanded. Holmes had turned away and was perusing her bookshelves.

'*Self Help By the People*. Samuel Smiles. Alcott's *Little Women*. Oh, and Flaubert. You are a woman of many parts, judging from your library.'

'And what of your own reading material, Mr Holmes? What is lying around your rooms?'

I could not help but laugh. Holmes shot me a look, annoyed.

'Crime, of course,' I answered. 'But also *Punch*, *Vanity Fair*, *The Illustrated Police News*. Chemistry, Pliny, Goethe, Marcus Aurelius, Shakespeare, of course, and Dickens . . .'

'Watson.'

Miss Wandley had at last cracked a smile. It was a lovely one. 'I may have many parts, but you, sir, are a splintered vase.'

'I suppose you are right,' said Holmes. 'I do not profess to understand women. My friend, here, is far more familiar with the fair sex. Watson has, in fact, known women on five continents.'

'Three, Holmes!' I was aghast at this indelicate and unnecessary revelation. But then, *quid pro quo*, I suppose.

Jane transferred her amused stare to me. 'Is that so? Women across the globe. Are you married?' She tapped her bare left ring finger and I nodded. 'Does that make you a serial philanderer?' she inquired sweetly, as though she were asking me if I took milk with my tea.

'No, I . . . He exaggerates,' I managed to get out, wondering why I was called to defend my feelings about the fairer sex in this simple inquiry. But then, Holmes had successfully managed to engage the young lady, and if a little privacy was the cost, so be it.

She turned her attention back to my friend. 'Why are you here, Mr Holmes? My sister killed herself after acquiring, for God knows what reason, that hideous tattoo.'

'You cannot possibly think that was her choice.'

She laughed. I felt a small chill as she did so. 'No, of course not. But in some way she must have asked for this. So I suppose you seek the criminal who tattooed her. But why come to me? This is hardly my milieu. I have no tattooists in my social sphere.'

Asked for this? What could this girl be thinking of her sister?

'A callous response, Miss Wandley,' said Holmes. 'And as illogical as it is uncaring. A tattoo is no longer the sole province of drunken sailors and convicts that it once was. Are you aware that Prince Albert sports one, as do other members of the Royal Family?'

'But not all over their faces. I would have killed myself as readily. Why don't you look for the tattooist?'

'We have found him. He is dead.'

The girl shrugged. 'What do you want from me? I am busy!'

Holmes did not move. 'Let us get to the point of our visit, Miss Wandley, so that you may return to your coffee and letter writing. I am charged with finding your sister's murderer.'

The girl went white. 'Murderer?' she exclaimed. 'But I thought she killed herself! That is what the court doctor said. I understood she either ran away or was kidnapped and tattooed. And then, seeing it, she . . . she . . . took her own life!'

'No, it was murder. Someone deliberately slit her wrists. But isn't the tattooing enough violence in itself to warrant your concern?' said Holmes.

'It is sad, to be sure. But she is dead . . .'

I marvelled at the brittleness of this young woman. She seemed so little interested in the fate of her sister.

'I would like to know if you are aware of any enemies your sister may have had?'

She sat very still, her eyes fixed upon my friend. She was entirely too cool for my taste. 'Besides myself, you mean?'

'No inference suggested,' said he.

'Let me guess,' said Miss Wandley. 'Peter Oliver told you that a fair amount of mischief transpired around the house after our mother's death.'

'He did mention that pranks were played. Something about a frog in a bed. India ink. But *mischief* was not the word he used.'

She sniffed. 'Harmless. We were children. Children play pranks.'

'However, it seems the pranks escalated. He said that you and your brother resented Jane's role as matron of the house and resented the restrictions she placed upon you. Some treasured recipes disappeared. Then . . . Jane's cat. I would call that more than "mischief". Did you or your brother harm an innocent animal?' asked Holmes.

Kate Wandley turned to ice. 'Peter Oliver was mistaken. It was Jane who behaved cruelly. And it was *my* cat who disappeared. We found him, eventually. I am convinced Jane hid him in retribution for disobeying her. She turned into a petty tyrant, if you must know.'

'I see,' said my friend, nodding thoughtfully. 'It seems, then, she gave you ample reason to dislike her.' Holmes appeared to believe the young woman, but I was less sure. There was something slightly strange about Kate Wandley, something less than savoury lurking beneath the surface.

'We got on well as small children. It was only later that . . .' There was a moment of silence. 'But if you think I was involved in her heinous . . . that terrible . . .'

'That is not my suspicion, Miss Wandley. But I do have a few more questions. Did your life at home improve after she took her position at the Palace?'

She laughed mirthlessly. 'No! I was charged to be nominal "mother". It is not a role to which I'm suited. Running the house accounts and the estate were easy for me, but frankly – the tasks of choosing recipes, arranging flowers, hosting tedious visitors, not to mention managing my relentlessly peculiar brother,' she gestured towards us, 'were not, shall we say, a good fit. Our father understood me not at all and kept trying to make a gentlewoman of me. He brought in a parade of eligible suitors. And so on.'

'I see,' said Holmes. 'Then you did not steal your mother's recipes and hide them?'

'What? Why would I?'

Holmes shrugged and smiled.

'Mr Holmes, you are wasting not only your time but my own. I have business to conduct.'

'It is my understanding that your father paid for you to attend Girton. And that now, he underwrites your life here in the city. You do not have to work for your living, correct? What *is* your business, if I may be so curious?'

The woman rose to her feet. 'Oh, you men! You may well be "so curious". But my business is my business. Good day.'

'Are you not interested in helping to solve your sister's murder?'

'I leave that in your capable hands.'

'What is your relation to Miss Emily Ferndale, by chance? She came for a consultation recently. She clearly has a challenging, if worthy, agenda. I can imagine that such a cause might very well suit a woman of your interests and abilities.' He smiled.

Kate Wandley stared at Holmes with outright malice.

'I have read of you, Mr Holmes. And I would wager that you know already that Emily and I are friends. Is that true?' She glanced around her. 'Oh, but of course!' She gestured to a table next to the sofa. 'Here is a stack of her pamphlets. I suppose you could have made your hypothesis from those. Nothing terribly brilliant in that!'

He nodded. 'Even simpler. I had been told. Both Miss Ferndale herself and Mr Oliver have mentioned your name to me. Mr Oliver said that your father is concerned about your activities. For your safety, I understand.'

'Balderdash! I don't care what Peter or my father thinks. The work I do with Emily does, as you say, suit me.

I enjoy having purpose. That is all I am prepared to say. Good day.'

'Are you aware that Miss Ferndale is concerned that there is someone within your organization who is undermining her?'

Kate Wandley tsked. 'Yes. She is needlessly suspicious. She sees conspiracies where I merely see incompetence.'

'Incompetence?'

'Some member mentions our upcoming plans to the wrong person. They have all been asked to keep silent, but no doubt some fool among them, perhaps by way of boasting, stupidly informs . . . as I said, the wrong person. I have told Emily to be more careful, and I believe she will be from now on. I suspect carelessness over treachery.'

'Nevertheless, perhaps you can keep an eye out. You seem to be an intelligent young lady. I would prefer your help, rather than hindrance, on the two problems which confront me. Odd that both, paradoxically, seem related to you.' Retrieving his hat from the table, Holmes replaced it on his head at a jaunty angle. 'Good day.'

He turned to leave, then turned back. 'Oh, one more thing. Do you know who stands to inherit your family estate, now that Jane is deceased? You are next in line . . .'

'How is that your affair?' she said. She advanced towards us glowering, and we exited the room, she following as though to chase us out. Near the front door, she paused for a parting shot. 'Mr Holmes, do not misinterpret me. While I did not love my sister unequivocally, I wished her no harm. But I am achieving good things here, and her lurid fate could erode my reputation and the security I need to be effective in my work with Emily.'

'You share a last name with the victim, Miss Wandley. It will be hard to maintain the distance you desire. Have the press not already paid you a visit?'

'I sent them away.'

'They will not keep away. What about the police?'

'No. I cannot imagine that I am a suspect.'

Holmes said nothing. She opened the door and gestured for us to leave. Holmes hesitated. 'Oh, let me bid you adieu,' she insisted, sarcastically.

'Miss Wandley, until we know more I suggest that you take care. We do not know the motive behind your sister's death.'

Her face darkened at this perceived insult. 'Take care, Mr Holmes! I am quite capable of looking after myself. But in the matter of my sister's death, perhaps you might look a little more closely at our brother. Now, out.'

Holmes and I crossed the threshold. Holmes turned back to the lady.

'Clarence. Ah, yes. What is so "relentlessly peculiar", as you put it, about him?'

'Meet him and you'll see.' She slammed the door with finality.

Holmes and I exchanged a look.

'What a family,' I said.

'Indeed. It makes one's own look positively sane,' he said with a smile. His brother Mycroft was hardly what I would consider normal. But then, of course, neither was Sherlock Holmes.

CHAPTER SEVENTEEN

Neptune

n hour later we found ourselves in Chelsea. Clarence Wandley lived in rather elegant digs in an area filled with artists and writers, benefiting from fresh breezes off the Thames, although it was quite chilly at this time of year. After a brief search for the house number, Holmes and I stood before the door. It was shiny and stood out from the neighbours' in bright, golden yellow paint. Centred on it was an enormous brass doorknocker . . . in the shape of intertwined serpents.

'Interesting,' Holmes remarked. Grasping the serpents, he rapped three times, loudly.

In a moment, the door was answered by a handsome, dark-haired man in his early twenties. Tall, strongly built with a mop of curly black hair extending to his collar and below his ears, the fellow had a long, sharp nose and dramatic cheekbones. He smiled broadly, his teeth a brilliant white. He put me in mind of some cross between a Roman statue and a carnival barker.

'*Buongiorno*,' said he. 'I am Neptune. Can I help you?' His accent was Italian.

'*Buongiorno*,' said Holmes, slipping instantly into Italian, to my surprise. '*Sono Sherlock Holmes, un detective che lavora per Sua Maestà la Regina, e questo è il mio amico e collega, il dottore John Watson. Siamo qui—*'

The man put his hands up in a kind of good-natured surrender. '*Grazie, grazie* – but please, English only. I must improve. If you don't mind, Mr . . . Holmes?'

'Certainly. Your surname, if you please?' asked Holmes.

'Bandini. I do not use. Neptune only. I am musician and, eh, this is enough.' He smiled and his personal charm was palpable. Holmes repeated our introduction, in English.

'The Queen, you say? You are detective?' Neptune's face grew sombre. 'I imagine of course why you are here. It is a very, very sad day for my friend, Clarence. The death of his sister, a very big shock. But naturally you wish to speak to him. Come in, come in, Mr Holmes. Dr Watson.'

Moments later, we stood in a large, airy room with tall windows open to the river breeze. Billowing white gauze curtains let in the light, and on the white walls, a variety of vivid green and gold paintings were hung. My eyes were drawn to the centre of the room.

There, an enormous, dark green velvet divan took up a quarter of the space. Prostrate upon it on it and surrounded by green and gold velvet pillows lay a young man.

He wore a long nightshirt of embroidered silk. One arm was thrown across his eyes, the other drooped off the side of the divan. At the end of this arm was a sketchbook, face down on a bright yellow Persian rug.

This theatrical presentation clearly belonged to the dead woman's younger brother, Clarence. His dark brown hair and delicate features were not unlike his sister Kate's. His mouth was distorted by grief. A long, low moan escaped his lips.

Although mindful of his family tragedy, I nevertheless found myself irritated by this display. While trying to shake this reaction and replace it with sympathy, I became aware of a faint rustling coming from somewhere in the room. I turned to look for the source and instead noticed Holmes staring, rapt, at a group of small paintings along one wall. I followed his gaze and received such a shock that I could not refrain from crying out, 'My God, Holmes!'

The first painting in the row was a careful, and delicate design of two snakes. And so was the second. In fact, *all* the paintings were of snakes. Some also contained leaves, one a female human hand, another bright flowers. But snakes. And more snakes.

We looked at each other in alarm.

Neptune had silently appeared at Holmes's elbow. 'I know,' he said. 'The snakes. It is a terrible – how do you say? – coincidence. The snakes on poor Jane's . . . You must understand. Clarence is an artist for the James Christie Atelier.'

James Christie, I knew, was a very successful designer of Arts and Crafts furniture, textiles and paintings. I knew this only because a young lady of my acquaintance liked their fanciful creations. His company was a rival to William Morris and was much lauded in the press.

'Christie, yes, of course,' said Holmes thoughtfully. 'Known for his designs based on the flora and fauna of the oriental countries. "Bring the jungle to Kensington". . . *that* James Christie. Clarence is an artist, then—'

'It is through his success that we live here.'

Holmes turned to eye the man called Neptune sharply. 'You live with Clarence? Are you boarding here?'

The man stiffened. 'We are friends, only. And I am a kind of assistant.'

'Friends for a long time?'

The man shrugged. 'Long time, yes.'

Holmes turned his attention back to the painting. 'Do all his works feature snakes?' he asked.

Neptune paused for a moment. 'I know that this look very, very bad for Clarence. But, yes, snakes. He loves very much.'

'Since childhood?'

'Yes! That is, he tells me this. He says the beautiful curves, the – how do you say? – iridescence of the skin—'

'Oh, stop!' cried the young man on the couch. 'Neptune, for God's sake. Words, words, words! The work speaks for itself.' He leaped to his feet. 'Now, you two. What do you want?'

'From the Queen. About your sister,' said Neptune with a frown of warning.

Holmes was fixated on the young artist. Clarence Wandley had landed on his feet awkwardly and staggered. But as he regained his balance, the young man displayed a very peculiar quality. Like my friend, he was excessively lean, but unlike Holmes, he had a kind of rubbery quality, so lithe and flexible did he seem.

From a sharp intake of breath from my friend I saw that he had torn his eyes away from the young man and stared down at the sketchbook which had landed open on the floor next to Clarence Wandley's feet. Holmes bent down to retrieve it. Wandley made a feeble attempt to snatch it back but the detective deftly pulled it away. He stared at the page with interest. I peered over his shoulder. And there I saw something that chilled me to the bones.

It was Clarence Wandley's pencil sketch of interlocking snakes. Each had its own tail being consumed by the head. A double ouroboros.

Exactly the design that had been tattooed across his dead sister's face.

CHAPTER EIGHTEEN

Clarence Wandley

ut that down!' cried Clarence Wandley, lunging forward to retrieve his sketchbook.

But Holmes neatly pulled it away from the young man and studied it further. Neptune moved closer to Holmes and held out his hand. Neptune was a large and well-muscled fellow. He was smiling, but there was menace under the friendliness. 'If you please, Mr Holmes,' said he. 'Yes, we know. It is similar to tattoo.'

Holmes continued to study the drawing. 'No. It is not *similar* to the tattoo. It is *exactly* the tattoo.'

The rustling sound grew louder, followed by a squeak.

'What is that noise?' I interjected.

'Would you care to tell us? It is coming from that box over there,' said Holmes, nodding towards the window. On a table nearby, the outline of a large box was visible under a drape of linen cloth the colour of ripe bananas.

'Nothing. We keep a bird. She is restless. The drawing please.' Neptune seemed to grow larger as he stepped even closer to Holmes.

Holmes studied the sketchbook a moment longer, then handed it to the Italian and turned to the younger man. 'Mr Wandley, how do you suppose this drawing ended up inscribed upon your sister's face?'

Clarence Wandley stood before us, peering up at Holmes with a dull malevolence. He seemed unsteady on his feet. I noticed the very peculiar way he held himself. He seemed intentionally to shift his weight from right to left and back again, his torso lagging a little behind, as in a kind of sinuous, shifting dance.

The subtle movement persisted as our conversation ensued. It was uncanny. And frankly unnerving. He was rather snake-like himself. I wondered briefly if opium or ganja contributed to the picture here. I could not smell any.

The rustling sound grew louder.

'Mr Wandley,' said Holmes. 'I will get to the bottom of your sister's death. You realize, of course, that this—' he waved generally towards the serpent paintings on the wall, 'and most particularly *this*—' he gestured to the sketchbook, 'puts you at the heart of the matter. I am surprised, in fact, that you are not in police custody.'

'Nothing to do with me.' The boy looked over at Neptune. 'Give it to me.' It was a command. Neptune handed him the book. The Italian then began to edge away from us. I felt uneasy, and it struck me that I needed to keep an eye on this man.

I felt in my pocket for my Webley. I had neglected to bring it! I caught Holmes's eyes upon me. He read my alarm and nodded nearly imperceptibly.

'I am willing to hear your side,' said Holmes, turning to the boy. 'Kindly explain.'

'I do not need to explain,' said Clarence, 'I am an artist. My design was stolen.' Holding the sketchbook close to his chest, he flopped himself back down on the divan, turning his back to us in the manner of a sulking child. 'Neptune. *You* explain,' he said.

Neptune was now standing near a large walnut desk. His hand was behind him, resting on a drawer – a drawer he was ever so carefully edging open. From my angle I could see his hand slither into the drawer.

'Holmes!'

'I see it, Watson. Flank.'

We quickly took up positions to the extreme right and left of the Italian. 'If it is a weapon you are attempting to pull from that drawer, Mr Bandini, I suggest you reconsider,' said Holmes. 'First, the police and the Palace both know we are here; we are acting on Her Majesty's behalf.'

As he spoke, Holmes slowly approached Neptune on his extreme right. I followed suit and did so on the man's left. Neptune looked nervously from one of us to the other, unsure of where to focus his attention.

'Even if you were able to dispatch us both and bury us in the garden back there,' continued my friend, 'you would be found, and in short order. Oh . . . that was not your plan? In any case, you would not be successful.'

Neptune closed the drawer and stepped away from the

desk, smiling sheepishly. 'You mistake me. So dramatic! No gun. Just I look for a pen,' said he.

'There's one, on your desk,' said Holmes, pointing.

'Ah, so there is.' Neptune took up the pen and stepped away from the desk.

Holmes turned back to the young man. 'Mr Wandley?'

Clarence Wandley lay on the divan, curling around his sketchbook like a kitten with a ball of wool. I was slightly repelled by the sight. 'Go away,' he whined.

Neptune pointed to the next room. 'Please. I perhaps can help you. Come with me.'

He left the room, Holmes behind him. Before following, I peeked into the desk drawer. There was no gun. However, there was a long and very sharp letter-opener.

We followed Neptune into a dining area, also painted a blinding white. A large, rough-hewn table with two long benches stood in the centre. French doors opened to a small, verdant garden at the back, crammed with flowering plants and tall foliage with enormous leaves. A jungle in the heart of Chelsea. A prolific and skilled gardener had been at work.

Holmes hesitated only a moment, then we both sat. A wind had come up and the greenery out back began to tremble and wave. An icy draft flooded the room and Neptune closed the French doors.

'Clarence,' he said softly, 'he is an artist, and you can see he is delicate. His work for James Christie, it is more than a year.' He joined us at the table with the pen and a small slip of paper. 'I write you here the address. Do you know this James Christie?'

'Of him, and only a little. Though I have the address. Tell me more,' said Holmes.

'Certainly. You know that he is famous for . . . a kind of Oriental style. It is – how do you say? – Flora and Fauna. There are collections. Collections with . . . themes. A jungle theme; a river theme; an elephant theme; and a snake theme. That one is Clarence's.'

'During Clarence's time there . . . has it *always* been snakes?'

'Yes. The paintings in our salon. You saw them. He design like this for two years. He love the snakes since he was a boy.'

'You seem to know your friend well,' said Holmes.

Neptune said nothing.

'But how do you explain the sketch we just saw being an exact match for the work that defaced his sister?'

'I am not so sure. It has upset Clarence very much. You see. But there is a story. The sketch you saw . . . the one that match . . . was basis for new series. It go like this. My dear Clarence draw many sketches and give to Mr Christie, who select. Then Clarence makes watercolour using different colours, beautiful colours – many different, er, variations, I think you say, of this sketch. Mr Christie then choose that which please him most. Then Clarence, he make a beautiful oil painting of the chosen colours. And fabric, or perhaps other goods for the home are created based on this painting.'

Neptune swallowed and glanced out at the garden. The wind had gained sudden strength and huge, heart-shaped leaves flapped wildly at the other end of the garden, the smaller plants shuddering in the breeze. It was almost as though nature were reflecting the unease of our situation, of this conversation. A small shed stood at the far end of this garden, nearly hidden by the verdant foliage.

'But what of this design?' said Holmes.

'They reach the final stages last month. Clarence, he make a magnificent painting. Exactly like the sketch. Like the tattoo. We deliver it to the atelier, and then . . . it disappear! Stolen!'

'Stolen? When exactly?'

'One month ago. Everyone so upset.'

'Anything else taken?'

'I do not know.'

'Go on.'

'James Christie, he was furious! The paintings on which his designs are based are sometime sold later at auction. Very, very high prices. But this one had not yet been, er, copy for the fabric design. It was – how do you say? – in work when the painting was stolen.'

'Was a report made to the police?' asked Holmes.

'Yes. And a sketch was provided.'

Holmes nodded. He and I exchanged a look. This meant the design could have been seen in many places and by many people in the last month. 'I will pursue this avenue of inquiry. That does not entirely clear your friend, as you can well imagine.'

'He had no to do with it. I was with him when he saw his sister's face,' said Neptune. 'Jane! He collapse with grief. The shock!'

I felt it odd for this man to use the dead woman's Christian name.

'Yes, yes. Upon viewing his sister's tattoo, I take it he failed to inform the Palace that it was his design?' said Holmes.

Here the man hesitated. 'He . . . he did not.'

'Nor did you?'

'No.'

'And so they have not yet made the connection with the stolen painting. Why did Clarence Wandley not reveal his connection at the Palace?'

'He could not stand the questions at that time. As I say, he collapse.'

Something about Neptune's demeanour was troubling me, but I could not put my finger upon it.

Holmes paused, calculating. His fingers drummed on the dining table.

'How long have you and Clarence Wandley been close?'

'I . . . uh, some years now.'

'How did you meet?'

I could not imagine the purpose of this line of questioning.

'Sir, how does this relate to your inquiries?' asked Neptune, who apparently could not, either. 'We are friends. For a long time. Clarence love the music. I play violin. He hear me at the restaurant and we talk about music.'

'Where do you play?'

'The Macaroni Palace.'

'He heard you at the Macaroni Palace? That has only been open for a year.'

'Er, no . . . He hear me at another restaurant I was before.'

'What restaurant is that?'

The smallest of hesitations. 'Nights of Napoli.'

'I have not heard of it.'

'It . . . it is closed now.'

Holmes said nothing but continued to stare at the man.

Neptune went on. 'I need a room. He rent to me and I help him. As you see, he is not a strong man.' He laughed. 'You know – artists, so emotional. They have trouble if alone too much.'

I have always thought of Holmes as an artist as well as a scientist, and although he was nothing like Clarence, whom I took to be a hothouse flower, Holmes also did better with the steadying influence of a friend. While I did not wish to overvalue my contribution to our crime-fighting activities, I had observed this quite clearly.

'Your violin playing – it pays well?' Holmes smiled and gestured at the elegant surroundings.

'I wish. But . . . not so much. I perform at a restaurant. The pay depend mostly from the people who dine. I am no wealthy man. This house, it is all the success of Clarence. The atelier pay him well.'

'I understand his father also contributes to his son's upkeep?' At Neptune's blank look, he continued. 'Mr Peter Oliver mentioned it to us.'

Neptune looked embarrassed. 'Clarence no longer need, but Sir James insist.'

'And so your friend supports you?' Holmes asked.

The man's face darkened. 'As I told you. We support each other.'

'Financially?'

'That is our business.'

'Why, yes, I suppose it is,' said Holmes. 'Enough, then.

I have a few more questions for Clarence. Let us hope he is a little recovered.'

We returned to the salon. Clarence Wandley sat morosely on the green divan, smoking a brown cigarette. The distinct odour of ganja filled the room.

'Mr Wandley,' said Holmes. 'I must ask you a few questions. It will be here or at the police station. Your choice.'

I smiled inwardly at this bluff. Holmes, of course, had no power to arrest anyone.

Clarence Wandley looked up with heavy lidded eyes. 'Here.'

'What was your relationship with your sister, Jane?'

Wandley snorted. 'Jane. She was . . . she was like a mother to us.'

'That does not tell me much. How like a mother?'

Clarence Wandley smiled, an expression that belied his next words. 'A tyrant.'

'Like your real mother? Was your real mother a tyrant?'

Clarence and Neptune exchanged a meaningful look. Odd, I thought.

'No, my mother was more of a quiet villain. Jane was a . . . a kind of petty tyrant.'

'Exacting? Strict? Authoritarian? In what way was your sister a tyrant?'

'She enjoyed humiliating us. Kate and me . . . both.'

'Peter Oliver, your father's assistant, described the opposite. He said that you and Kate tormented Jane. Was he incorrect?' Holmes was relentless.

'Not exactly. It was a kind of war. Jane had the upper hand. But we gave back, Kate and I.' He smiled. His canine teeth were large and pointed. It was a sinister smile on such a young, undeveloped-looking person.

'You realize, of course, that your resentment of your sister gives you ample motive for her murder?'

For the first time, Clarence seemed startled. His eyes went wide as he choked on his smoke and coughed violently for a moment. Regaining his composure, he said, 'She killed herself. *Jane killed herself!* The Palace told us that.'

'They were mistaken. She was murdered. One more thing, Mr Wandley. What is your personal theory for how your very particular design came to be tattooed on her face?'

'It was stolen!' He turned to Neptune. 'Didn't you tell . . . ?' The taller man nodded, and sat beside him on the divan, putting his arm protectively around the younger man's shoulder. 'Beyond that, I have no idea. Please leave me alone.'

'I suggest you remain in London, Mr Wandley. If you are innocent, the police will get to the bottom of it. But they must, you understand, follow up on the matter of this painting.'

'Please go.'

'When I am satisfied, I shall leave you. But first, I need your exact whereabouts for the last week – every minute of every day and night.'

'Here,' said Clarence. 'I was here. I eat, sleep and live always here. In my studio. Or in my garden.'

'He was here all the week,' said Neptune. 'I cannot drag him even to the market, although he is very particular about his food. No, I cannot make him go out.'

'But *you* go to the market? When?'

'Twice weekly. Tuesday and Friday. In the morning.'

'And you play violin at the Macaroni Palace. Is that every night?'

'No. Only Friday and Saturday nights.'

'Southwark, I know it. It is very popular with young people,' said my friend. I smiled at this. Holmes and I were in our early thirties. How young were these people, I wondered? Of course, I had heard of the restaurant. It was reputed to have a slightly romantic, if decadent, atmosphere and excellent food, inexpensive. Macaroni of various shapes served with Italian sauces. I had always meant to try it.

'Then you were out of the house on those evenings . . . at what hours?'

'From five in the afternoon until quite late.'

'You cannot vouch for the whereabouts of Mr Wandley, then. Or during your visits to the market.'

'Clarence does not leave the house alone.'

'Why not?'

Neither man answered.

At length Neptune volunteered, 'Clarence has been a kind of target. He is . . . he has . . . an appearance that occasionally, I think you say, provokes remark.'

That last statement was entirely believable.

Holmes took up his hat. 'Oh, one final thing. How many snakes do you keep?'

Snakes? Dear God. My eyes flew to the floor.

'We keep no snakes,' said Neptune.

'Nonsense. You keep them in that shed at the back. You have furnished it with steam heat.' He nodded toward the shed. Of course, the plumbing was visible, but I had not noticed it.

The two young men exchanged a look of pure guilt.

'Just one snake,' said Neptune.

'Three,' said Clarence Wandley.

Holmes waited, expectantly.

'All right, six,' said Neptune. 'A rattlesnake, a baby python, a viper, a boa, a cobra and a mamba. Yes, in the shed. We have a special enclosure. Each separate. They are not friends. But very good models for Clarence. How did you know?'

'The pipes for the heat *snaking* through your garden was one indication. But I already knew it from this room.' He moved over to the box covered with the yellow cloth. With a flamboyant gesture, he tore off the cover to reveal a cage of at least thirty live brown mice. This was, of course, the source of the small noises we had been hearing.

'Lunch, Watson?' Holmes said with a smile.

My stomach lurched.

'We must be off. Good day, gentlemen,' said Holmes.

We left to a cacophony of squeaks.

Despite the brisk wind, Holmes suggested we walk along the Thames for a while. 'The fresh air will help me think,' said he. He usually preferred stillness and a pipe while thinking, but instead we trudged along for some minutes. It was nearly three o'clock, and the wind had further picked up and had a distinctly icy edge to it. I suggested we head back to Baker Street and a nice fire, as we had, in fact, missed lunch.

'I prefer to walk, Watson, to clear my mind. This is a very strange case. Something about the relationship of the siblings is highly concerning. And inconsistently described.'

'What a very unusual young man that Clarence is, don't you think?'

He laughed. 'Unusual does not begin to describe him.'

'He must be involved in some way! That drawing . . .'

'That drawing was clearly the basis for the tattoo. But whether or not he was involved directly, I cannot say,' said Holmes.

I could hear a sudden squawking of seagulls. Their travel into London usually heralded a storm. Holmes walked on in silence. Then, 'Watson. There is something underlying this story. Something deep below the surface. I am afraid we have some digging before us.'

'Could it be someone attempting to blackmail, or implicate him for some reason or other?' I murmured. 'Look! There's a pub serving roast chicken!'

Holmes walked right past it. After another ten minutes of pensive walking during which the temperature dropped precipitously, he stopped and consulted his pocket watch.

'Ah, at last, it is time! We have one more visit today, Watson.' At this, he signalled for a cab. 'We are for Tooting!'

I laughed. But he was serious.

'The Christie Atelier, Watson. They are expecting us. I arranged it last night.'

'Before we met with Clarence Wandley? *How? And, why?*'

'I found some clippings about Wandley's snake-themed work.' He smiled at me. 'That was enough for me.'

'Rather a lot, I'd say!' I marvelled. He still could not have known it was the precise design that had been tattooed on the dead girl's face.

CHAPTER NINETEEN

Christie's Kittens

oon we were en route by carriage to the famed Christie studio, across the Albert Bridge towards Tooting, a name which in sunnier times always made me laugh, and into the greener spaces further south.

We arrived at last at a long, low brick building that must once have been some kind of warehouse. Above worn loading docks, enormous two-storey windows had been cut into the walls.

A receptionist was expecting us, and we were ushered into the studio to await the proprietor. This was a large, airy space incorporating the floor-to-ceiling windows we had seen from outside, and the room was further lit by skylights. The air was thick with the smell of turpentine, sweat and coffee. Clustered near the windows were three easels, with two men and one woman painting at them.

As they worked, music filled the air. I looked around for the source. Off to one side, a middle-aged pianist with garishly dyed red hair played a desultory tune on a cottage piano, with the listless languor of one long past being interested in the world or its doings.

The musician was a surprising touch. I supposed some artists did their best work inspired by such a soothing background.

I turned my attention to the three painters.

All perhaps in their mid-thirties, they had surrounded themselves with props. The woman, a tall, angular young lady with auburn hair carelessly knotted at her neck and a denim apron covering a paint-stained black frock, riveted her attention on a large tin pail set up on a stool. It contained a profusion of what looked to be tropical blossoms in autumn colours of gold, vermillion and yellow-green.

Next to her, another tall figure, also with auburn hair which stood on end in a chaotic halo around his sallow face, stared with fierce concentration at a cage in which there were two monkey-like creatures. I would guess they were lemurs. Every so often, one of these would shriek.

The third painter, a stocky, prematurely balding man, was engrossed in a minute study of the taxidermized and disembodied foot of an elephant. Photographs of elephants were pinned to a board, propped up near his feet.

Enormous potted plants with a distinctly jungle-like look clustered on either side of the tall windows, surrounding the painters. Some of the plants were of the kind I'd noticed in Clarence Wandley's small garden.

The receptionist who had brought us to this room

departed, and seconds later the proprietor of this atelier, Mr James Christie, appeared before us.

Christie was a corpulent man of perhaps forty, in the prime of life, with a cheerful countenance. His sleek brown hair was parted in the middle, swooping down past his ears, and was pomaded to a high sheen.

'Mr Holmes, Dr Watson,' he beamed. 'Welcome to my Jungle of Primitive Delights! James Christie, at your service. I am delighted to make your acquaintance. I have followed your adventures, Mr Holmes – penned, I believe, by you, Dr Watson? It would seem, just as I am an artist of furnishings of the home, so Sherlock Holmes is an artist of the solving of crimes. It is all in the details, is it not, sir? All in the details!'

'Indeed,' said Holmes with a smile. 'Details are to crime solving as pencil sketches are to artistic design.'

'Surely not?' said our host. 'I thought details came last. Rather to confirm the detective's theories of a crime. The final brush strokes to refine and complete the picture, so to speak.' He smiled modestly. 'I read quite a bit of crime, you see. It is a hobby of mine.'

'Fascinating. That is the common theory, but no. Only amateurs theorize ahead of the evidence. No, Mr Christie, useful premises arise only *after details have been collected*. In a good sketch, the pencil lines explore before honing in on only those details which are true. From these assembled lines or shapes *one then begins to see the entire picture*.'

The phrase 'art in the blood' came to mind, which Holmes had used to describe both himself and his brother Mycroft.

'Ah, well, you are the expert, I suppose,' said Christie,

with a shrug. 'I understand that you are on a mission for Her Majesty. Though shrouded in some mystery, I gather it may pertain to a certain possession of mine which was recently stolen?'

'Yes.'

'Then I welcome your inquiry, sir! Police have made no progress in finding the painting in question. I am hoping you will. Its restoration to the atelier would mean a great deal to me. It is the latest in our serpent series. A remarkable work—'

'Even if found, Mr Christie, the painting most likely will be retained by the police. It has a direct bearing on a larger case. A case of murder.'

'Murder! My painting would be retained, you say? Why on earth?'

'That is for a later discussion. Perhaps it will come back to you. But tracing the theft will serve both Her Majesty's – and your own – wishes, Mr Christie,' said Holmes, whose annoyance was evident, at least to me. 'Now, if you will kindly answer a few questions . . .'

With somewhat less bonhomie than that with which he had welcomed us, Christie assented. He led us to a table in the centre of the room. On it were a platter of biscuits and sandwiches, and a tall pot of steaming liquid that smelled like Turkish coffee.

'May I offer you a refreshment?' Christie asked.

Holmes waved his hand. 'I see that at least some of your artists seem to do their work here in the atelier,' Holmes said, gesturing toward the three painters near the window. 'How is it, then, that Mr Wandley works at home?'

Christie paused.

The tall red-haired artist approached on silent feet and began to pour himself a cup. I noticed he was wearing carpet slippers. As he put the pot down, the man left a smear of red paint on the handle.

This did not escape our host.

'Paint, Rufus!' cried Christie. The artist noticed his error and wiped off the handle with a paint-flecked cloth hanging from his belt. He grinned at us.

Christie attempted to herd us away from the table. 'Come. My office is this way. As to why Clarence Wandley works at home, he—'

I heard a sudden hiss. Behind us the painter Rufus continued to busy himself with his coffee, his back to us. He turned to glance at us with a mischievous smile.

'Rufus!' cried Christie.

Rufus turned to face us. 'Snakes,' he said, then shivered theatrically. With a final shrug, he returned to his easel, biscuits and coffee in hand.

'Mr Wandley insisted on working with live specimens,' said Christie.

The lemur or whatever it was shrieked again. 'So does Rufus, I see,' said Holmes.

'Yes, but snakes! They bothered the other artists. One escaped once, and—'

Over at the window, all three of the artists, still at their easels but clearly still listening, began hissing. The woman giggled.

Christie looked skyward. 'Artists! Children, all. It is like trying to pull a sled with kittens in the harness.'

I laughed.

Holmes glanced at me with a frown. 'I would like to learn more about Clarence's work,' said he to our host.

'I am happy to advise. Please. Let us continue in my office,' said Christie.

CHAPTER TWENTY

The Theft

oments later, seated behind a grand desk in the whimsical Arts and Crafts style of Bohemian high society, Christie described the theft of Clarence Wandley's painting.

How the thief entered was unknown, as no locks or windows were broken, but he had ignored many other paintings in progress as well as other finished paintings and had gone straight to a small stack of recent paintings awaiting Christie's approval. Only Wandley's was stolen.

'The thief knew his way around,' said Holmes.

'Many people do. I have given tours here to various collectors, arts organizations and benevolent societies. Schoolchildren, even.'

As he spoke, I could not help but notice his decorative waistcoat, featuring a profusion of leaves with mysterious eyes peering through them intermittently.

'And was anything else taken?' asked Holmes.

'No.' The designer noticed me staring at his waistcoat. 'Ah, do you like the fabric you see on my waistcoat, Dr Watson? I see that you are a man who pays at least a modicum of attention to current fashion. Your waistcoat has a subtle connection in hue to your tie. Well chosen, my good man!'

Holmes tsked in impatience. But Christie was not to be deterred. He tapped his pocket square. 'What do you think of this small addition, here, the pocket square? It has gained some traction in certain circles. Oscar Wilde, for example, wears them. The fabric is ours, of course. You will be seeing these soon on everyone.'

He took in my more conservatively attired friend. 'You, on the other hand, while certainly elegant, could indeed find a pocket square adding a bit of cachet.'

'I am not here for fashion advice, Mr Christie,' said Holmes rather testily. 'Let me impress upon you the severity of the situation. The precise design of your stolen painting – down to the colouration – was found reproduced in a particularly detailed and horrific manner upon the body of a murder victim.'

'On the body, you say? How—?'

'Tattooed. You need not know the details. When did the theft occur?'

'I . . . I am not sure. I noticed it gone the morning after a party. Presumably sometime during the event . . .'

'Anything else taken?'

A small hesitation. 'No.'

'We will come back to that,' said Holmes. 'How large was the painting?'

'Not so very large. Our fabric designer needs only a relatively small—'

'*How* large?'

Christie held out his hands to indicate. 'Perhaps two by three feet.'

'We understand from Mr Wandley that once a design and a set of colours is decided upon, the fabric designer then adds his final touch?'

'Yes. *Hers*, in our case. She must then create a repetitive design, one that can extend over yards and yards of fabric or wallpaper. That design was already in work, but incomplete. Come, I will show you.'

He led us to another room which featured another bright window, but of a normal size, and sitting before it, a large, slanted drafting table. On it were various sheets of vellum paper with tracings – of snakes! A cup of sharpened pencils, some scissors and other cutting tools were arranged nearby in neat, precise rows, in direct contrast to the writhing, twisting figures on the vellum.

But there was no one present. 'Where is the fabric designer?'

'She is home with a cough. But you say this design, or something like it, was tattooed, on a victim's body?'

'It was an exact copy. It may well be related to the theft. The criminal could have worked from it.'

Or from Clarence Wandley's materials at home, I thought, but said nothing.

Christie went pale. 'Grotesque! All the more reason to find it, I would think.'

'Surely you will not release this snake design in your collection?' I blurted.

'On the contrary. I will most certainly! And capitalize on the popularity of the serpent in the public's imagination. I have already invested hundreds of pounds in the development of this design.'

'What is the production significance of the stolen painting, Mr Christie?' asked my friend. 'How much delay has this introduced to your process?'

'Frankly, rather small, as I have colour notes, here—'

He moved to a side table and opened a large folder. Inside were a number of studies of sections of Wandley's design, rendered in delicate ink and watercolour – some bright and almost garish, others more subtle and earthy.

Holmes eyed them all, rapidly paging through the sheets of watercolours. He stopped at one and pointed to it. 'This one, here . . .'

'Yes, that is the one I chose!'

'Why Holmes, that is . . . that looks very like the colours on the young lady's face!' I said.

Holmes frowned at me. 'No, Watson it is not *very* like. Those are *exactly* the colours.

'On a lady's face?' exclaimed Christie. 'Someone tattooed a snake *on a woman's face?*'

'Yes, Mr Christie, someone tattooed Clarence Wandley's precise design on his sister's face. With those colours.'

'There must be a mistake. The young lady – you say she was a *sister* of Clarence Wandley?' The man was frowning, trying to make sense of the outré details.

'Yes, Mr Christie, but if you would kindly ignore our indiscretion and forget you heard the name and the specifics, if you please? Here is a question for you. Was it the oil rendering of this design in precisely these colours that was stolen?' Holmes continued.

'Yes.'

'When you sell these paintings after your designers are finished with them, how much might you expect to receive for such a work?'

'Several hundreds of pounds,' said the man. 'In one case, nearly a thousand.' He shook his head. 'Dear God, her face!'

Holmes stared at him for a moment as if trying to calculate the veracity of the statement. He stood up. 'Very well, then. Can you show me where the paintings were kept?'

'Right here, in my office. This stack, here, by the door.'

'Is your office normally locked?'

'Yes.'

'And this particular night?'

'I . . . no . . . I think I may have forgotten to lock the door. That day we were celebrating a recent lucrative commission. We had a small party for the family.'

'The family?'

'Everyone at the studio. We have no workers. No management. We are all family.'

The kittens in harness notwithstanding, I thought.

'Where was this party?'

'In the studio we were just in, gentlemen.'

'Could someone have slipped away from these festivities, come in here, and moved the painting to a waiting carriage or recipient in the alleyway visible outside this window?'

He swallowed. 'Yes, I suppose so.'

'Did you check on the painting before leaving that night?'

'Well, I looked in and nothing seemed amiss.' The man paused. 'It was late. I had had rather a lot of wine.'

'Then you are not sure the painting in question was still there?'

'No.'

'When did you discover the theft?'

'The next morning.'

'As the police report shows no evidence of a break-in, it might conceivably have been taken during the party.'

'I – I suppose so.'

'Nothing else was missing?' asked Holmes.

'No.' The man swallowed, and rubbed his eyes 'But—'

'Go on.'

'I have since remembered. One other thing was missing.'

'What was that?'

'Oh, just a small thing. A silver filigreed pen. Not terribly valuable, but unique.'

'Describe it,' said Holmes

'There is no other pen like it. It was a design struck when I was considering offering desk accessories some years ago. Oh, I was greatly vexed to discover that pen missing. It was a personal favourite – in the shape of an alligator. Quite witty, in fact.'

'Do you have a photograph of it?'

'I am afraid I do not. Though I could sketch it for you.'

'Please.'

Christie sat down at his desk and took up pen and paper.

Holmes resumed his perusal of the room. 'How many people attended this party?'

'Eighty or so, I would say.'

'All by personal invitation?'

'Yes, either by me or by the artists.'

'Do you have a final guest list?'

He finished his quick sketch and held the paper up. Holmes was busy at the bookcase so I took it, eyed it briefly, and placed it in my pocket.

'Somewhere, I suppose, let me see.'

'Did the artists submit to you their list of invitees?'

'Yes.' After a brief rummage Christie procured it for Holmes. Four separate pieces of paper, one with paint smears visible to me from several feet away.

'I see that Clarence Wandley invited his father to the showing. And his sisters. Jane Wandley and Kate Wandley,' said Holmes. Did they come?'

'To my knowledge, the father did not. Clarence was not the most sociable of beings. Only one of the sisters came, a rather forward young lady.'

'Describe her, please.'

'Slender. Angular face, black hair, full lips. A bit sullen, perhaps.'

'Kate Wandley, the younger sister. Yes, here she is on the list. Visiting alone?'

'Well, she was with someone. A young man. Was she the sister who—?'

'No. Describe the young man she was with, please.'

'Oh, dear. I only saw him across the room. He was entirely unremarkable.'

'Oh, come now, Mr Christie. You are a visual artist. Height? Build? Moustache? Spectacles?'

'Ah, well, let me see. He was clean shaven, middle height,

perhaps your age, medium build, light brown hair, unremarkable tailoring. Wearing spectacles.'

'That could be anyone. What was your impression? A professional man? An aristocrat? A working-class fellow?'

'None of those precisely. Educated, perhaps? Though I am not sure why I say that. He did not speak in my presence. I am sorry. He was entirely unremarkable. I was rather distracted by the young lady.'

'And what was interesting about Miss Kate Wandley?'

'She was most irritating. She seemed amused, almost mocking about the art she saw. I remember hoping she'd leave quickly. And fortunately she did. One snide viewer at a gallery showing can poison the atmosphere, you see. I had a number of small works for sale that evening, and . . . well, you understand.'

'Yes. Might any of your guests have wandered back through that door and into your office?'

He nodded sadly. 'Yes. I suppose I should have been more careful. Much more careful, Mr Holmes. Anyone could have gone in there.'

PART FIVE

TANGLED STRANDS

*'Just as a snake sheds its skin, we must shed
our past over and over again.'*
—Gautama Buddha

CHAPTER TWENTY-ONE

Heffie Reports

s we headed back to 221B in a hansom cab, night settled over us. A full moon pierced through the heavy clouds and the temperature had dropped precipitously. It was one moment when I wished for the relative comfort of a four-wheeler, but none were to be found in the neighbourhood of Christie's. A lap blanket that looked like it had recently lined a barn stall remained on the floor.

'Both siblings grow more interesting, don't you think, Holmes? Clarence's design was tattooed on the girl's face. And Kate had the opportunity to steal the design, to be sure. What are your thoughts?'

Holmes shook his head. 'I have not enough data for a theory, Watson. What, for example, does either sibling stand to gain from Jane's disfigurement?'

'Revenge for her presumed good luck? Or perhaps they

predicted she would kill herself? Then . . . more inheritance?'

'Illogical, Watson. Why not simply poison their sibling, if that last was the motive? No, this perpetrator bore an extreme grudge against Jane Wandley. Or what she represented.'

'I suppose.'

'It was intended to make some kind of statement. But to whom? What was the intended result? And where did the murder then figure?'

Holmes closed his eyes. I supposed that alternative scenarios played out in his mind as they did so often in the past. I often thought of his mind as a kind of combination lock, his keen imagination spinning the dials, again and again, until the right sequence unlocked the solution.

'Suppose, Watson, that the tattoo was a message. A punishment. A threat of worse to come.'

'What could be worse for a beautiful young woman?'

'Use your imagination,' said he.

'I cannot imagine,' I said after a moment. And truthfully, I could not.

'Slavery, for one,' he said at last. 'A return to the family seat is in order.'

'The father, do you think?'

'His evasion, given the circumstances, is puzzling in the extreme.'

Holmes would not engage further on the subject. After our freezing ride back to Baker Street, we welcomed the warmth of 221B.

There we discovered Heffie, standing before the hearth,

bending down to rub her cold-reddened hands nearer the coals. She had come to give us her report on Miss Ferndale's group and her hunt for a purported traitor.

Mrs Hudson soon entered with tea and roast beef sandwiches for all. Heffie dived in eagerly.

'It's quite the – what-you-call-it? – *fractious* group,' she said. 'Is "fractious" a word? Well, anyways, Emily Ferndale is not pushing violence. Not at all, is my impression. No, indeed. In fact, she's the voice o' reason.'

'Well, that's a relief,' I said. I had had the disturbing worry about repercussions if it transpired that Holmes was inadvertently supporting mob violence.

Of course, 'inadvertent' was a concept one could rarely apply to him.

'What of the members, Heffie?' asked Holmes.

'Lots of very angry young women, Mr 'olmes. Used to doing without, an' tired of it. Some of 'em 'ave 'ad some pretty awful experiences – unwanted attention an' the like. Some violent, even.'

'Personal beauty is most certainly a liability in their world,' I said.

Heffie snorted indignantly. 'Sometimes. Not always.'

'Any who stand out as possible traitors?' asked Holmes.

'Several of 'em would rather lead than follow. A couple of 'em would gladly step up if Miss Ferndale even left the room to relieve herself, which she don't because she knows it. Well, I exaggerate . . .'

'Tell me about them, Heffie.'

Heffie pushed some wayward curls out of her eyes and took a deep breath. 'Early days. Firstly, all them girls want more to do. Or say they do. Emily is strugglin' to think up tasks for 'em to make 'em feel important. So she has 'em go an' spy on places. Investigate like they was detectives, findin' out when factories open an' what doors do people go in an' out of, stuff like that.'

Holmes paced by the window. I sensed he was holding back his impatience.

'You said a couple were ready to step up, Heffie,' I prompted. 'Can you elaborate?'

'You two ain't goin' to like this.'

'Ain't we?' snapped Holmes.

I did wish he'd let up on the girl sometimes.

'You *are not* going to like this.'

'Go on.'

'There's two in a different class from the rest. One in particular. She is already second-in-command.'

'Her name?'

'Kate Wandley.'

Holmes ceased his pacing and turned to Heffie with keen interest. '*Kate Wandley?* You're sure of that name?'

''Course I'm sure. S'why you hire me, ain't it? *Isn't it?*'

'Just to confirm: black hair, blue eyes, looks French?'

'That's the one, Mr 'olmes.'

'You say second-in-command. What does that mean, precisely?'

'She helps plan. They go off together an' do that. This Wandley girl's the only one wi' brains enough for the task. Emily seems to have really took 'er in. She came in recently. But . . .' She paused.

'But what, Heffie?

'I don' like the way she looks at Emily when Emily ain't – *isn't* – lookin' at her.'

'How?'

'From underneath, like this.' Heffie looked down at her boots then her eyes flickered up at me surreptitiously, then away.

Much as I did not care for Kate Wandley, still this observation seemed slim to me. 'Oh, come, Heffie!' I interjected.

Holmes held up a hand to me and turned to the girl. 'No, Watson. Tell us more, Heffie,' said he. 'I trust your instincts. What precisely is Miss Wandley's role as second-in-command?'

'She picks the times and places,' said the girl.

Holmes nodded, considering. 'And a second young woman? You said a couple caught your eye.'

'Girl named Laura Benson. She used to be Emily Ferndale's favourite, so far's I can tell. Not exactly upper class but a cut above the rest o' the girls. Special friend of Miss Ferndale, I think. She hates this Kate girl something fierce. There ain't nothin' hidden about it.'

'Jealous, then?'

Heffie nodded. 'Guess Kate Wandley kinda stepped between 'er and Miss Ferndale.'

'How so?

'This Laura, she's the one used to help choose the places.'

'To disastrous effect, obviously,' I said.

'Now Miss Ferndale and Miss Wandley are keepin' it secret, even from the other girls. I mean women. On account of the troubles past.'

Holmes smiled. 'But I'll wager you know where,' said he.

Heffie grinned. "Course I do. S'why I'm 'ere now. It's tomorrow. Before dawn. Five in the mornin', in fact. 'Ere's the address.' She handed Holmes a small slip of paper.

'How did you find out, Heffie?' I asked.

Heffie just smiled mysteriously.

'It is why we employ her, Watson,' said Holmes. 'When I can steal her back from her police work.'

'You always come first, Mr 'olmes.'

'Keep an eye on Miss Benson and Miss Wandley, would you, Heffie? And do remind me when this case is over. I'd like to send you off for a bit.'

'Off?'

'Yes. A summer course in Switzerland. Or perhaps Italy. Expand your horizons.'

'Don't think I need no expandin'. If it ain't – *isn't* – in London, what do I need it for? Everythin' is here.'

'Trust me, Heffie. Some enrichment will make you a better detective.'

She sniffed. 'Detective, eh? Don't remember no commitment about that.'

Holmes smiled. 'Or whatever is your eventual career, Heffie. Trust me.'

She laughed, but gave me a wink and was out of the door.

As soon as the girl had left, he called for the page, with instructions to deliver a hastily scrawled message to a Mr James Chudley in Islington.

'Who's that?' I asked.

'Help. And now to bed, Watson. We have business before dawn.'

CHAPTER TWENTY-TWO

A Smelly Business

 hus it was that we found ourselves, well before dawn the next morning, loitering in a dark alley near the docks, with a view of the entrance to the Berkeley Brothers Fish Cannery. The pungent odour of sardines permeated the icy air. After my hastily consumed coffee and eggs, the smell rendered me queasy.

A feeble streetlamp barely illuminated a growing crowd of young women clustered nearby. Some held signs, others flyers. Emily Ferndale, elegant in a dark green wool coat, stood in the centre of this gathering.

As we joined the group as the only two men, tension stiffened their movements. Everyone except Miss Ferndale eyed us with frank suspicion. I caught a glimpse of Heffie, playing her role as a part of the group, seeming to regard us with the same hostility.

Kate Wandley was nowhere to be seen. Where, I wondered, was she?

Emily Ferndale quietly addressed the attending group. 'Ladies. These two gentlemen are here by my invitation. This is the esteemed detective, Mr Sherlock Holmes, and his colleague, Dr Watson. They are here to protect our interests—'

'Not *protect*, Miss Ferndale,' corrected Holmes. 'Merely to observe and substantiate your lawful protests. Which, I emphasize, *must remain peaceful at all times.*'

'Of course. And that is our goal. Mr Holmes is here on our behalf, ladies,' corrected Miss Ferndale. 'And at my behest. Now, I ask you all to raise your mufflers and cover the lower half of your face. If there are any photographers here today, they will not be rewarded with our pictures.' Half the group, given the foetid air, had already raised their scarves.

The rest complied, including Holmes and myself. We now resembled a group of marauding pirates. Holmes, towering above the ladies, peered over the top of the group and said, aside to me, 'Watson, look! It's Pettifer, the infamous "umbrella moment" photographer!'

I followed Holmes's gaze towards the factory entrance. Sure enough, a tall, muscular fellow was setting up his camera equipment with the help of an assistant. Sporting a dye-darkened moustache and mutton chops, Pettifer had the look of a sinister circus barker.

The photographer felt our stare and turned to peer into the alley. The dawn light was breaking through and we were likely becoming visible through the murk.

'Why, hello, ladies!' he called out. 'We meet again!' There were murmurs of disapproval, even hostility.

'Ah, the nerve!' I said.

'C'mon out. Let me see your pretty faces!' called Pettifer.

Emily Ferndale waved the group forward. 'Ladies. You know what to do.' The women emerged from the alley and stood across the wide entrance to the factories. Some held leaflets, others carried signs. All kept their scarves up.

As we followed them out, I spotted Kate Wandley to the left of the factory gates. Her muffler covered the lower half of her face, but those distinctive eyes gave her away.

'Holmes!' I whispered.

'I see her.'

Kate was threading her way toward Pettifer and his camera. She noticed us and started in surprise. With a frown she turned back to her task, whatever it was.

'Take off those mufflers and smile for me, would you? For a moment of fame?' Pettifer called out to the young women. 'A moment in the public eye for the strike for women's rights? Your mum will appreciate your courage, even if your 'usbands don't.'

Emily Ferndale waved them forward, and *en masse*, the group moved towards the photographer. I could sense his sudden unease.

'You can just 'appily get lost,' said one surly young lady, as another, a short, heavyset girl, approached and in a sudden move appeared to trip and fall heavily against the camera tripod, upending it. Pettifer and his assistant barely caught his camera before it crashed to the ground. The girl backed away and melted into the crowd.

'Break this camera and I'll see you in the clink for that, you little harlot!' Pettifer snarled, his bonhomie shed faster than a snakeskin.

The crowd of women parted as Emily Ferndale stepped forward and approached the photographer. Drawing him aside, she conferred with him. We were too far away to hear her words, but it evidently was the voice of reason, of charm, for the man shrugged and cracked a smile, entranced.

Next to me Holmes chuckled. 'Ah, she's very good. She has convinced him that she doesn't know he was the perpetrator of the famous "umbrella attack" photograph.'

He nodded towards the group. Two of the prettiest young women had moved in. Having lowered their scarves, they were all smiles, chatting animatedly to the photographer's assistant. Kate Wandley had edged in unnoticed, taking up a position close to the camera lens.

As the photographer and his assistant were thus distracted, Miss Wandley deftly pulled off the camera lens cover, withdrew a small tin from her voluminous coat pocket, opened it, and appeared to daub something on the lens, deftly smearing it around. She replaced the lens cover.

'What on earth?' I wondered.

'Vaseline,' Watson,' said Holmes. 'That will be the devil to get off that lens. Whatever happens, he'll get nothing here.'

'Unless he has a spare lens,' I said, recalling the resourcefulness of wartime photographers I had encountered in Afghanistan.

Heffie had sidled up next to us. 'Look!' whispered Heffie,

tugging on Holmes's sleeve. We both turned to follow her gaze to a severe-looking young woman standing off to one side. A tall redhead, with handsome, angular features and a look of deep-seated anger, she glowered at the scene. Like Kate Wandley, she was clearly of a different class than most of the group. She kept herself slightly apart from the other women, and unlike them had not covered her face with her scarf.

She stood frowning at the scene, while others around her gestured and pointed surreptitiously at Kate Wandley's manoeuvre.

'Laura don't care 'oo sees 'er,' said Heffie. 'Ain't that something?'

'That is Miss Benson, then?' said Holmes.

'That's 'er.'

As we watched, Laura Benson pulled her muffler up and eeled her way into the throng of young women.

A long horn sounded and echoed out over the Thames.

The gates to the factory opened up and a crowd of female factory workers, their hair covered in kerchiefs or mob caps, began to emerge at the end of their night work. Soon they were flooding out of the opening, their faces, to a one, pinched with exhaustion.

I was then jostled from behind and turned to see an oncoming tide of shift workers, which had appeared out of nowhere, heading toward the same gates, ready to take over from the departing girls. The empty street was suddenly filled with women.

Threading through this mingling throng, Emily and her cohorts had moved away from the photographer and took up their positions, forming a kind of phalanx, some facing the entrance, some away. They withdrew placards from their coats and held them before their chests like shields. 'EQUAL PAY' and similar phrases were written thereon. With another hand, each began distributing flyers.

Confusion took over as the arriving, departing and demonstrating women began to tangle into a complicated mass.

As Emily Ferndale's masked line of demonstrators effectively slowed this transition, the area in front of the factory became jammed with bodies, pushing through. The tension was palpable. My hackles were raised. The situation was messy, far too crowded. I sensed an oncoming disaster.

CHAPTER TWENTY-THREE

Watson Strikes Out

oments later, chaos ensued. A police whistle cut through the air, followed by a shout. 'Oi! Oi! Move off, ladies!' Away to the right, several burly policemen ran towards us.

Another blew his whistle. 'Step aside ladies, you are blocking the way!' he shouted. The two with him repeated the command.

'Someone must have leaked the plan to the police,' remarked Holmes. He peered around, worried. 'Where is my man?'

I knew nothing about any 'man' but turned my attention to Miss Ferndale's small line of demonstrators, standing firm. Several shoved flyers at the workers, those both departing and arriving. Some of the workers angrily tossed them to the ground, but others took them up and paused to read, and the factory entrance rapidly became clogged.

More police whistles.

Behind me, I heard a roar of anger. 'Bloody hell! My lens!' Pettifer had no doubt discovered what had been done to his camera. The crowd noise rose in volume.

Emily Ferndale's voice rang out: 'Positions!'

On cue, her group began to thrust their stacks of flyers into the nearest workers' hands, and formed a distinct line, joining arms to further block the entrance. Kate Wandley was right in the thick of it; Laura Benson as well. '*Today. Fair play. Look! Look at what you pay!*' cried one of the women. I could not see which. Her voice was joined by others.

'*Today. Fair play. Look! Look, at what you pay!*'

Caught on either one side of this line of protestors or the other, the arriving and departing factory workers all began to mill about in confusion. The crowd grew in size and density.

'Damnation! Where is Chudley?' cried Holmes, looking about.

'Who is Chudley?' I asked. A young woman backed into me, treading on my foot with her sharp heel. Holmes and I were becoming hemmed in. I did not like the situation. Trouble was brewing, the air was electric with it.

'Watson, back to the alley! We can do no one any good if we are caught up in this.'

The chants continued and grew louder. The policemen once again blew their whistles, joining the echo of other whistles farther away, and I noticed a group of five more policeman racing in our direction.

Then I heard the high-pitched neigh of a nervous horse, and a carriage drew up with a clatter just outside the throng, nearly knocking aside three young workers on the edge of the crowd. From it emerged another photographer and two assistants, laden with equipment.

'At last!' cried Holmes. 'And not a moment too soon.' At my puzzlement, he added: 'Percival Chudley. He's one of us, Watson.'

The chanting, the whistles, the shouts – all grew louder. Bodies pressed in on all sides, and I became separated from Holmes. Chudley and an assistant elbowed their way through the crowd to set up a camera near the entrance to the factory. But where had Holmes got to?

I felt a hand on my arm. 'This way, Watson. Be quick!'

I followed my friend as he threaded through the pressing, noisy crowd and back down another nearby alley. We took shelter in a doorway. I looked back and could see, in the sliver of a view outside, what I reckoned would soon be pure pandemonium. Heffie was nowhere to be seen and I felt a sudden pang of worry for the girl.

'Stay put, Watson. We can do nothing of use there,' said Holmes, reading my mind as usual.

'But Heffie—'

'The girl can handle herself, do not fear.'

'I don't like this, Holmes.'

'She has explicit instructions. She will be safe.'

'As if Heffie always follows your instructions!'

'She will. It is a good thing that second photographer arrived.'

'How so?'

'Because I engaged him. And he's been hired to document any manhandling of young ladies by the police.'

I shook my head. 'We cannot just stand by and watch!'

'Come, Watson. All will be well. There are four other young ladies there who were hired and instructed by Heffie to help calm things down.'

But the scene before us was far from calm. Muffled shouts emerged as the crowd grew denser and more frantic. I could not imagine Heffie and her girls managing to dilute the pulsing energy of this scene.

'Holmes! Those girls are in danger. Crowds like this can go wild!'

But Holmes turned and headed down the alley, away from the fracas.

I looked back at the growing chaos. I once had been caught up in a stampede in a crowded bazaar in Afghanistan. A fire had broken out in a cooking stall and ignited a series of festive banners strung above the main thoroughfare. Crowds in a panic take on a powerful life of their own. A trip or a fall could mean trampling and sudden death.

Women's shouts and a single piercing scream broke though the commotion. Perhaps Holmes had never experienced the horror of a rampaging crowd. But I had, and could not, in all good conscience, leave our Heffie there.

'I'm going back!' I shouted and ran back toward the surging masses.

'Watson, no!'

For once I did not heed Sherlock Holmes. A mistake?

Leaving Holmes in the alley, I burst through the melee without a clear plan except to find Heffie and, if necessary, convey her to safety. I hoped that Miss Ferndale had managed to escape harm, but I was less concerned, perhaps uncharitably, for the unpleasant Kate Wandley. But I could see none of these three in the churning mass.

As I had feared, the crowd of mainly young women, both demonstrators and factory workers, had been compressed and panicked by the arriving police. In the ensuing surge, even with my strength and determination, I was knocked off balance and fell to my knees.

To my right, two young women had also hit the pavement, and as I watched in horror, several others stepped on them, a third tripping and landing on the first two. We were seconds away from a fatal crush.

With a mighty shove, I righted myself and, using every ounce of strength I had, I elbowed clearance around the fallen girls and hauled them both to their feet.

Immediately we were jostled and pushed, hemmed in by struggling bodies. Panic electrified the crowd. And the noise! The shouts and whistles of the police blended in with the chant of the protestors, which grew weaker as more of the young women were subdued by the increasing aggressions of the bobbies. Cries and curses competed with moans around me as the crowd compacted and writhed.

Despite my relative size and strength compared to the young women who surrounded me, I was nevertheless nearly crushed. Knocked from all directions but still on my feet, I planted myself and scanned the crowd for Heffie, Emily Ferndale and Kate Wandley.

Instead, I saw Laura Benson. Some ten feet away, she faced a policeman, shouting up at him and gesticulating. Spotting me, she pointed straight at me. The constable nodded and started pushing toward me.

Behind him, Laura Benson caught my eye triumphantly, then turned away, melting into the crowd.

All around me, flashes of dark blue came into view as the policemen raised arms and billy clubs and pushed their way into the crowd. I was a lone male in the sea of female protesters. Laura Benson's copper pointed at me and shouted, 'That bloke! 'E started it!'

As if I were the instigator.

'Get 'im!'

I ducked and squeezed through an opening, only to face two more men in blue. As they spotted me and raised their clubs, I turned and elbowed my way past four of the demonstrators, who were still valiantly trying to hand out leaflets.

Whether it was my war experience, a sixth sense or divine providence, what happened next altered the course of events. Out of the corner of my eye, an object on the ground nearby drew my attention. Something that did not belong there. A black package, the size of a rat, rested at the base of a plinth, just to the right of the factory entrance.

Next to it, something orange flickered against the grey of the pavement.

A flame, a lit fuse.

A bomb!

It was a mere ten feet from where I stood. And placed to do maximum harm.

I shoved violently through those surrounding me in the crush, unfortunately knocking aside two of the young women I had recently rescued. But I had to reach that bomb at all costs. Dozens would be killed or maimed if it were to explode.

Just then a young constable, his billy club at the ready, leapt into my way. His face filled with fury. 'Awright you!' he shouted, raising the club to strike me.

Pushing past him, I dived, landing on my chest, two feet from the bomb. Less than an inch remained on the fuse! I reached out, took it up in my bare hands and pinched down, hard. There was a searing pain in my hand and I felt, or heard, the sizzle of my own burning flesh. I pulled the thing into my chest and curled around it without a thought, shielding the crowd with my body.

Had I succeeded? I did not have the chance to find out for at that moment I felt a blinding pain in the back of my skull.

All went black.

CHAPTER TWENTY-FOUR

Gaol

ometime later, consciousness gradually returned. Was I dead? My eyes opened, closed, and opened again. I was in a small room. Pain. My hand. My head. I was stretched out on something hard and very cold. A bench.

Raising my throbbing head, I looked around me. My surroundings went out of focus, then more or less back in. A very small room, barren, another bench nearby. Above me was a stained ceiling and off to one side a small, barred window.

Not the afterlife, then. Gaol.

But how had I arrived here, and why? I remembered nothing of being arrested, nor of being transported. Closing my eyes, I tried to dredge up what had happened. Vague images appeared. Some kind of crowd. Noise. I had seen a bomb. A lit fuse. I dived on top of it, had to stop it!

I squinted at a dirty bandage on my right hand. I touched it and it slipped away to reveal a small, deep burn. Evidently, I must have succeeded in extinguishing the fuse with my bare hand, but I had been arrested anyway. The irony of this struck me deeply.

One might presume that if I had been caught *extinguishing* the fuse of a bomb, I could hardly be thought to be the instigator of it. But the details of this event – the where, the why – were clouded. Nevertheless, here I was.

A wave of nausea and dizziness swept over me and I thought it might be wise to lie back down. Except I was already lying down.

I must have dozed but awoke to the sound of familiar voices. I became aware that the door of my cell was open.

There was Holmes, wet, dripping from the rain. Beside him stood a slim young man with a thatch of sandy blond hair. I didn't recognize him. A larger man loomed behind them. Holmes's eyes swept over me, taking in everything at a glance.

'Watson, I have returned with help. How are you now?'

'Returned?' I had no recollection of him having been there before.

'I was here two hours ago. We spoke about what happened. Don't you remember?'

'No.'

I tried to sit up, but a wave of dizziness swept over me and my surroundings seemed to be moving. 'Head is hurting,' I murmured. 'My hand.'

'I've brought a doctor to see you,' said Holmes. 'You were quite confused about the riot.'

My head spun. *The riot . . . ? The riot!*

Holmes gestured toward the blond fellow. 'This is Dr Patrick Sheehan of Harley Street. Let him have a look.'

The newcomer kneeled beside me and looked deeply into my eyes. He began to examine me, thoroughly and with a gentle touch. He quickly assessed my condition, noting the various bruises including the contusions and cuts from the earlier fall at Clapton's Dry Goods. As he handled my bruised forearm, I flinched.

'Too many adventures, doctor?' said Sheehan. 'What happened here?'

'Fell through a floor.'

'At least you remember that,' said Holmes.

'And today, an encounter with a billy club,' said Sheehan. 'My God, man, you really must be more careful. Keep this up and your brains will be cheese. Follow my finger.' He waved it slowly before my eyes. 'Yes, good. Now let me take a look at that hand.'

Suddenly, the third man loomed into view behind Holmes, startling me. It was Mycroft Holmes, my friend's older brother. Enormous, taciturn, immaculately dressed. Unreadable. Mycroft made me instantly uneasy, as he always did. What was he doing here?

'What did you see, Dr Watson?' Mycroft said. 'Who set the bomb?'

'Give us a moment, Mycroft,' said Holmes, with irritation. 'Watson?'

'Bomb,' I said, finally. I sounded like an idiot to myself. 'Er, I didn't see.'

Mycroft tsked and looked skyward. 'Good God, man,

try. You were right there.' He turned to his younger brother. 'If you request my help, Sherlock, you must give me ammunition.'

'I have told you, Miss Ferndale is being sabotaged. This is yet a further example. All I am asking is that you keep it out of the papers until I can sort this out,' said Holmes.

'Little brother, I have pulled every string to keep the Windsor events from igniting the public imagination. You are asking too much with this one. That photographer Pettifer is out for blood and is a close friend of the editor of *The Times*.'

Mycroft when annoyed was slightly terrifying, I will admit it. I hoped he would leave soon.

'We made sure he got no photographs.'

'That may be so, but your man Chudley did. Are you aware there have been two attempts already to steal your photographer's negatives?'

Holmes looked startled. Mycroft, even more than his brother, had an uncanny access to what seemed like everything. The photographers floated back into my memory. Fuzzy, however.

Holmes looked alarmed. 'Mycroft! You must protect them at all costs. And help us find Miss Wandley.'

Kate Wandley he meant. It was filtering back, slowly. The sister of the tattooed murder victim . . . but why *find* her?

'Sherlock, that is for you to arrange. The Royal Family come first, and there I shall concentrate my efforts. May I suggest you get your friend here to remember what he saw? I'll wager he knows who set that bomb.'

'No, I don't know!' I cried. Then, 'Ouch!' as Dr Sheehan opened out my hand to look at the burn from the fuse.

'Well, I say you do,' said Mycroft. 'Get it out of him, Sherlock. I'll do the other.' He turned on his heel and left.

Holmes shook his head in frustration.

What *other*, I wondered. Holmes moved to my side and peered at me with concern mixed with impatience. Some vague thoughts swam before me. 'Heffie . . .' I said. I had gone into the crowd to find Heffie. 'Is she all right?'

'She is fine. Arrested with the others but released an hour ago, once they learned of her police work,' said Holmes.

'Arrested. Yes, of course.' Memories began to flood in. 'A demonstration at the cannery led by . . . our client, Emily – Emily, er . . .' I struggled for her surname.

'Emily Ferndale. Lady Summers. It's coming back to you then, Watson?'

'What of Miss Ferndale?'

'Arrested but released immediately. A number of her compatriots have been detained. My photographer will be of assistance there, providing he can keep hold of his negatives. The police were extremely aggressive, to put it mildly. An investigation is underway to determine who planted that bomb. No one saw it. Miss Ferndale and her group are not yet free from suspicion.'

It came back to me in fits and starts. Miss Ferndale's group. Ah, yes, of course. The bomb. But . . . why? A sudden thought. 'She would never have planted that bomb and endangered her own girls,' I said.

'Indeed, you and I know that,' said Holmes.

The doctor had moved behind me and I could feel a

sudden sharp pain in the back of my head. 'Ouch, can't you numb that first?' I asked.

'Apologies, but hold still,' said Sheehan, continuing his work. 'A couple of stitches. Won't take long.'

'The bomb?' I murmured. 'I must have stopped it. But the young ladies. How—?'

'Fourteen arrested. No one seriously injured. Nine are free already. My photographer captured enough evidence that Miss Emily Ferndale, with her connections, will be able to free the five young women who are still detained.'

'This will still look bad for her.' I said. 'Ouch!'

'Stop moving,' said Dr Sheehan.

'Regrettably, there is still that danger. Despite what he said, Mycroft will suppress news of the bomb, Watson. I know my brother. Regarding the bomb, it's the newspapers acting as a megaphone that will inflame the populace. Rage will be focused on the protestors. The bomber, whoever he or she is, is counting on it. We need to know who set that bomb. It is possible you may have seen something.'

'I don't think so.'

'Watson, I would like to hypnotize you. It may help you to recall. Will you agree?'

'Where on earth did you learn that?' I said. Holmes was proving to be even more encyclopaedic than I had imagined.

'Never mind. Yes, then? Lie down, please.'

Sheehan came around to where I could see him. He looked keenly interested. 'Fascinating,' he said. 'I have been wanting to learn this.'

'Dr Sheehan, we are short on time. Please go and sit down over there and don't make a sound,' said Holmes.

The doctor reluctantly complied.

'All right, Watson. Let us proceed,' said Holmes. 'Lie down and close your eyes. And listen to my voice.'

I doubted that this would do any good, but Holmes was insistent. I reclined back onto the bench, being careful not to lean on my cut. Out of the corner of my eye I saw the doctor settling himself on another bench.

Holmes's voice grew soft and gentle. 'Watson, listen carefully. At this moment, it is all about my voice. *Listen to my voice . . .*'

And here is where I had to consult with Holmes about what happened next. Naturally, I could not relate it otherwise. The following is a transcript he provided me. A condition of its inclusion here was that I include it verbatim, with no edits:

Watson, I will attempt here to mimic your rather lurid style of storytelling to relate what transpired during your trance.

You were a largely cooperative subject. No one can be hypnotized against his will, as you know. But you were highly motivated, and you trusted me not to have you stand on one leg and quack like a duck.

All right, I jest. But trust is key. As a medical man, you are aware that, while the general public looks at hypnosis as a source of entertainment, this has practical applications, including pain control, hysteria and recovery from temporary memory loss.

I began with instructions for you to roll your eyes skywards, while slowly closing the lids. Then to breathe in and out, relaxing the eyes, and to feel your body floating. I will not elaborate further, you can read of these techniques. You arrived smoothly into a trance state.

I directed you to return to the riot in your mind. Then to focus on the seconds leading up to when you saw the bomb and, in a moment of extreme self-sacrifice, leapt upon it to extinguish the fuse to keep it from exploding.

Both Mycroft and I wondered what had made you look over at the entrance to the cannery at precisely that moment and to spot that very small object in the chaos surrounding you. Something or someone, out of reach of normal memory, may have caused you to look there. Perhaps you saw the bomber and could identify him . . . or her.

But I would need to lead you into that moment. It went more or less like this:

I said something like, 'You are in the press of people. People all around you. I need you to answer me, Watson. *What exactly do you see?*'

'Bodies. It is like . . . a war,' you replied.

'A war. Chaos, then?'

'Chaos. So many bodies. A crush. Danger.'

'Watson . . . two women near you are on the ground. Can you see them?'

'Yes.'

'What do you do?'

'I . . . I help them up. To their feet. I . . . oh, no . . . they don't stay and . . .'

'And what? What do you hear?'

'Shouts!' Then, 'A policeman shouts at me, raises his club!'

'And he hits you?' I asked.

'He misses me. I dive. Dive away from him. I trip and am instantly on the ground.'

Here you paused, Watson, searching for the image. Finally you said, 'Heffie! I am looking for Heffie!'

At this point, most irritatingly, you opened your eyes, and I had to take you under again. But not before assuring you that Heffie was safe. I brought you back to the riot. With some effort, I focused your attention on the very moment just before you noticed the bomb. A bobby had attacked you with his billy club but you escaped by pushing through the crowd. You then told me, 'But there are more. More men in blue.'

'What makes you look at the entrance to the cannery?' I asked you.

'I . . . I . . .' Here you fumbled around for a bit.

'What was at the entrance to the cannery?'

'Someone . . . I . . . I . . .' More fumbling.

Credit me with some patience here. I know it's a rare commodity, for me, at least. Finally I asked, 'What makes you look? You are looking for Heffie. Is she there?'

'No, but—'

'What else are you looking for?'

'Men in blue. Dark blue. To avoid them.'

'What did you see?'

'There was . . . there was a man in blue there.'

'Describe him.'

'Like all the others,' you said, Watson.

I next asked you for detail, hoping you could identify this mystery figure. Sorry to say, you replied as follows: 'Can't see. Hat. Moustache. I cannot see his face clearly. He moves away and then . . .'

'Then, what?'

'I see the little grey shape. Like a rat. But . . . but with a bright orange tail . . . It is a spark. A fuse. *A bomb!* I see it then . . . and I . . .'

And here you roused yourself a final time. You opened your eyes and cried out, 'A policeman! *A policeman set the bomb!'*

And here Holmes's accounts ends.

As I came out of this trance, the reality of everything came into sharper focus. My head hurt. But memories flooded back. I'd seen *a man in blue who very likely placed the bomb.* Something I had not been able to remember on my own.

Holmes had skilfully dredged up a memory that had been just out of reach.

'This is very helpful, Watson,' he said.

'It was all you, Holmes.'

'No, Watson, you are the hero today. There is more going on here than a snake in Miss Ferndale's organization. A policeman set that bomb. I need you on your feet. We have work to do.' He turned to Sheehan. 'Doctor?'

Doctor Sheehan was sitting on a bench against the wall. His eyes were shut and he was breathing as though asleep.

'Dr Sheehan?' said Holmes. There was no response.

'Holmes, you've hypnotized him!'

My friend crossed to Dr Sheehan and knelt beside him. 'Dr Sheehan. Doctor! I will count backwards from three, and on one you will hear a clap and open your eyes and you will be right back with us. Ready now: three, two, one!' He clapped.

Sheehan's eyes popped open. 'I'd like to tend to that burn briefly in Harley Street,' he said. 'Perhaps you'd like to hypnotize him there. It will be most interesting.' It was as if the last several minutes had not happened. As if he'd never been in a trance himself.

Holmes and I exchanged a look of surprise.

'No need,' said Holmes. 'Watson remembered.' Holmes next leaned in close to help me up, 'I must be careful with that technique,' he whispered.

I laughed. 'I'll say.'

The gaoler arrived with the announcement that I was free to go.

'Come along, Dr Watson,' said Sheehan. 'A quick trip to Harley Street.'

I stood up, and it felt as though my brain was rattling in my skull. The room seemed to tilt slightly. 'I don't think I need—'

'Step to it,' Holmes commanded. 'Harley Street. For that hand. Don't dawdle.'

'Stop ordering me about. Damned lucky I didn't listen to you back in that alley.'

'I will give you that,' said my friend. 'Dozens are alive who would be dead, Watson. Take comfort in that, but now do as Doctor Sheehan says.'

CHAPTER TWENTY-FIVE

Recovery

t his surgery in Harley Street, Dr Sheehan completed his ministrations, and I returned to spend an uncomfortable night at 221B. The next morning, I dressed and came down, only to find an empty sitting room. I was soon dozing on the sofa.

I awoke to see Holmes standing next to me holding out a cup of steaming liquid. It was late morning. A gentle tapping had begun to sound at our windows.

'Holmes? Is it hailing?'

'Yes. How are you feeling, Watson?'

'I feel like I've been kicked in the head by an ass.'

'Well, you were struck on the head by one. Coffee.' He handed me the cup.

Holmes returned to his desk and began flipping through what looked like a stack of small photographs. I tried to stand, but the room swayed. I sat back down.

'Stay there, Watson. You are unwell,' he said.

'Says the man who complains that I state the obvious.' I took a sip. 'You forgot my lump of sugar.'

He ignored this, returning to his photographs.

And I ignored him and moved woozily to the breakfast table to add sugar and milk to my coffee. I could feel the cold seeping in through the windowpane, and outside the air was white with hail. The rattling grew louder. The new daffodils in Regent's Park would be taking a beating.

'The ladies wisely staged their demonstration in advance of this weather,' I remarked.

Through the mist and hail I could see an elegant carriage parked across the street, a thin white crust accruing on its roof. A matched pair of horses snorted and stomped to keep warm. Dark green blankets topped with waxed cotton had been strapped onto their backs, even extending, like a child's hooded jacket, up over their heads. I could just make out the familiar crest on the carriage itself.

'Holmes!' I felt dizzy again but shook my head. 'The royal carriage!'

'Yes, yes. Sit down, Watson, before you fall down.'

'But why are they here?' I asked.

'The Palace has grown impatient with my investigation. They inform us that Sir James Wandley has at last returned from abroad and I am asked to interview him without delay.'

'Er . . . right now?'

'I shall do so when I am ready.'

My friend was not one to have his investigations directed by others. He continued to leaf through the items on his desk.

'Holmes, are those the photographs from yesterday? So soon?'

'They are, Watson. My man Chudley earned his fee and more.'

'From that silly little box camera he brought? How did he take so many?'

'That silly little camera is a remarkable invention. American. He was able to shoot in a series, rapidly.' Holmes continued to shuffle through them, then laid down his magnifying glass and pounded the desk in frustration.

'I miscalculated, Watson. I did not expect a bomb. Yet, upon reflection, I see the perverse logic of it.' He shook his head. 'Dear God, if you . . . if Heffie—'

'No one could have seen that coming, Holmes.' He may have felt that he had made an error, but I did not.

Holmes returned to his examination of the photographs. I moved behind him and looked over his shoulder. 'I do not see Heffie in these,' I said.

'I told her that narrow entrance where the incoming and outgoing workers crowd each other would naturally be the nexus for any violence. And to stay away from it.'

'Thank goodness she followed your instructions!'

He picked up his lens and peered closely at one, then a second photograph. The pictures were small, only about three by five inches.

'Do the photographs reveal who placed the bomb?' I asked.

'I am working through them now. Chudley kindly numbered them, as I had asked, to convey the sequence. Look at this, Watson.'

He pulled one from the stack and laid it next to a second and then a third.

'You see?' he said. 'Before the crush, there you and I are standing near the entrance, and there is no bomb. But in this one, we are gone . . . still nothing. In the next, nothing as well. Then the melee begins . . . and moments later, *there it is*!'

'Then it was placed shortly after the police descended! But who is the man in blue that you helped me to remember?'

'I hope to see . . .'

'Do you think the same person who alerted the police to the demonstration also placed the bomb?' I asked. '*Disguised* as a policeman? Or perhaps an actual policeman? I saw Laura Benson conferring with one of them. The one who came after me. In fact, she pointed me out to him.'

'Interesting,' said Holmes. 'She is looking more like the serpent in Miss Ferndale's group,' he mused. 'But complicity with the bombing and also the police does not add up. A number of the men in blue would have been killed as well. Despite your memory, this makes the culprit being an actual policeman *less* likely.'

'Could it be that the bomber was a woman, then—?'

'Possible, but improbable, I think, based on what you saw. Perhaps a man disguised as a policeman.'

'Well, I didn't see him place the bomb. Only that he was there. Right before I noticed it. What is your theory, Holmes?'

'I was hoping these photographs would tell us.' He continued to inspect them. 'This was well planned. The placement was ideal for maximum impact. A death knell to Miss Ferndale's movement.'

He took a sharp intake of breath. 'At last! Here is our murder victim's charming sister, Miss Kate Wandley.' He picked up his magnifying lens and leaned in to examine one of the photographs closely. 'And very close to the entrance!' he exclaimed.

'Could she have placed the bomb? Perhaps she put on a policeman's jacket? And then took if off?' The thought energized me. 'Kate Wandley! I wouldn't put it past her!'

'Watson, hold off your assumptions!'

'I do not like that girl.'

Holmes continued to study the photos. 'Look at this.' He handed me his lens, pointing to one of the photographs. 'There is Kate Wandley, as I said, near the entrance. You see the bomb there, already in place. And now this, seconds later. There she is, holding a sign aloft and not even looking at the bomb, although she is within striking distance.'

'Perhaps she knew how long the fuse was, having lit it herself,' I said.

'Unlikely! Any sane bomber would be making a beeline away from there as fast as possible.'

'Assuming the bomber is sane.'

'I don't think she knew it was there.'

I was not quite ready to give Kate Wandley the benefit of the doubt.

'Still not convinced, Watson? Look at this one. It is only a moment later, the same two girls near her have not moved. But now Kate Wandley's sign is on the ground, and she is off balance, on one foot only.'

'Running away, then!'

'I would say stumbling,' he continued. 'She has a look of surprise, perhaps fury – it is hard to read – on her face. These images are so small!'

He placed another photograph next to it. 'And in this next photo she is only half visible. She is mostly hidden behind this woman, here. Falling perhaps.'

'Or slipping away? Ah, here I enter the scene!' I saw myself as a blurred figure, diving for the bomb. 'Where is the next photograph?'

Holmes sighed in exasperation. 'It was here that my man ran out of film.'

'How unfortunate!' I exclaimed.

Holmes pulled a thicker lens from a drawer. But before he could continue his study, we heard footsteps clambering up the stairs to our sitting room, and Heffie burst through the door. She had not removed her coat and was covered with a fine dusting of ice crystals.

'Ah, Heffie! Glad to see you were unharmed!' I cried.

'Of course! And I got my girls out o' there when the police came,' she said to me. She pulled off her cap, sending a sprinkling of frost to the rug. 'But Mr 'olmes. I done what you asked last night. When Miss Wandley didn't return home, I checked wi' every police station in the city. She ain't in none of them. Nor in gaol.'

'She must be,' said Holmes. 'I must ask you to try again, Heffie. She was still not at home this morning.'

'How do you know that?' I asked.

'I went by.' Once again, Holmes had slept little or not at all.

'Sir, you forget, I works for the police now, thanks to

you. An' I'm tellin' you, she weren't arrested. Which is really odd, because—'

Mrs Hudson's voice penetrated the room from the hallway below. 'Madam, please! They have a visitor!'

Having evidently pushed past our good landlady for the second time, Miss Emily Ferndale appeared at our sitting room door. She, too, had kept her coat and hat on. Everyone was in quite a rush this morning. Miss Ferndale was at least dry. She snapped her expensive umbrella closed and dropped it into Holmes's tall china vase with a resounding click. She suddenly noticed Heffie. 'You! What are *you* doing here?' she said sharply. 'You were to warn us of any plots against me. Now look what has happened!'

'Given time, she would have,' said Holmes. 'What have you come to say, Miss Ferndale? I see your father prevailed yet again for you to be out of gaol very quickly.'

'Why is that a surprise?' she said. 'But my father has washed his hands of me, Mr Holmes. That bomb has effectively put an end to my organization and to all my efforts. It did not even need to detonate! I intend to find the culprit, and the signs must point to someone. What have you found, Mr Holmes?' She gave him a penetrating stare. 'If anything?'

Holmes shook his head. 'In time, Miss Ferndale. We have our suspicions.'

'Well, you have missed your opportunity. If you think I'm going to pay you for—'

'It is not about my fee, Miss Ferndale. At least three women in your group knew of the planned demonstration.'

'No one knew the details of the location of our demonstration until late in the evening before. That would have been too late to pull together the bomb and the police raid. I say no one . . . except Kate Wandley. That's one only. But she could not possibly be at fault.'

'I do not agree. Others knew.'

Miss Ferndale drew a breath. 'What others?'

'*Me*, for one,' said Heffie. 'That's why Mr 'olmes and Dr Watson 'ad that second photographer there!'

Miss Ferndale turned to stare at the girl. 'No, Mr Holmes knew because *I* informed him via messenger. I did so because you had not made any headway.'

'Well, I came by here an' told him in person!'

The lady turned back to Holmes. 'Nevertheless, not one of you saw this coming. You do not merit your reputation, sir!'

'You oughta to take a look at that third one who knew,' said Heffie. 'Laura Benson.'

'Oh, nonsense,' said Miss Ferndale. 'I know her mother.'

'Yep? Well I knows her father! 'E's a copper.'

This gave Lady Ferndale a moment's pause. 'To her mother's great regret, I am sure. She is a cultured woman. I believe they are separated. No, you simply overheard me, you little spy. Though I don't know how. I was so careful.'

'It is why I pay her handsomely,' said Holmes. 'And the police find her indispensable.'

Miss Ferndale rounded on Heffie. 'You work for the police, too?' she cried. 'Then it had to be you!'

'No,' said Holmes, 'Heffie did not notify the police, did you, Heffie?'

Heffie snorted. 'O' course not!'

'Tell me about this Laura Benson, please,' said Holmes.

'She's a sneaky one, I tol' you. Something not right,' said Heffie.

'Never mind Laura Benson. I need to find Kate!' cried Miss Ferndale. 'She missed our tea today.'

I laughed, then abruptly stifled myself. Tea? How varied was the life of a civilized provocateur!

'What exactly did Kate Wandley miss today?' asked Holmes.

'Today we were to meet with the Duchess of Claremont and the wife of a judge. They mean – meant – to add public support to our movement. Kate was to host them this morning for tea at her home. I am worried about her.'

'Ha!' I said. 'Riot one day, tea party the next. Just the ordinary life of a lady of leisure!'

'Quiet, Watson. Miss Ferndale, continue, please. I share your concern.'

I had difficulty doing so.

'Kate did not return from our demonstration. Her house-keeper was angry, having made preparations for the tea. I, on the other hand, worry that she has met with mischief.' Miss Ferndale's face softened. 'I will give you another chance, Mr Holmes. Find her and I will pay you handsomely. If she is at fault . . . well, that is another question. Miss Benson seems to think that Kate Wandley is the traitor in our group.'

'There is, of course, a third possibility,' said Holmes. He glanced up at me. 'Should we not check the hospitals as well, doctor?'

'I suppose it is possible Miss Wandley was hurt,' I said. 'So, yes indeed.'

'Heffie?' said Holmes. The girl stood up, at the ready. 'Note, please, that it may be that Miss Wandley has not been admitted under her name – if she came in unconscious, for example.'

Heffie nodded. 'I knows that, Mr 'olmes. If she's there, I'll find 'er. Can I borrow some o' your Irregulars, sir? There's a lot o' ground to cover, and I ain't connected to the hospitals like I am the police.'

'Certainly.' Holmes dashed a note on a slip of paper and handed it to Heffie. 'Find Wiggins here.'

Miss Ferndale withdrew her umbrella from the vase and gave Heffie and Holmes another serious look. 'Well, then, I suppose I shall leave you to it. And I hope you are more successful now than previously.' The lady departed, and Heffie and I looked at Holmes in mutual curiosity.

'Mr 'olmes, there's somethin' I wanted to tell yer. But not with Miss Ferndale 'ere. I . . . think I saw a copper drag 'er off.'

'Drag Kate Wandley off, you say?'

'Yes. Maybe. Somethin' half-way between draggin' and leadin' 'er off.'

'Can you be more specific?'

'No, I can't. I weren't that close. Remember? Your orders.'

'Yes, yes, I understand. Can you describe him?'

'Not exactly. Tall. Dark moustache. Looked like they all look. Hat was low on his face. It were madness just then.'

Holmes considered. 'Even so, Heffie, check the hospitals for Miss Wandley. What precisely has happened to her is unknown.'

'Ah, Mr Holmes. It ain't very likely—'

'Heffie, it is what I need you to do.'

Reluctantly the girl left. A puddle of water stained the rug where she had been standing. I was doubtful that she would find Kate Wandley in a hospital somewhere, but Holmes never left a stone unturned. He returned to the photographs, picking up his strongest lens.

'Watson, come and look at this. On Kate Wandley's arm – what do you see?' He handed me the lens.

There, on Kate Wandley's upper arm, a large hand had a firm grip. A man, unseen behind the others, was pulling at her.

'Well, just as Heffie said. It's a copper, that's all,' I said.

'Then why, Watson, is she in no gaol? Anywhere?'

I had nothing to offer.

'I'm going to talk to Lestrade.' This was, of course, Holmes's closest contact in the Metropolitan Police. 'Mrs Hudson, call us a cab!'

But Holmes had forgotten what awaited us outside, and at that moment, so had I. As he and I pulled our scarves and hats from the hooks on the landing, a tall fellow in royal livery bounded up the stairs, grim determination written all over him. He put up a hand as though to stop traffic.

'I'm sorry, Mr Holmes, but your two visitors have left and now the Palace must prevail. I'm to see you off to the Wandley Estate. *Now.* The carriage has been waiting some time.'

Holmes paused and I saw his jaw muscles twitch. But he said nothing. And soon we were hurtling up Baker Street, past Regent's Park, and north to the Wandley Estate.

You cannot argue with the Palace. Not even if you are Sherlock Holmes.

PART SIX

THE SERPENT'S NEST

'O serpent heart hid with a flowering face!
Did ever a dragon keep so fair a cave?'
—William Shakespeare

CHAPTER TWENTY-SIX

Sir James

e mounted at once into the sleek carriage loaned to Holmes by the Palace. After a relatively smooth ride through alternating bouts of hail and cold sunshine, we arrived at last at the remote and foreboding castle that was the Wandley family seat. Holmes inquired of the butler if Kate Wandley had returned home but was referred, stuffily, to Sir James.

We were ushered into a gloomy room somewhere at the back of the building. Unlike the richly appointed salon in which we met the man's private secretary on that first day of this case, today we found ourselves instead in a dimly lit and somewhat shabby study.

The fire burned hot in a messy grate and a very old grandfather clock stood beside it, stopped at two thirty-four. Three empty dog beds were aligned under a window looking out onto an unkempt garden, and a worn tartan blanket was tossed over a chair, next to which was a chipped Turkish octagonal table with a pair of reading spectacles atop a pile of books. There was a distinct air of disconsolation.

I found it curious that we were received days ago by the secretary Peter Oliver in a reception room designed to impress, but our meeting with the patriarch was to occur in this much humbler, almost seedy place. But the room reflected its occupant.

Sir James, the father of the slain girl, was slumped in his chair by the fire. His long legs were stretched out before him. He was a tall and once powerfully built man clad in ancient country tweeds, but in contrast to his faded, loosely fitted jacket and scuffed boots, a crisp white shirt collar stood up under his jowls, with a perfectly knotted silk tie and gold stickpin. Deeply worn by time and circumstance, his craggy countenance, no doubt handsome in his youth, was marred by tragedy.

Holmes displayed little empathy. 'Sir James,' he said. 'Now that you have consented at last to meet with us, I have a few questions for you. First, your daughter, Kate—'

'Questions for *me*, young man?' he retorted. 'Well, first you must answer mine. I will hear a report on your investigations. The Palace tells me that we are in good hands with you, yet I do not hear of any arrests. Sit down and tell me all.'

Swallowing his impatience, Holmes sat, and I followed suit. He recounted a severely edited summary of our investigations to date – questioning members of the Palace staff, Lady Jane's fiancé, the specialist at the London Zoo and finally his discovery of the tattooist and the place where he had done the work. But to my surprise, he omitted our visits to the younger daughter Kate Wandley and her subsequent disappearance, and left out the rather telling visit with the dissolute artistic son, Clarence.

The father listened, none too patiently. 'Is that all? How is it that a young woman can be kidnapped and desecrated in this manner, returned to Windsor Castle, and no one seems to have seen or heard anything? What does it matter that you discovered the tattooist? This led you nowhere!'

'My investigation is ongoing,' said Holmes. 'And now, I must ask *you*—'

'Ask me? *Me?* Don't be ridiculous. I say someone at that Palace knows something.'

'Sir James,' said Holmes, 'I have reason to believe that the perpetrators of this heinous crime will not be found within the Palace walls.'

'Nonsense! Of course, someone at the castle is to blame. Jealousy. My daughter was beautiful beyond compare. Nothing like this would ever have happened had she remained here, where she belonged. But her vaunting ambition . . . Well, you clearly have missed something. Another man would have had the culprit in irons by now.'

'I doubt it. And you, sir, have delayed my investigation by refusing to meet with me.'

'I was unwell. And then I had urgent business abroad.' He sipped at a whisky but offered us none. 'But you are here now. What do you want?'

'If you would kindly answer some questions about the relationship of your three children. I understand Jane, as the eldest, stood in for her mother after Lady Wandley's untimely death?'

The man snorted. 'She did. And an excellent job she made of it. So what?'

'Please elaborate.'

'If you insist. With Jane here, the place ran like clockwork. Meals on time, servants in line—'

'How did this arrangement suit her younger siblings? Were they jealous of their sister's new position?'

'Oh, those two were always jealous of Jane. The girl was vastly superior in every way. A stunning beauty . . .' The man's eyes misted over at the thought.

It occurred to me that the girl may well have fled her home for a variety of reasons other than 'vaunting ambition'.

'But what of sibling animosity?' insisted Holmes. 'Pranks. Arguments. Anything?'

'Childish pranks. From a very early age. I say now, you are not suspecting my children of plotting against their sister? I have been told you are some kind of genius, but that is a damned fool notion!'

'Calm yourself, sir. I must follow every possible pathway. Jealousy does not always inspire murder, but I must assess the battlefield and all the players. After she left, presumably Jane's younger sister Kate then took on the running of the household?'

'Useless girl. A rebel from the cradle. Kate fumbled her responsibilities and ran away to do God knows what in London. Some women's club, I hear.'

'I am familiar.'

'Then you have interviewed her?'

'Yes. Have you seen her of late?'

'No.'

Holmes leaned forward in his chair. 'You provide your younger daughter financial support, do you not?'

'I see that Peter has disclosed rather a lot of my personal business to you. But yes, she receives an allowance. I will not have a Wandley living impoverished in London. What would that say of the family?'

What indeed would he think if he knew the full details of Kate's activities?

'When is the last time you saw Kate? I presume she visits upon occasion?' asked Holmes.

'No.' There was a pause. 'I mean yes, she does. But not recently.' The old man seemed to have nothing more to say on the topic.

I expected Holmes to continue down this path, but he surprised me. 'And your son, Clarence?' he asked.

Sir James sighed. I followed his wandering gaze to the right side of the room where the drinks table stood, laden with cut crystal decanters and glasses. It occurred to me that he was waiting to be served, and that a second drink might move our conversation along. But before I could rise to get him one, Holmes read my mind and frowned, shaking his head almost imperceptibly. I stayed seated.

'Clarence is a disappointment to me,' continued Wandley. 'I had anticipated handing the estate to him, but he shows no aptitude and wastes his time with drawing and dissipation. I brought in several suitable girls for him, each with their own estates, but they failed to interest him.'

'He, too, moved to London. Do you subsidize him as well?' asked Holmes, already knowing the answer.

'Clarence has recently refused my support. I am told that

he is well paid for his scribbles these days and is proud to deny my offer. Who could imagine that painting lessons would have paid off for my own heir? But really, it is an embarrassment to think of him in some trade.' Sir James shook his head sadly, and once again glanced at the drinks table.

Holmes leaned in. 'Sir James,' said he, 'I beg your forgiveness, but my investigations require my next line of questioning. With respect, sir, I need to know the exact circumstances of your wife's death many years ago.'

The father sat up in his chair, his face flushed in anger. 'What has that to do with this?'

'I cannot know until I have more information.'

'That was twelve years ago!'

Holmes's patience was reaching its end. He stood. 'Sir, you will answer my questions, or I shall be forced to—'

Wandley arose from his chair. He was a tall man, taller even than Holmes.

'I do not like the tenor of your questions. I do not like you. It has been five days since my darling Jane was killed. You have, I see, discovered very little. I am of a mind to dismiss you from the case.' He rang a small bell on the table and a butler appeared instantly.

'Escort these gentleman out.'

Holmes did not move. 'I am afraid you cannot dismiss me from the case, Sir James. I am engaged by the Crown, and you would do well to answer my questions or you will be brought up on charges of interfering with the law.'

'How dare you speak to me in this manner!' Sir James seemed to swell in size and took a step toward Holmes. We were seconds from violence.

'Sir, if I may interject—' came a soft voice from behind us.

We turned to see that the butler had been replaced by Peter Oliver, who had entered the room silently and stood near the door. 'Gentlemen, Sir James is deeply disturbed by the events, as you might well imagine. Perhaps I can be of help here?'

He moved to the drinks table. Without being asked, he poured a second whisky for his employer and handed it to him. Wandley took it and looked at it with a frown. He then downed the liquid in two large gulps and handed the glass back to Oliver, who refilled it.

Wandley took the drink and sat down with a sigh.

Peter Oliver turned to us. 'May I offer you gentlemen a glass?'

'No,' said Holmes and turned back to Sir James. 'Sir, if you please. I find it odd that you, her father, did not deign to travel to Windsor to identify Jane's body, nor to meet with those who are tasked to discover the murderer. You have blocked me from this interview for several days, and—'

'Won't you please sit down, Mr Holmes?' said Peter Oliver. 'Perhaps I can answer for Sir James.'

'I will interview this gentleman myself, and alone,' said my friend, remaining on his feet.

Peter Oliver hesitated, but upon a nod from his employer, bowed graciously and departed, closing the door behind him. Holmes moved to the window, giving our host some breathing room. I sat down again.

'All right,' said Wandley. 'I'll answer your questions.'

Peter Oliver, I noted, had thankfully restored a bit of sanity to his employer.

'Sir James, returning sadly to the circumstances of your wife's death . . . I have been told by Mr Oliver that she died of a heart attack and that it was unexpected.'

Apparently somewhat mollified by drink, the man gave in. His voice dropped and he slumped back in his chair. 'That was years ago. It can have nothing to do with this.'

'I shall be the one to determine that. What were the precise circumstances of her death?'

'It was in late September. Unseasonably warm. She was in the prime of life. All was well in our little world. She collapsed in her room one evening after a special dinner.'

'In what way was this dinner remarkable?'

'She had requested the cook's speciality: Beef Wellington. She wished to celebrate.'

'What were you celebrating?'

'I said *she* was celebrating. Oh, sit down, would you?'

Holmes ignored this. 'And what, sir, prompted this celebration?' I could sense his impatience.

'Silly, really. Well, ugly, perhaps. As I recall, she was happy that a band of ruffians who had illegally encamped on our land had recently vacated the place. Their camp had gone up in flames a day or so before, and the remaining band of undesirables scattered to the winds.'

'Can you tell me more of these "undesirables"? What caused the fire, for example?'

'How would I know? But it did not surprise me. Those people cook over open flames, you see. Vagrants. Quite a primitive life, of their own choosing, of course. But my wife could not abide them. She was very happy that they . . . well . . . after the fire, that the remaining ones took off.'

'Where did this group of indigents go?'

'Come away from that window. I cannot see you against the light. How should I know? What does this have to do with anything?'

'Did anyone die in this mishap?'

'Later I heard there were deaths. They were probably drunk.' This seemed to affect Sir James not at all, but his eyes wandered back to the drinks table.

It has often struck me that we most despise what we fear in ourselves.

He turned back to Holmes and squinted. 'Two died, I think,' he added, raising his empty glass to his lips and draining the last drops. 'A shame about that, I suppose.'

'A tragedy,' said Holmes. 'And yet your wife found reason to celebrate?'

'We didn't know about the deaths then. Sit down, I say.'

'Was arson suspected?'

'No, I don't think so. The cooking, as I said. It was a rowdy crowd. Dissolute.'

Holmes moved away from the window to stand before a bookcase. At least our host could see him, now. But my friend refused to sit. 'How did you hear of the deaths?'

'From the police the next day. The local man went over there. On the night of the event they had called in the fire brigade, but they were too late and several of the caravans went up in flames. The police sent us a letter the next day.'

'Caravans? So this was a Gypsy encampment? Did an investigation ensue?'

'Why are you asking me all this? How is this relevant to my daughter?'

'I cannot be sure until I have the facts.'

'Yes, they were Gypsies. I don't know about an investigation. The police do not waste much time with matters such as this. In any case, my wife's death soon after overshadowed all.'

'The Gypsies on your land . . . I understand this encampment was at the distant end of your northernmost field. Quite far from the house and not visible to you?'

'That is correct.'

'And yet it bothered your wife very much. Did she feel unsafe, perhaps? Did any of the Gypsies approach the house?'

'Not that I know of.'

'No contact at all?' asked Holmes. 'They often trade in knife sharpening, rags, small kitchen items, and are known to ply their wares and services at large country homes.'

The man shrugged. I could see he was growing tired of the questions. 'Maybe they sold small goods. But I think these people were entertainers of some sort. We've had other groups camping on our land in the past. We are on some kind of route. I don't really pay attention. You might ask in the kitchen.' He waved his hand dismissively.

'Well, perhaps your wife—'

'I said, *ask in the kitchen*. I am tired now. This interview is over. Good day.'

Holmes and I headed out but my friend paused at the door. 'Has your daughter Kate been in touch with you in the last twenty-four hours? Might she have come for a visit?'

Wandley looked up, startled. 'I told you, no. She rarely comes here. Why are you asking me this?'

'Sir James, your younger daughter has gone missing in London.'

The man looked up blearily. 'Oh, really?' He seemed uninterested.

'She vanished yesterday.'

The man shrugged.

'Are you quite sure that she did not return here without your knowledge?' Holmes persisted.

'To what purpose? No. But what is the worry if she "vanished", as you say, only yesterday? That hardly qualifies as "missing".'

'Miss Kate Wandley was involved in a demonstration. There was violence and the police were called in. Her disappearance is troubling. And in light of what happened to your eldest daughter—'

Sir James shrugged. 'Those two travelled in different circles entirely. I doubt this has any bearing, and if you would kindly concentrate on finding the villain who . . . ah . . . Jane . . . my sweet Jane.' Overcome with emotion, the old man covered his eyes.

Holmes glanced at me in frustration.

Immediately the butler arrived to show us to the kitchen.

CHAPTER TWENTY-SEVEN

Stirring the Soup

 stooped but vibrant man despite his age, the butler escorted us downstairs. En route, Holmes inquired about the missing younger sister.

'We have not seen Miss Kate, sir,' replied the old man.

'No chance she could have arrived in the night?'

'I assure you, I would know, sir,' said the butler. 'She is not here, thankfully. The master is most irritated when she does appear.'

We were ushered into a spotlessly maintained kitchen which boasted a modern stove as well as a very old open fireplace. A large iron pot of richly fragrant soup hung over the fire, and on a long wooden table, a plate of scones steamed in the chilly air. Seated at this table was a heavy-set older woman nursing a cup of tea.

A young scullery maid greeted us and introduced us to

the cook, Mrs Prunella Brown. It was often below stairs that Holmes would learn the intimate details of the goings on in grand houses such as this. Sometimes it required intimidation but more often sympathy and tact. With a jockey's instinct for the opening, Holmes always found the inside track.

He sniffed the air. 'Leek and potato soup! My favourite!' he exclaimed. I knew him to despise the stuff. 'And are those fresh scones?' The older woman looked up from her tea with a smile.

Moments later, we both sat across from her at the table over steaming bowls of soup and scones. And, yes, Mrs Brown had been in service there twelve years earlier at the time of Lady Wandley's death.

Holmes began by asking Mrs Brown about the wanderers who had camped on the estate and whose settlement was destroyed on the night of the fire. Unlike Sir James, she was hardly sanguine about the event.

'It was terrible, I thought. Simply terrible. It was a hot night, clear, with so many stars visible. A young page boy, Charlie, was outside fetching spring onions for the morning's omelettes when he came running in. "Fire!" he cried. "Up at the north end!" I remember racing out of the back door, and way up there—' she nodded towards the window, 'I could see the orange glow of a huge blaze behind a row of poplars. I knew there was a Gypsy encampment back there, families with children, and it was that which must have been ablaze.'

'Gypsies, you say. Did you sound an alarm?'

'I ran to tell the Master, and it was then that I saw my

lady in the library, standing at the window, looking north, her hat in her hand.'

'What time was this?'

'Perhaps eleven.'

'Was it unusual for the lady to be about at that hour?'

'Well, yes.'

'Where was Sir James?'

'Long asleep by then. He's an early-to-bed gentleman.'

'And the children?'

'Must have all been asleep. I don't attend the nursery.'

'And Peter Oliver?'

'He were new to us back then. Just twenty, I would say. He did not have a room in the house then. He'd have been down at the factory.'

There was a pause.

'Back to Lady Wandley, then,' said Holmes. 'She had her hat in her hand, you say? She had been out, then?'

'Why, yes, I suppose she had.'

Holmes glanced at me, confirming my sudden thought that the woman may have set the blaze herself.

'What happened next?'

'The police and fire brigade were summoned. But I believe the Gypsy camp suffered great losses. A woman died. And a baby.'

'A baby!' I exclaimed.

'What was the reaction of your master and mistress?'

'At breakfast the next morning, my lady was positively bouncing with joy.'

'How do you know this? Do you typically serve breakfast to the family?'

'No, sir, I do not. A maid does. But Lady Wandley called me in, special, to compliment me on my French omelette. With the sautéed onions. I could see her happiness then.'

'What of the others? Sir James? The children?'

'Sir James spoke little that morning, but then he never did. The children did not breakfast with their parents. Oh, but now I recall little Clarence went missing that morning.'

'Missing?'

'Yes. They later found him at the north barn, hiding in a small fort he and another child had built of hay. Boys will do such things. Worried his mother something awful.'

Holmes moved his spoon in his soup but did not eat any. I thought it was excellent and said so.

'How long after this event did Lady Wandley expire?' asked Holmes.

The old cook shook her head, saddened by the memory. 'It were not long. Less than a week.'

'What were the circumstances of her death?'

The cook looked down at her mug of tea. She sighed. 'Dropped dead one night in her own bedroom, an hour or two after dinner.'

'In her room? Did anyone witness this?'

'No.'

'And the cause of death?'

'The doctor said 'twas a heart attack. On account of it being so sudden. But . . . well, the police were not sure. One of 'em thought she'd been poisoned. I thought so, too, but I didn't say it.'

'Why not?' I blurted.

'Well, because I'm the cook, you see.'

'Yes, but why did you *think* it?' asked Holmes.

'Because I saw her dead body. And she had a little bit o' white . . . white foam around the mouth. Me father died of a heart attack when I were ten, but nothing like that happened. There weren't no foam. And she had her hand to her throat, not her chest.'

'Very observant, Mrs Brown. How is it that you are familiar with poisons and their effects?'

'I read the *Illustrated Police News*,' said she, with a sly grin.

'Of course you do.' Holmes turned to me. 'Doctor? The symptoms described?'

'Poison is a distinct possibility. Arsenic perhaps,' I said.

'What happened next?' Holmes asked the woman.

She shuddered. 'The young copper who thought about poison came to the kitchen and tested the food. But of course – no poison. Not from here, anyway. I were with my cooking every minute.'

'If she had been poisoned, how might it have happened then?' Holmes seemed to read something in her eyes. 'Please, Mrs Brown, I believe you have a suspicion.'

'Box o' chocolates. Came a day or so before.'

'From whom?'

'That's just it, there weren't no note attached. I frankly suspect it.'

'I see. Did you mention these chocolates to the police?'

'I did. I took the coppers up to my lady's room. Pulled 'em down from where she had 'em hid. An older policeman came in and called me an old fool. Took a chocolate and popped it in his mouth. Old fool, indeed! Talk of pot calling the kettle black!'

'That sounds like the police,' I said.

'What happened?' asked Holmes

'Nothing. So he ate another one. Nothing again.'

'So, not poisoned, then?' I said. Though that fellow had certainly taken a chance to prove a point.

'It only takes one,' said Holmes. 'Mrs Brown, if only *one* of the chocolates were poisoned, then the poisoner would have had to be certain the lady herself would eat it. How might they—?'

'My mistress loved her chocolates. She were known to hoard 'em, not share 'em, and keep 'em in her bedroom high up in her wardrobe, so fond of 'em she was.'

'Was this common knowledge?'

'Among the servants, yes. The children, no. Well, maybe Clarence. He didn't miss much.'

'Clever,' said Holmes. 'And Peter Oliver? Where was he at this time?'

'Oh, he were still fairly new to the establishment. Not so much inside the house as he is now.'

'But sometimes?'

'Yes, an' lucky too. Anyway, the Missus were mostly hiding her chocolates from the little ones, who would steal 'em if they had the chance. Especially Master Clarence – he were a deft hand at stealing cake from the larder. And his mother's chocolates, even when she hid them.

'But not this time. Or else he was lucky,' said Holmes.

The old cook shrugged. 'You ain't eating your soup, Mr Holmes. You're only stirring it round, just like Master Clarence used to do with his vegetables he didn't want none of.'

I laughed. I once witnessed Holmes surreptitiously toss a sandwich out the window on Baker Street after Mrs Hudson had been unduly insistent that he eat.

'And so the police dropped their investigation and concluded it was a heart attack?' asked Holmes.

'Yes. The doctor they called in agreed.'

Holmes glanced at me.

'Most doctors have had little experience with poison,' I said. 'Though it is certainly covered in the literature.'

'Back, then, to this terrible fire,' said Holmes. 'Gypsies, you say? Are you certain of this?'

'Oh, yes.'

'Sir James mentioned they were entertainers of some kind.'

'They were. Snake charmers.'

Her comment hung in the air for a moment. Holmes leaned forward in his chair.

'Tell me more, Mrs Brown. Was their profession the reason for Lady Wandley's extreme aversion?'

'Well, partly.'

'What else?'

'I think Master Clarence was friends with a boy from that camp.'

'Was that boy harmed in the blaze?'

'No, I don't think so.'

'When Clarence was found hiding in the barn the next day, it was in a fort he had made with another child. Was this by chance the Gypsy boy?'

'Yes. Master Clarence was not quick to make friends. But this boy was different. Saw him once . . . big, handsome boy. But underfed.'

'You met him then?'

'Only once. He were afraid to approach the house. I gave Master Clarence sandwiches to take to him.'

'This boy's name?'

She shrugged. 'Don't know.'

'Try, Mrs Brown.'

She shook her head.

Holmes glanced at me. He turned back to the woman. Before he could speak, she added, 'Oh, now I remember. It was this boy's mother who died in the blaze. And little sister.'

A chill shot up my spine. Holmes gave nothing away but appeared only slightly interested. He nodded. 'What happened after the fire?'

'Never saw him again. Supposed he moved on with the rest right after that. Clarence, he was inconsolable. They pulled him out o' the barn and he ran to his room, locked the door, and wouldn't let no one in. For days, as I remember.'

'Days! How did Clarence survive, then? How did he eat?' I asked.

Mrs Brown looked out the window with a slight smile playing on her lips.

'How did you get the food to him, Mrs Brown?' asked Holmes.

She beamed at him, delighted to be understood. 'Peter Oliver, all in secret, set up a pulley system, and we sent baskets up via a rope to his room. Couldn't have the poor lad starve to death.'

Holmes nodded. 'Well done, Mrs Brown! You and Mr

Oliver have more sense than the family. What happened, eventually?'

'Just the strangest thing. No one would guess.'

'I might. But do tell us, dear lady.'

'Well, Sir James insisted, and finally Peter Oliver were called up an' took the door off its hinges. The maid rushed in and fainted dead away.'

'Why?' I asked.

'Let me think,' said Holmes. 'Could there have been a snake in the room?'

'Three of 'em!' cried the cook.

'Loose in the room? Poisonous snakes?' I blurted.

'Nobody waited to see. There was a suit of armour in the hall with a hatchet. What I hear was it was Peter Oliver who ran and took it up and cut off their heads, one, two, three!'

'Brave man. And little Clarence?' said Holmes.

'Devastated. Loved the beasts, apparently. Didn't speak for weeks.'

Holmes nodded, considering the grisly tale. 'And you heard nothing more of his young Gypsy friend?' he asked at last.

The woman shrugged. 'Moved on with the rest, I suppose. And . . . frankly, I was glad, too. No one wants bloody snakes hanging about. I mean, do they?'

CHAPTER TWENTY-EIGHT

The Factotum

olmes looked up towards the doorway and I followed his gaze. It was Peter Oliver, eyeing the plates on the table. 'Oh, Mrs Brown, you are too kind! Gentlemen, may I escort you? I will have your carriage brought round. That is, if you have completed everything to your satisfaction?'

Holmes paused and turned to the factotum. 'Mr Oliver, if you do not mind, before we leave, I'd like to interview *you* privately. In your quarters, if I may?'

The young man looked momentarily surprised, but instantly recovered.

'Certainly, Mr Holmes.'

Minutes later, we were in an upstairs bedroom on the third floor of the main house. The room was modest, connecting to a small sitting room. Few personal effects were in evidence: a dresser; a desk with a single notebook and pen; a seafaring novel open on a chaise longue; a pipe, unused, in a holder. No photographs, no personal mementos.

We glanced into the spartan bedroom. The bed was precision made, almost military. It felt like a hotel or, oddly, like a stage set.

'You do not spend much time here, do you, Mr Oliver?' said Holmes.

Oliver smiled. 'True. No rest for the weary! My duties keep me busy.'

Holmes smiled. 'No rest for the *wicked*, you mean? As Calvin said.'

Oliver laughed. 'I suppose some of the servants might say so.'

'Mrs Brown seems to like you.'

'It is a land divided,' Oliver smiled. 'But you are right – the cook and I are friends. My duties have been so expanded in twelve years. I sleep very little,' he said.

There was a pause.

'And your office?' asked Holmes.

Oliver smiled. 'I have a work area in an old building past the kitchen garden out there.' He gestured vaguely.

'And do you sometimes sleep there?'

Oliver seemed puzzled by the question. 'Well, yes, sometimes I do.'

Silence.

'Well, mostly I do,' he admitted with a smile.

'It is obvious. Will you show us, please?'

'I am terribly sorry. I really cannot invite people into that area. Sir James's orders. He is extremely protective of his trade secrets. His special dyes are world renowned and . . .'

'I must insist.'

'I apologize, but he is quite adamant on this point. He simply will not allow visitors there. Not even any staff from here, either. No one.'

Holmes smiled. A gauntlet had been thrown. This would be interesting.

'You mean *you* will not allow.'

'I serve Sir James. It is his decree.'

'Mr Oliver, unless you would like me to return with Palace officials and the local police, I suggest you accommodate my request. Otherwise, this situation will escalate in a most unpleasant manner, and you will be held responsible for the incursion of any number of policemen, who will be brought in to see what you could quite simply show to me, privately, now.'

Oliver capitulated, and with some reluctance led us to it.

His office was located in a very old outbuilding some thirty yards behind the house, down a slight hill and well hidden by a grove of trees. To reach it, we had to traverse a walled kitchen garden which stood between the main house and this building. Spring had not yet touched this garden. The bare branches of fruit trees, the spindly arms of a number of dormant rose bushes and blackened remnants of herbs gave it an eerie, forlorn look. In the far wall was a gate, opening to a gravel path leading through the trees to a large, single storey stone building, at least as old as the main house.

Peter Oliver unlocked the door and motioned us in. His resentment was in check and he exhibited no outward emotion. A smooth character, I thought. But I suppose one had to be, to deal with the oddities of this family.

In contrast to the weather-worn exterior of this building, the interior was surprisingly finished to a pleasing, if idio-syncratic, degree. A short entry hall was crisply tiled in chequerboard flooring. On the right, a rack hung neatly with a winter coat, scarves and hats, with rubber boots and clip-on ice cleats stored underneath on a shelf. On the wall next to this was mounted a very large, full-length mirror. It was French – ornate and gilded – and looked like it belonged in a lady's boudoir.

Odd, I thought, but perhaps Peter Oliver checked his appearance before going to the main house. The man certainly kept himself in trim. I wondered briefly if he'd been in the military, before I remembered his introduction to us during our first visit. He had come straight from university into the Wandley's employ.

High on the wall to the side of the door was a small bell, with a wire disappearing into the doorframe. It seemed to be the kind of newly electrified summons one found below stairs in the grand houses, and I presumed Sir James or members of his family used it to send for Oliver.

His exact position was still unclear to me. It appeared to be a mix of glorified servant, trusted business colleague, and yet something else as well. His familiarity with Sir James made him seem almost like a member of the family. I wondered if Holmes intended to probe this relationship.

Oliver had remained silent throughout, then proceeded down the hallway to a heavy door. Unlocking it, he stepped aside, gesturing us to enter. 'My office,' he said, flatly. If he was cross, he was hiding it well.

It was not what I expected. We entered into an enormous

room, with a vaulted ceiling and a row of windows placed high up on the far wall. The floor was made of ancient stone slabs. Below the high windows stood three long tables, each covered with a very different collection of objects: the first appeared to be chemistry equipment, including a Bunsen burner with a gas hose to the wall; the second were blueprints, notebooks and drafting tools; and the third books, pens, a ledger and unidentifiable clutter. The room had been electrified and large lamps hung down to cast a bright light on each of these tables.

A bare, polished wooden desk faced these, and next to it stood a large blackboard, similar to Holmes's own, with dates and notes scrawled in chalk. Given that Peter Oliver ran both the house and Sir James's businesses, the whole room put me in mind of an army command post.

Standing irreverently out from all of this was a bright bouquet of early daffodils, perched on one corner of the desk.

Peter Oliver let us take it in without interruption. Glancing back at him, I noticed he was carefully observing Holmes.

'You are a polymath,' said Holmes, clearly impressed by the room itself. 'I can see myself spending many happy hours in such a room.'

I laughed, hoping to lighten the mood. 'That is certainly true. Mr Holmes has a passion for chemistry as well, Mr Oliver. That is quite a remarkable laboratory you have over there.'

'May I?' said Holmes, approaching the first of the three tables without waiting for permission. 'You may be assured

I have no interest in revealing trade secrets. Or any secrets at all.'

Oliver seemed to have melted just a little. 'I suppose,' he said, 'yes, be my guest.' He followed.

This chemistry table even exceeded Holmes's in 221B. In addition to the Bunsen burner, charts and notes were aligned precisely alongside beakers and tubes.

'Impressive,' I said.

'Of course, you are the lead chemist,' said Holmes.

'Yes, sir. It was the reason for my being hired.'

'I remember.'

Of course, he remembered everything.

'Mr Holmes is a quite accomplished chemist, himself,' I said. 'In our sitting room, we have—'

'Watson, please. And here, the aniline dyes which you mentioned earlier!' Holmes had picked up a beaker and held it up the light. It lit up a beautiful royal purple.

'Did you know,' asked Oliver, warming at last, 'that prior to the discovery of these chemicals only twenty years ago, purple was a very costly hue? Hence, "Royal purple". Long ago, wearing purple as less than a Royal would land you in prison!'

Holmes nodded vaguely, set the beaker down and moved to the middle table. The blueprints spread there revealed a complex, multi-roomed structure. Drafting tools gleamed in precise rows. Books and notebooks were stacked neatly around the edges.

Holmes smiled. 'And what have we here? It looks as though an extension is planned to Sir James's factories. Am I correct?'

'Indeed,' said Oliver. Pride had seemed to have overridden his initial reluctance. 'We have flourished in recent years. That new factory and workshop will house future developments in dyes. Artists will be employed to further develop the colour range, along with the perhaps less aesthetically minded chemists.'

'Sounds a propitious mix,' said Holmes, 'Are you in charge of managing this expansion of the physical property in addition to its operation?'

'Yes, I am,' said Oliver modestly. 'I apprenticed with an architect before Cambridge.'

'Where you matriculated at a very young age. A precocious boy, then.'

'I suppose so, sir. But, I may add, this expansion is also a secret, for now.'

'I assure you of confidentiality, Mr Oliver,' said Holmes. 'I see you intend to level this raised hillock. Dynamite, I suppose?'

Oliver nodded. 'That has been done already.'

'Hard to keep such a thing a secret.'

'There's no one within hearing distance, Mr Holmes.'

The large room was comfortably warm, and I turned to regard a fire that burned cheerily in an enormous fireplace at the far end.

'That is quite a fire you have there,' I remarked.

'This is the former kitchen,' said Holmes, nodding toward it. I only then noticed a system of racks and hooks above the flames.

'Yes,' said Oliver. 'In the past, the kitchen was always separate from the house. All of the cooking and laundry were once done in this room. The high windows were opened to let out the heat,' he added.

'Quite useful in the summer even now, I expect,' said Holmes.

'Indeed.'

Holmes seemed to be fishing, but for what, I could not ascertain. Bored by the building plans, I wandered over to the third table and began to peruse it. The objects in this collection were harder to classify. They included a large ledger book open to a half-filled page, a stack of what looked to be art books, another of cookery books, a calendar, a journal, a pot full of expensive pens, and some wallpaper samples.

Holmes followed and seemed to find this last table intriguing. I wondered what he found interesting. It appeared as though Peter Oliver had taken over the running of the domestic end of the main house as well.

Holmes picked up the wallpaper sample, a floral, leafy design in delicate colours. In doing so, he managed to upend the pot of pens which clattered onto the floor. Peter Oliver stiffened in alarm.

'Oh, forgive me,' Holmes said. 'So clumsy of me!'

It was indeed, and out of character. I stooped to help Peter Oliver retrieve them. The pilfered silver alligator pen from the Christie Atelier came to mind. Surely Holmes did not suspect Peter Oliver? In any case, nothing like that was there.

Upon rising, I looked more closely at the wallpaper sample in Holmes's hand.

'That is lovely,' I said.

'A Christie design,' remarked Holmes. He set the sample down. I knew him to be little interested in such domestic detail. He picked up a small box and opened it. 'And this box of ashes?'

Oliver started. 'Oh! that belongs on table one. We are looking to create some new inks, some rich blacks.' Oliver took the box from Holmes's hand and walked it over to table one.

Holmes returned his attention to the third table.

'And you have the running of the house as well, I see. Cooking, everything.'

Oliver nodded.

Holmes lingered at this table. I lost interest and once again took in the entirety of this unusual space. Peter Oliver was a well-rounded man. I could easily imagine that if I had such a large estate and so many businesses, the master of this office would be just the man to run them all.

'Sir James is a lucky man,' I said.

'Thank you,' said Oliver.

'As you said, then, little rest?' said Holmes.

Oliver laughed. 'Very little rest, indeed.'

'May I see the wine cellar below, then?'

Oliver seemed surprised at the question. 'Ah! Both the kitchen and wine cellar are in the main house, now. As you saw, a modern kitchen, with the latest inventions. Sir James is not fond of wines, preferring spirits, so the cellar is quite small, and is located near the kitchen there.'

'But there must have been one here at one time?' said Holmes. 'They were always near, and usually under the kitchen. A large one, considering the size of this room.'

'Very astute, sir. It flooded some years ago and I had it fitted with drains and filled in. We cannot risk the documents in this room.'

'I see,' said Holmes. 'Will you show me please?'

'I cannot. The stairs have eroded away, and the place is filled with earth and stones. There is nothing to see.'

'Just the stairs, then?'

Oliver was puzzled but acquiesced. 'If you like.'

We entered a narrow hallway, from which I got a glimpse of a very small bedroom, almost a closet, but yet looking well used. A stack of books and a wall-mounted light told the story. At the end of this corridor was an old wooden door sealed with a padlock. Oliver withdrew a key from a ring on his belt and opened it.

Derelict stone steps led steeply down to a wall of dirt and broken bricks, impassable by any means. It looked exactly as described, an unused old cellar, now filled in.

'Thank you, Mr Oliver,' said Holmes.

We returned to the main room. Holmes coughed slightly. 'The dust,' he remarked. My friend then nodded towards the far end of this very large room where the fire was burning. 'I could use a refreshment,' he said, amiably. Only I knew how out of character was this request, and surely not a social one, knowing Holmes.

Oliver smoothly guided us to the area before the fire. There were three mismatched and worn leather armchairs with a threadbare rug thrown below them. Castoffs from the main house, I thought. A few more books were strewn about and reading lamps stood near two of the chairs. Oliver brought us each a whisky.

All in all, together with the worktables, the room conveyed a strange combination of crisp efficiency and, at this end, a kind of domestic comfort. I wondered briefly whom he might entertain in this place where 'no one was allowed'.

CHAPTER TWENTY-NINE

A Convivial Whisky

olmes took a sip of his whisky. 'Ah, an excellent Highland choice. Glenmorangie, is it not?'

Oliver seemed to bask in the compliment. 'My favourite.'

Holmes was successfully soothing our host. 'I would be quite happy here, in this workshop, I think. All that is missing is music. Is that a gramophone . . . ?'

I followed his glance to a side table on which rested one of those very new cylinder gramophones and some wax cylinders.

'Yes! I have recently purchased that device.'

I had seen only one prior to that date. Holmes stood up and moved over to inspect the cylinders. Oliver seemed suddenly nervous.

Holmes picked up a cylinder and read off one of the titles: '"The Virtues of Raw Oysters". Well, that is a piece I have never heard. Would you play it for us?'

'The machine does not quite work yet. I am going to take it back to the seller. I am sorry, I cannot serenade you just now. But do come back and hear some Wagner. Next week, perhaps?' Oliver indicated the easy chairs.

'Delighted,' said Holmes returning to his seat. 'It is a pity that so few will enjoy your hospitality here.'

'Indeed. It was my intention to entertain, but of course Sir James's wishes prevail, and I am prevented.'

The two settled in again. Holmes smiled. 'I will need just a little more of your time, Mr Oliver. You spoke to us earlier about the three Wandley children. Privately, here, I hope to learn more about the household. You must have been quite young when you joined the family?'

Oliver blushed. 'Well, not the family. The firm. I was a very junior employee, straight from Cambridge.'

'Your age then?'

'Just nineteen. I graduated early,' said Oliver.

'I see. You have done very well for yourself,' said Holmes. 'Were I in your shoes I should never like to leave this building. I take it you prefer to sleep here?' he asked, gesturing at the hallway we had traversed earlier.

'Yes, I do spend every available minute here. And often grab my forty winks in the little room adjoining this space. I am always here when Sir James is away on travels. I only stay in the main house, in the suite you saw, when he is at home and specifically demands it.'

'Are there not a butler, housekeeper and numerous servants to attend to his needs?'

'There are, but it is his preference to call on me.'

At Holmes's stare, he pressed on. 'I know this is unusual.

We have already lost one housekeeper over this. She was happy to take the meal and household orders from Miss Jane or Miss Kate, even as children, but bristled at a young man ruling over her.'

'Ruling?' asked Holmes with a smile.

Peter Oliver laughed. 'Well, "ruling" is the wrong word. It only seemed so to her. "Directing", perhaps.'

'And now?'

'I have since hired replacements for both that lady and the head butler. We have settled into a nice rhythm.'

Holmes nodded. 'I see. Regarding the Wandley children, I am hoping that perhaps you can speak more candidly away from the house. Bluntly, even. Anything more you can tell us about Jane, for example?'

The young man ran his fingers through his curly hair and hesitated. Clearly he was uncomfortable with being indiscreet. 'Jane was not only the eldest, but the most mature. She had a calming way about her, and a natural instinct for people. I understand that she was well liked at the Palace and was due for promotion.'

'Where did you hear that?'

'From Jane herself. But it fitted exactly with my observations of her.'

'You always called her by her first name?'

'She insisted.'

'Go on.'

'Well, she was a lovely girl. Few shortcomings, really. Perhaps a certain vanity, but it is to be excused in one so young and so beautiful.'

He smiled sadly.

'You liked her, then?'

'Very much. When her mother died and her father handed her the running of the house, she had large shoes to fill. She was too young, in my opinion. But Sir James was – is – very particular about everything being a certain way, down to the very smallest details. How his shirt collars were to be pressed, how his eggs were to be cooked, exactly – Jane was familiar with all of that, and an extremely competent girl. She soon had the house running as before. To be frank, this surprised even me.'

'Even you?

'Yes. The level of detail. In one so young.'

Holmes nodded to the three tables. 'You seem to have a head for details yourself,' he said.

A flicker of sadness appeared in Oliver's eyes. 'Attention to detail is the hallmark of the scientist. And the detective, too, I imagine?'

'To be sure!' I said. 'It is. Although you wouldn't say so from the chaos in our sitting room.'

'Watson.' Holmes frowned good naturedly at me for this non sequitur and turned back to Oliver. His expression broadened to a smile. 'I take it you have the management of the collars and the eggs now?'

Peter Oliver laughed. 'I have trained the staff.'

There was a pause as Holmes considered.

'Another whisky?' offered Oliver, nodding to the bottle nearby.

To my disappointment, Holmes shook his head in reply, then said, 'The gold mirror near your front door – is that from Jane's room, by chance?'

Where on earth had he pulled this from?

Peter Oliver was startled but smiled at the memory. 'Why, er, yes, it is! One day, as she was preparing to leave for Windsor, I chanced upon her with her father. He took me to task about some detail of my *habillement* – oh, something – my own collar, I think. That night, she had the footmen bring the mirror down to me here with a note. "To keep my father happy and you *perfectly* attired". She had quite a sense of humour, did Jane.'

Holmes laughed. 'The master and his collars, I see.' His face darkened as he continued. 'But about the siblings. Kate is an unusual girl.'

'Ah, an angry one, that,' said Oliver.

'You know, I will have that second whisky, thank you.'

Oliver obliged. As he did, Holmes swiftly pocketed a small slip of paper from the table next to his chair. What, I wondered?

'Not much for running the house, then?' continued Holmes.

'No. Parliament, maybe. Not the house.' He laughed. 'Kate is not a domesticated creature. The master assumed Girton would absorb and transmute her wayward tendencies.'

'That is not what I have heard of Girton,' said Holmes. 'You don't, by chance, know what has become of her in the last day or so? Has she made an appearance here? Sent word?'

'Why, no. Is she missing?'

'Yes. And I worry.'

'Worry? I would not. Kate Wandley is often adventurous.'

'Yes, but given the highly unusual features of her sister's

death, it has occurred to me that there might be a villain with a vendetta against this family. If so, he may have extended his view to the younger sister.'

Peter Oliver started at the notion. 'My God! Do you really think—?'

'Mr Oliver, it is not the time to hold back. Do you have any idea whatsoever where Miss Kate Wandley might be?'

'Well—'

'I thought perhaps there was something you did not wish to say with Sir James present.'

Peter Oliver nodded. 'All right then, yes. Kate Wandley is a sore spot with her father. She vehemently declined his recommendations for marriage. I know that she loves France. I believe she has a young man there – in Paris. Quite against her father's wishes.'

Of course! I was not wrong in my detecting a certain French quality to Kate Wandley's dress and mien. Lovers often adopt the style or characteristics of their amours.

'Have you a name? An address?' said Holmes.

'Pierre . . . Pierre Brouillard. No address, only that he lives in the Fifth Arrondissement.'

'Wealthy, then. How do you know this?'

'I caught a glimpse of an envelope before Sir James burned it.'

'Thank you. Very observant. We shall follow that up. But again, I must understand in more detail her relationship with her older sister.'

Peter Oliver considered. 'Adversarial, but not precisely competitive. The two girls wanted different things in life.'

'Can you elaborate, please?'

'Hard to pin down. Jane concerned herself with beauty, elegance, prestige.'

'Possessions? Or in herself?' asked Holmes.

'Both. She took tremendous pride in her appearance.'

'And Kate?'

'Power, I suppose.'

'As her namesake in *The Taming of the Shrew*!' I interjected, referring to Shakespeare's heady protagonist.

Peter laughed. 'Not unlike.'

'My impression as well,' said Holmes, sharing a smile. 'And now, candidly, what of Clarence?' Holmes asked.

'A sad case that. He was a difficult child. Lonely. A talented artist with a strange passion for insects, frogs—'

'And snakes.'

'Yes.'

'Now, Mr Oliver, I was made aware of your role – heroic, actually – in killing the snakes found in Clarence's room after the unfortunate fire.'

Peter Oliver flushed modestly. 'I was merely in the right place at the right time to be of service.'

'Brave, nonetheless. Now – you may probably have surmised this already, but Clarence's love of snakes puts him quite in the picture regarding Jane's disfigurement and death. And yet I have trouble with the direct connection.'

'I am not sure I can be of help.'

'Anything whatsoever you can offer regarding Clarence, perhaps? Do not mince words, Mr Oliver. Did you know that it was precisely his design for the Christie Atelier that was tattooed upon Jane Wandley?'

'Why, no. I cannot fathom it.'

'But it is the case. What, then, do you think is the likelihood of his direct involvement?'

Peter paused and shrugged. 'It is not for me to say, Mr Holmes. There was no love lost between those two, Jane and Clarence. They were oil and water.' Here he closed his eyes and tried to shake off the image. 'But how Clarence's own design came to be tattooed on her head like that, I cannot imagine.'

'Yes, indeed,' Holmes remarked, and stared into the fire for a moment. Peter Oliver shifted in his chair uncomfortably. I sympathized. It had been a serious shock even for me, and I had seen much violence in recent years.

'The exact duplicate of this design in the form of a painting was stolen from the Christie Atelier some time before the crime, Mr Oliver. It was taken during a party – a party in which Miss Kate Wandley and an unidentified man were present.'

Peter Oliver's face registered shock. 'Who, I wonder?' he said.

'It is interesting, to be sure. Christie was focused on Miss Wandley and could not describe her companion.'

'Then surely he . . . or perhaps they . . . stole the painting . . . ?'

'The case is muddied. Because a coloured facsimile of this design was present at the atelier and was later circulated to the police to help them find the painting, a great number of people could have seen and noted that exact rendition before the events at the Palace.'

Peter Oliver slumped in his chair. 'That is unfortunate! The view widens then, does it not?'

Holmes nodded and sipped his Scotch. 'Sadly, yes. Do you have any idea who might have accompanied Kate Wandley to that party?'

'Perhaps you should ask her,' said Oliver.

'If I could find her, I would.'

'There was a long pause. 'I feel I am being indiscreet,' said Oliver, 'but my suggestion would be to look to . . . Paris?'

Holmes stood up to leave and I followed suit. 'Thank you, Mr Oliver, so kindly for your insights. And your excellent whisky.'

Peter Oliver accompanied us back through the garden, into the main house and to the front entrance, where our carriage awaited.

Holmes paused before embarking. 'You will let us know if Kate shows herself, or communicates with anyone here?'

'Certainly, Mr Holmes.'

Holmes gestured me to proceed him into the carriage. As I climbed aboard, he said, 'Oh, and one more thing. Who stands to inherit the estate now that the eldest, favoured child, Jane, is deceased?'

Peter Oliver stiffened. 'I understand it to be the two remaining children.'

'Not you, then?' Holmes said with a smile.

'Oh, indeed not. In the event of Sir James's death, I am contractually obligated to carry on in my position, if desired by the heir or heirs. And if not, then to receive a generous stipend.'

'It is good that you are well looked after,' said Holmes. 'Please look after your master well, Mr Oliver. There is a darkness that surrounds this house. I do not think the Wandley family has seen the end of its woes.'

'Oh, I sincerely hope you are wrong, sir,' said Peter Oliver.

CHAPTER THIRTY

The Macaroni Palace

he royal carriage rolled at great speed over the bumpy roads leading from the grand house towards the capital. The hail had long since stopped, but dark clouds hung low in the sky as dusk folded in around us. Holmes seemed lost in thought, and I was loath to disturb him.

The missing Kate Wandley weighed heavily on my mind, and I wondered how Holmes would choose to follow up this Frenchman, Pierre Brouillard. But more compelling was the news we had gleaned from the cook – a Gypsy encampment possibly set afire by Lady Wandley some years ago, then Lady Wandley's sudden death a week later, possibly by poison. One might easily conclude that our present-day case was a matter of retribution. And members of the Gypsy encampment were snake charmers! How could this not be related to her daughter's recent mutilation with snake tattoos?

Finally, I could stand the silence no longer.

'Holmes, are you thinking what I am thinking?'

'That is highly unlikely, Watson.'

'Well, don't you want to *know* what I am thinking?'

'The obvious, Watson. You are thinking the obvious.'

Holmes's arrogance could occasionally rankle. 'All right then, *what* am I thinking?'

'You are thinking that there is some Gypsy connection to Jane Wandley's death after the tragic history of that fire.'

'Well, it does appear—' I began.

'You forget that Jane Wandley was a child when her mother presumably – and we do not know this with any certainty – set alight that Gypsy encampment the cook described. You are startled about their profession as snake charmers, and are thinking that Jane Wandley's heinous disfigurement might be some kind of continuation of this ghastly tale. Perhaps part of a vendetta. The Gypsies must be behind it. That somehow this all connects.'

'Well . . .' I did not want to admit it, but he had voiced my thoughts, precisely. 'But come now, Holmes, it must be!'

'Watson, of course it may connect. But consider this. Whoever perpetrated this crime was far more devious than you perhaps give him – or her – credit. And there was money involved.'

'Not likely within the purview of your average Gypsy, then?"

'Your prejudice does not serve you well, Watson. While many are poor, there are Gypsies in all strata of society. I know of both an Oxford don and a Member of Parliament with Gypsy blood.'

'Surely not—'

'Well-hidden, as you may imagine.'

I shrugged. I could not bring any to mind, but that did not mean there weren't any.

'But yes, we must follow up the lead of this particular Gypsy group – where they went, what they did next, and where they are now.'

'All right, then,' I exclaimed, grasping at a touch of vindication where I could find it.

'But then . . . there are the oysters,' said my friend.

'What?'

'That wax cylinder recording. I have heard of it, Watson. It is not music!'

'What are you talking about?'

'There is an underground market for recordings and performers of a very specific type, Watson. Performers who create jokes, stories, limericks of a highly salacious nature, and sell them on cylinders like the one in Mr Oliver's sitting area.'

'Salacious! You mean risqué?' I laughed. 'You jest, of course.'

'No. And more than risqué.'

'Perhaps Peter Oliver is in need of some humour? I would be, having to serve *that* family,' I mused.

'Perhaps. But grist for the mill, Watson, that is all.'

There was a silence.

'What kind of jokes, exactly?'

'Let us drop the subject. I am sure one of your gambling friends can fill in the details.'

We rode on in silence toward the city. I felt myself begin to doze when Holmes broke in. 'And there is this.'

He withdrew an envelope from his pocket and stared at it thoughtfully.

'What have you got there, Holmes?'

'Something I took from Peter Oliver's third table.'

So that was why he had upended the pens. 'What is it?'

'Sadly, just the envelope. Addressed to Peter F. Oliver from the Nobel Dynamite Trust Company. Manufacturers, obviously.'

'Nothing surprising, then, is there? You already know he had ordered dynamite.'

'True. But it, too, was on the wrong table.'

'Trivial, don't you think?

Holmes shrugged. 'I wonder what the "F" stands for? Peter *F*. Oliver.'

I could not imagine this was at all significant. I feared my friend was suffering from overwork. Or grasping at straws. I was on the cusp of mentioning this, but we rode on a little further in silence.

'Watson, it may surprise you to learn that I am very hungry. What do you say we try out a new restaurant this evening?'

Now that was indeed a surprise, and so very out of character. A good meal held a great deal of appeal to me at that precise moment, and perhaps over a glass of wine Holmes might open up further about his thoughts on the case.

'On this we agree!' I volunteered. 'In fact, there is a new Indian restaurant on Paddington Street—'

'No, Watson, I have my heart set on a little place in Southwark . . .'

In two hours, we found ourselves in that very neighbour-hood, facing the strangely named 'Macaroni Palace'.

I had been foolish to think Holmes might be taking the evening off. The man was relentless. Of course, this restaur-ant was where Clarence Wandley's handsome Italian friend Neptune played the violin on certain evenings each week. Fridays, in fact.

Tonight.

There was nothing the slightest bit palatial about the Macaroni Palace. Unprepossessing on the outside, inside it had a certain seedy charm. Worn red velvet curtains cupped round individual, chipped black tables, providing small, semi-intimate spaces. On each table, candles with brass shades sent a soft glow into the faces of what appeared to be mostly very young couples. I caught the briefest impres-sions of moon-eyed stares and fingertips gently caressing outstretched palms. A haven for trysts, no doubt. However, another attraction of the place was soon in evidence. It was the food!

Waiters in brightly coloured shirts with long, flowing poet sleeves danced between the tables, bearing large oval platters piled high with pasta shapes of various kinds, long spaghetti strands, and others which I would be hard pressed to name – tubes, spirals, little shells – and on top of these, mounds of various sauces ranging from bright scarlet to deep purple and brown. The aroma of tomatoes, onions, mushrooms and browned meat perfumed the air.

The whole impression was richly Bohemian and unabash-edly romantic. I could imagine the possibilities for courtship here, if the food tasted as good as it promised. But there was no sign of Neptune and his violin. Perhaps he had taken the evening off.

Without asking for our preferences, a waiter placed three small plates on our table, one with olives, one with blanched almonds, and a third with simply a pool of viscous green liquid. Before I could wonder about that third dish, another waiter brought a basket of steaming bread, cut into crusty chunks. Noticing my confused stare at the liquid, he mimed taking up a piece of bread, dunking into the green pool and taking a bite. He grinned and moved off.

'Olive oil,' said Holmes. 'Try it.'

I did. It was delicious. I gave over the ordering of food to Holmes, and soon we had our own steaming platters of noodles and red meat sauce.

A single bite told me I had travelled to culinary heaven. A sudden violin flourish sang out over the crowd and the general hubbub quietened a little. Standing near the door to the kitchen was Neptune, in a flowing white shirt, tight black trousers and tall suede boots. With his long hair sweeping back from his forehead, he cut a dashing figure as he began to play.

The music was dark, romantic and heartfelt. He moved first to a table near the kitchen and began to serenade the young couple sitting there. It was a sweet, poignant melody.

'Is that some famous aria? Puccini, perhaps?' I said, bluffing by naming the only Italian composer I could bring to mind.

An opera aficionado, Holmes would surely know. Instead, he was signalling the waiter for our bill. Why? We had barely had time to touch our food. 'No, Watson,' he whispered.

Holmes could be quite a pedant on the subject of music. 'Well, what then?' I said, slightly irritated. 'A re . . . recitative, perhaps?' I was proud of myself for dredging up this musical term from my limited knowledge of the subject. I took another bite. Yes, I would return, to be sure.

'No.'

The music arched and soared, passionate and thrilling. Even I was stirred by the sheer emotion of it. Neptune was quite the fiddler, I thought.

The low hum of conversation had ceased as the entire restaurant gave over to listening.

'Oh, come, Holmes,' I whispered. 'It must be some Italian opera – perhaps one even you do not know?'

The waiter arrived and Holmes threw down some coins to pay. The waiter departed and he stood up. 'It is not Italian. It is not from any opera. Come!'

Without further words, he slipped quickly towards the exit. Frustrated, I tossed down my napkin and followed. I had not had time to eat more than a few bites of what had promised to be an excellent meal.

PART SEVEN

EVEN A DRAGON

'*When someone criticizes or disagrees with you, a small ant of hatred and antagonism is born in your heart. If you do not squash that ant at once, it might grow into a snake, or even a dragon.*'

—Rumi

CHAPTER THIRTY-ONE

A Close Call

n a moment, we stood outside the door of the restaurant. A thick fog had settled over Southwark since our arrival.

'Holmes,' I cried, 'what the devil—?'

'Neptune is no Italian.'

'What?'

Holmes glanced up and down the street. There was no cab nearby, no traffic at all, just a long dark cobbled road, gradually becoming obscured as the fog rolled in.

'The music, Watson! It was pure Romani. Just as I thought.'

'*Gypsy* music?'

'Yes.'

I shivered. Of course! The larger picture swam before me: Clarence as a child; the Gypsy boy he had befriended; their 'fort' in the barn; their present-day friendship. *Snakes.*

Holmes had taken off at a fast walk down the wet pavement, his figure nearly vanishing into the fog a few feet away. I had to run to catch up.

'Neptune! Of course, *he* was the young boy—'

'Ah, Watson, the light dawns,' said Holmes. 'There is no doubt he is a survivor of the tragedy at the Wandley home. Clarence's childhood "little Gypsy friend". All this fits together.'

'But how could this be?' I shook my head. 'I thought you spoke to him in Italian?'

'Only a few words. Frankly I had my suspicions, although I was thinking perhaps he was Greek,' said Holmes. 'We did not yet have the Gypsies in view at that time.'

'He must be our man, then?'

'There is no "must" about it.'

'But the motive, Holmes! If his mother and baby sister were killed by—'

'Motive to kill Lady Wandley, perhaps, but as a small child, then, he would not have had the means. However, a long simmering desire for revenge on others in the family? Very possible . . .'

He paused at an intersection and looked about him, triangulating our location. Holmes never failed to astound me with the virtual map of London he carried about in his head. 'This way! We shall have a better chance for a cab at Borough Market.' It was beginning to rain again.

And so we set out in a rush, our collars turned up as the stinging icy droplets pelted us. Springtime in London, I thought sourly . . . when Holmes grabbed my arm and pulled me abruptly into a dark, narrow alley.

'What?' I whispered.

'Shh. We are being followed.'

Holmes seemed to have some kind of peripheral vision, which I had noted before, but for it to function in the darkness and rain? That surprised me. A moment later, his instinct was borne out when a very tall, muscular man garbed in black, a hat pulled low over his face, appeared in the street and paused at the entrance to the alley, just six feet from where we hid in the shadows. He turned to look back the way we had come, and the streetlamp briefly illuminated his face. His swarthy skin and sharp features were not unlike Neptune's. A relative, perhaps.

A sharp cry sounded behind me and I turned to see Holmes, only barely visible in the darkness, with hands to his neck, locked in mortal combat with a bulky figure attempting to garrote him. The silence of this attack had surprised even my friend!

I leaped upon them with such force that all three of us fell to the ground, enabling Holmes to break free. We sprang to our feet and Holmes turned on his attacker.

But the sounds had alerted the man in the street, who dashed into the alley and set upon me as I rose from the wet pavement. In that instant, Holmes and I, back to back, fought for our lives in that slippery, black alley.

As I have related elsewhere, Holmes was a skilled street fighter, and I am no easy victim myself. It was too dark to see clearly and the four of us fought silently, with only the sounds of fists upon flesh and the grunts of pain echoing in the alley as the murky figures approached and fell back again and again.

But these two were soon outmatched. A police whistle sounded nearby. And as quickly as they appeared, our attackers were gone.

Holmes leaned against a stone wall and coughed.

'Holmes?'

He continued to cough, still unable to speak.

At the end of the alley a policeman appeared with a lantern. 'Hold up!' he cried, raising his billy club. 'Who goes there?'

'I am Dr John Watson,' I cried out. 'And this is Sherlock Holmes. We have been set upon!'

'Approach!' said the copper, unwilling even with a lantern to venture into the darkness around us without a backup. I took Holmes by the arm and pulled him forward.

Our gentlemanly attire, even muddied as we both now were, worked in our favour. After a brief exchange, we managed to convince the constable that we were in fact the victims, not the instigators, of the fight he had come upon.

Some thirty minutes later, after a chilly ride home, we reached Baker Street and now sat, boots off, warming ourselves by the fire at 221B. Mrs Hudson, who had uncharacteristically waited up for us, had been alarmed at our appearance and taken our wet outer clothes with some concern. She noted the red mark upon Holmes's neck and clucked about him, but he waved her off.

'Holmes,' I said, 'under normal circumstances, you would not have been surprised in that alley.'

'We *both* were surprised,' he said, his voice gravelly from the attack. 'The man was remarkably silent.' Here he was cut off by a cough.

'This is precisely what I meant about over-confidence,' I said. 'You have slept little since this case began. Or rather, cases. You take on too much, thinking yourself some kind of man made of metal. You risk collapse, I tell you!'

'Oh, pish posh, Watson! You enjoyed yourself immensely just now. Your face is flushed and you positively swaggered as Mrs Hudson fussed over us.'

If I was not flushed before, I must have become so at that moment. I was embarrassed to admit he was right. I was, in fact, exhilarated.

'And we have made progress on the case,' said Holmes. 'Was it Neptune in that alley? With a friend, perhaps?'

'I did not get a good look. But likely, don't you agree?'

'Do you suspect Neptune of the tattoo and murder of Jane Wandley?' I said. 'If Neptune is indeed the Gypsy friend of Clarence Wandley when both were boys, then could he not harbour a well-founded grudge—?'

'Except why, then, organize a tattoo of precisely Clarence's design? Not only does that defy logic, but it is a complex plan which required cunning, not to mention a great deal of money to execute. He is a suspect, but not, for the moment, at the top of the list.' Holmes was suddenly overtaken by a fit of coughing.

Mrs Hudson entered precisely at that moment with tea and honey, her face a mask of concern. 'This should help your throat, Mr Holmes. Honey will soothe.'

He opened his eyes, about to wave her away a second time, but I rose and took the tray from her. 'It is not that sort of sore throat, Mrs Hudson,' I said. 'But this may help anyway. Most kind of you. I'll see that he drinks it.'

I had already had a quick look at the injury. Holmes had been lucky. The man who had tried to garrote him had not managed to crush the trachea, otherwise we would not be sitting here now. He was nothing more than badly bruised. I was less injured, having suffered only a few blows to the ribs. But my burned hand did still pain me a little.

I would hazard a guess that the villains tonight had emerged in worse shape. 'No glimpse of the second man?' I asked.

Holmes shook his head. He put his hand to his throat and tried to clear it.

'Best to let it rest, Holmes. I warrant you'll be all right in the morning. Or the next day at the latest.'

The bell sounded below. It was after midnight, and we were surprised when Heffie entered the room, rain-dampened but glowing.

'Sit down, young lady. You have news, I see,' said Holmes, his voice raspy.

'True enough. Firstly, Kate Wandley ain't in any 'ospital in London,' said she. 'Wiggins was a big 'elp, and 'e put two of 'is best Irregulars on it with me. Including a new girl. Did you know you 'ave girls in the Irregulars? Well, unofficially anyways.'

'Never mind that. What is your news?' said Holmes.

'You better sit down.'

'I am sitting down.'

'I mean Dr Watson.'

'Do get on with it, Heffie, we are quite fatigued,' I said.

'Not you,' she remarked, looking me up and down. '*You* are lookin' right pleased wi' yerself – an' like you drunk six cups o' coffee.'

Holmes chuckled. 'You are right, Heffie. Watson has always found a bit of fisticuffs invigorating.' He turned to her. 'So, Kate Wandley has vanished. We have just learned tonight that she may have fled to France.'

'I got no connections there, sir,' said Heffie.

'No matter. I do. Eventually, young lady, I would like you to expand your horizons. A bit of travel perhaps, when this case is solved. What else did you find?'

'That Laura Benson I tol' you about? A copper friend o' mine let on as she's the one who flagged the police, just like I thought! I went to have a word with that li'l traitor, but turns out she's left the city. Came into some money, 'er landlady said, and *pouf!* Gone.'

Holmes looked pensive. 'Then she *was* the traitor,' he said. 'I don't like it.'

'Sorry I don' 'ave more,' said the girl.

'What was so exciting that you wanted us to sit down for it, then, Heffie?' I asked with some irritation.

'Oh, yeah, I almost forgot. Lash, me little buddy 'oo was kicked out of the Irregulars and later drowned—'

'Yes. Lash Burton, right?'

'Wiggins confirmed the name, and 'e were Gypsy for sure. An' here's the thing. There's a camp of Gypsies hangin' out just now near Battersea. Some of 'em name o' Burton, too.'

Burton. *Burton!* The name of the Gypsy troupe that were snake charmers. The photograph on Dr Flackett's wall swam into my mind.

'Holmes!' I cried.

Holmes and I exchanged a quick look and he nodded.

Heffie did not miss it. She smiled, sensing she'd been helpful. 'Good, eh?' she said.

'Do you know their exact location?' Holmes asked her.

'No, but I'll 'ave it for you in the mornin'.' Heffie left, but not before Holmes scribbled a note and handed it to her. He asked her to send off a wire.

Moments later, we sat sharing a late-night whisky. It had been a very long day. I could hear that it had begun to rain again, quite hard.

'Poor Heffie, in this weather,' I said.

'She runs between the drops, Watson.'

Indeed, Heffie knew well how to look after herself. We sat in silence for a moment.

'What about this Pierre Brouillard fellow?' I asked, thinking of Kate Wandley's possible paramour. 'If we can't find Kate Wandley, do you think a trip to Paris is on the cards?'

'I rather think not. But we'll know soon enough. I just wired our old friend Jean Vidocq to have a look.'

'Vidocq! Not that scoundrel?' We had had a number of dealings with the notorious French detective, Jean Vidocq. Granted, some of these had been felicitous, but more often were they complicated in unpleasant ways. The fellow claimed to be a descendant of the famous Vidocq who started the Sûreté, but we both knew he was nothing of the sort. And he was very jealous of Holmes.

Nevertheless, he was sometimes useful, and I hoped in this case he would be. I felt uneasy about Kate Wandley, and yet conflicted. One moment I thought she might be somehow complicit in the heinous crime against her sister, the next I wondered if she were in danger. I looked up to see Holmes staring at me over his whisky.

He read my thoughts, as he so often did. 'Kate Wandley?' he said. 'Yes, she concerns me, too, Watson.'

'Not an easy girl to like, that Kate,' I said. 'And yet . . .'

'Irritating or not, she is quite possibly an innocent. And, if so, in danger.'

'As part of a larger revenge plan?'

'A visit to the Burton clan may offer us the information we need.'

'But aren't they the likely villains, Holmes? They certainly have reason to carry a grudge against the entire Wandley family.'

'If they are, they have friends in high places. Or at least friends with money. It is time to stir that snake's nest.'

CHAPTER THIRTY-TWO

The Gypsy Camp

he next day passed without incident. In the morning I left Holmes still sleeping and visited a former patient currently hospitalized nearby. I returned to dine with Holmes, but he had gone out without explanation, so I ended up with a cold roast beef sandwich alone by the fire at 221B. I retired before ten.

The following morning, I came downstairs early to find Holmes fully dressed, visible through the door to his bedroom. He peered into his mirror, doing something I could not discern to his ear. He heard the clink of my coffee cup and joined me at once.

There was something decidedly 'off' about his appearance. For one, his hair was combed differently: loose and curling about, untamed. Also, he was wearing an uncharacteristically bright red handkerchief in his jacket pocket.

Rather insistent gold cufflinks gleamed a bit obviously at his sleeves. It was not the sartorially conservative Holmes I knew well. I laughed. 'Well, Holmes, what is on the docket for today?'

'A visit to Battersea, Watson. Or thereabouts. I now have the precise location of that Gypsy encampment, thanks to Heffie.'

I glanced into a tureen of scrambled eggs, and another of porridge, both untouched. 'You have eaten nothing!' I exclaimed.

'I have had coffee, Watson. Eat up, and be quick about it.'

I served myself and began breakfast. I have often wondered how he maintained his breakneck pace during long investigations without fuel to run the engine. It was not medically advisable, but he would hear nothing about it, claiming digestion robbed his brain of clarity. It was a habit that would undermine his health eventually, of that I was sure.

That and over-confidence, which of course were quite connected.

'Where were you last night, Holmes?'

'Many places, Watson. While you breakfast, I shall fill you in. I paid two visits, one quite late, to Chelsea, confirming that one of our attackers was indeed Neptune.'

'Holmes! What a damned fool thing for you to do alone.'

'Your concern is appreciated, Watson. Neptune did not return home after the attack. Neither he nor Clarence Wandley answered the door all day. A neighbour thinks they left the city.'

'In the middle of the night, after the attack?'

'Possibly.'

'I see. But still, you should not have—'

'Eat up, we have work to do. Despite my failure to locate our errant fiddler, the rest of yesterday was fruitful. Not only did Heffie deliver, but our friend, Monsieur Vidocq, did as well!'

'Jean Vidocq? I hardly expected him to jump to attention.'

'It is merely a matter of applying the right combination of threat and, er, substantial reward. Vidocq can be remarkably effective when motivated.'

At my look of doubt, Holmes continued. 'He employs a group of young scallywags, not unlike my Irregulars. I have used them myself. And he has connections in high places. Between them, here is what they found: there are three Pierre Brouillards in Paris—'

'He found this in one day?'

'Yes, of course, Watson. The first is a baker with six children in the Sixteenth; the second a thief in Montmartre, whom he knows personally; and finally, a septuagenarian retired judge in the Sixth. No likely lover, and no Brouillard at all in the Fifth.'

'Perhaps Peter Oliver got the name wrong?'

'I doubt Mr Oliver gets very much wrong, Watson.'

'What then, Holmes?'

'It seems more likely to be a subterfuge of some sort, perhaps by our missing Miss Kate Wandley. In any case, France for the moment is a dead end. Are you finished with those eggs, Watson? Can we not head out?'

'You are going out like *that*?' I smiled, indicating his unusual presentation. With the simplest of changes, he had acquired an uncharacteristically flamboyant aspect. The artist in him, I thought, with every attention to detail.

'Precisely like this,' he replied with a grin. And then, to my astonishment, he reached into a pocket and popped in a cap onto one of his canines, turning it into a gold tooth. He grinned convincingly.

'Good heavens, Holmes!'

En route in our cab to an address near Battersea, Holmes explained that we would be visiting this extended Burton family of Gypsies who had, late yesterday, received a letter from a Gypsy solicitor known to them.

'There are Gypsy solicitors?' I said.

'There are Gypsies in all walks of life. Many of them do not reveal their identity, for obvious reasons. They suffer from even more discrimination than our dear Heffie. In any case, they are expecting a visit from "Professor Handel of Lonsdale College, Oxford". I am an anthropology professor with Gypsy antecedents and am writing a scholarly thesis on Gypsy culture, one which proposes to elevate this usually despised group in the eyes of academia.'

'Oh, come, Holmes! An Oxford scholar with a gold tooth? And you think they will believe that?'

'I know they will.'

I stole another glance at my friend's unusual attire and noted the dot on his earlobe.

'Did you . . . did you pierce your earlobe, Holmes?' I often wondered at the lengths he would go to with his various disguises.

'Does it look like a piercing, Watson? To your trained medical eye?'

I peered closely. 'Yes, it does.'

'Ha! It is merely the dot of a pen. I am glad it is passing.'

'Am I to accompany you?'

'Yes.'

'In the guise of what?'

'Not a Gypsy, have no fear. You are a trusted colleague who will be photographing at a later date, if they give their permission.'

'But there will be no later date, I presume?'

'If all goes well . . . no.'

We departed at once for an area near Battersea. The road wound past piles of refuse from factories. Stained and broken pieces of wood and metal, shredded rags and mounds of less recognizable materials lay about, some of which steamed unknown vapours into the damp, frigid air. It was an altogether inhospitable place.

The Gypsy encampment was reported to be concealed by a grove of trees behind a row of factories.

We followed a path into a denser area of woods and rounding a tall stand of birch trees came at last upon a large clearing. A vibrantly colourful set of Gypsy caravans and several tents put up in a ring stood out in the bleak landscape like a bright set of children's toys dumped onto a refuse heap.

There was a certain comfort in the cheerily decorated caravans, the rich aroma of meat and spices cooking, the bright clothes of the Gypsies, the laughing children. Despite the dank forest surrounding the place it had a charm, a kind of homeliness. And yet I could not shake the sense of danger.

Some ten or twelve people were moving about, several drawn round a metal canister in which a fire had been built and over which several chickens were roasting.

We were instantly spotted. A woman dashed inside the largest caravan and a tall, swarthy man of indeterminate age, but perhaps in his sixties, hopped down and approached us with an aura of forthrightness, bordering on belligerence.

With a snap of his fingers, he was backed by three young men, large and well-muscled. Around us I could feel the stares of a number of others who had emerged from the caravans and tents, and several young men elbowed to the forefront of these.

It was not a friendly welcome.

Although I had never personally had a harmful encounter with a Gypsy, I felt a frisson of alarm. I imagined this moment of entering their camp might be akin to British settlers of two centuries past meeting for the first time a group of indigenous residents in the American colonies. There was a visceral, tribal bond surrounding us, and I was struck with a sense of danger.

Do not generalize, Holmes had repeatedly warned me. Yet I knew my soldier's instincts should not be ignored.

Automatically, I reached into my pocket. But at Holmes's behest, I had left my Webley at home. I did not realize at the time the mixed blessing this might be.

The leader drew closer, then stopped, eyeing Holmes with curiosity. 'Dr Handel of Oxford?' he said, staring closely at Holmes.

He was focused on Holmes's right ear, touching his own,

which sported a gold hoop. Holmes smiled and touched his earlobe.

The dot. An inspired touch.

'Hiding your Romani roots, I see,' continued the Gypsy leader.

'Never completely hidden,' said Holmes, extending his hand in greeting and smiling to reveal his own gold tooth. 'And you are Mr Esau Burton, I presume?'

The two shook hands. I sensed, rather than saw, the young men nearest us lowering their guard, if only slightly. The leader gestured to me.

'My photographer, Mr Mendelssohn,' said Holmes pleasantly.

'No photographs!' said the man forcefully.

'Understood. In any case, he has no camera today,' said Holmes.

'Fine,' said Burton, but stood fast, as though waiting for something. Holmes took his cue, and reaching into his pocket withdrew a small suede pouch, which jangled with coins as he handed it to the Gypsy leader. 'On behalf of myself . . . and Oxford University,' he said. 'We are grateful for your cooperation.'

Esau Burton opened the purse and I glimpsed a mound of gold coins!

'Come,' he said.

CHAPTER THIRTY-THREE

Jez Burton

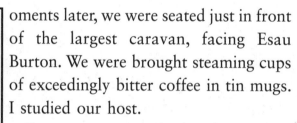oments later, we were seated just in front of the largest caravan, facing Esau Burton. We were brought steaming cups of exceedingly bitter coffee in tin mugs. I studied our host.

Burton was a swarthy, handsome man, attired in exuberant, brightly coloured clothing, topped by a ragged yet once costly frock coat, and wore one gold hoop earring dangling from his right ear. He smoked a large Meerschaum pipe featuring a stained ivory bowl carved into what looked like intertwined snakes, from which emanated the aroma of an incongruously expensive tobacco. When he smiled, his gold front tooth glistened.

Holmes was in an expansive, jocular mood, one which I'd seen him employ to good effect before. After exchanging a few pleasantries and establishing a kind of wary rapport by a shared mockery of the Metropolitan Police, which I knew to be genuine if perhaps conveniently exaggerated, Holmes began his interview.

First, he informed Burton that within his article, he hoped to feature the rarefied world of 'Gypsy snake charming', with an emphasis on the cleverness, courage and mystique of this vanishing art form. Having gained a measure of rapport, he dived in.

'I have come here under the impression that your particular family is, or was, carrying on the tradition of your ancient Indian forebears in this thrilling entertainment. I understand that you had dominated the trade – a rare one, or so my research informs me – for fifty years, but that you no longer pursue this.'

'That is right.'

'How long has it been,' Holmes wondered, 'since the Burton family practised the art of snake charming?'

'Not for many years,' said the elder.

Holmes nodded, interested. 'And why did you drop the snakes?'

'Fewer of us were interested in the risk. One of our family was bitten, an expert who should have known better. Cobras are very dangerous animals.'

'Highly venomous, I understand. But I can well imagine why they might be the snakes of choice,' said Holmes.

'Cobras were very much the crowd pleasers. So big! The dramatic hood, the thrill of the threat. "Stand back!" we warned our audiences. They loved it,' said Burton, with pride. He clearly relished the memory.

'Did you not first milk the venom of the snakes that were used in your act?'

'Some of our people did on occasion. We didn't. It's hard to do, and not always effective.'

Holmes nodded and pretended to consult a small notebook.

'I see. What do you use for income since you have eliminated this profession?'

'That is our business.'

'Yes, but *what* is your business? Now, I mean.' said Holmes.

'I will only say that we trade in small items. And horses, but only seasonally. We help on farms near London at this time of year. Why do you ask?' The question had made our host uneasy.

'Mr Burton, I know that the traditional life of our people is a hard one. And made even harder by rampant prejudice. I have suffered it myself and have had to hide my Gypsy heritage. But you . . . well, I had heard tell of a fire suffered by your group some years ago. Near an estate belonging to a . . .' Holmes consulted his notebook '. . . a Sir James Wandley. I understood there were deaths.'

The man stiffened. 'This news made a small paragraph only, in a local newspaper,' said he. 'You do your research well.'

'Oxford would not have me otherwise,' replied Holmes. 'The danger of your lifestyle may indeed help generate sympathy. Can you tell me about this accident?'

'It was not an accident.'

'Might you tell me more, as a matter of interest?'

The man hesitated and looked from Holmes to me, as if re-evaluating us. He evidently decided in our favour. 'There was a terrible fire. We lost most of our snakes, and the man who performed was badly burned. Others, including members of my own family were killed as well. After this, we lost the taste for this profession and we moved to other things.'

'Not an accident, you say,' prompted Holmes, 'but an act of pure aggression. Arson, then?'

'We saw them set the fire. A woman and a younger man. Their faces were covered, but we knew who they were and reported it. No action was taken by the police.'

'In any case, you would not have been believed. This, of course, makes my point.' Holmes made a note. 'Did you and your family not seek revenge?'

Some boundary had been crossed, because Esau Burton's affability vanished. 'No. And on reflection, Professor Handel, the account of this incident may not go in your book. It was a tragedy which we do not wish to relive, as it may kindle other flames.'

Holmes closed his notebook and nodded. 'Understood. Struck from the record. But as a matter of curiosity, and off the record, a Romani violinist who uses the name "Neptune Bandini" is now friends with—'

'That is an Italian name, not Romani.'

'I have reason to believe the fellow is of Gypsy birth. In any case, this Neptune is very interested in snakes. And he is friends with one of the family members involved in that incident. Do you know this Bandini fellow? If so, was he present at the fire? He would have been quite young.'

Burton's face had hardened. 'Your line of inquiry is most curious. I know a man named Neptune. He is dead to us. What is it you are after?' He gave a sharp glance to someone or something behind us.

Holmes put his notebook away and adopted a different tone. A sympathetic one.

'I am sorry if I offended. I am trying to help, Mr Burton, by documenting the prejudice and lack of regard towards our people. In that light, I read that an unidentified Gypsy boy was fished out of the Serpentine the other day. It was in the papers. Was this young boy known to you? Perhaps another family member?'

Suspicion clouded our host's features. 'What is that to you?'

'Naught. Except as an example. I suppose the police didn't care.'

Burton signalled to someone behind us. I was uneasy and eager to depart. I glanced at Holmes. Behind him hovered a small figure, just outside the firelight. A second glance told me this child was keenly interested in the conversation.

'The point being,' continued Holmes affably, 'that prejudice is rampant. I simply wish to highlight it in my book, with, as I said, the intention of describing the conditions under which you live.'

Esau Burton leaned toward Holmes with a peculiar smile. '*Hmmm . . . Baxt hai sastimos tiri patragi. Kaj si toalet?*' he said softly.

Holmes was startled but recovered instantly and laughed. 'Easter greetings to you, as well. Although it is a little early. And . . . no, I do not know where your toilet is.' He smiled. 'But please, my accent is so terrible, may we continue in English?'

Holmes was full of surprises. I could not imagine when he might have learned some Romani.

Burton relaxed a little at this response. I became aware that two boys had begun kicking a ball between them very near us. The ball escaped and rolled toward me, bumping my foot and settling there. As I bent down to pick it up, the boy who had been listening closely ran up to me to retrieve it.

'Watch yourself, Mendelsohn,' murmured Holmes with a smile.

What harm could this small child do? Just as the boy arrived, he tripped and nearly fell, but I righted him and handed him the ball. I was rewarded with a toothy grin.

I noticed Burton smiling at me in somewhat sinister amusement.

Holmes was less amused. 'Your pocket, my friend.'

I felt in both pockets. My new silver vesta was gone! I had paid a fortune for this new and stylish silver case only last week and it was the envy of my friends. Damnation.

'That was little Jez. He's our best,' said Burton. 'Eh, Jez!'

Jez Burton. The brother of Lash Burton, of the Irregulars. A prickle of worry travelled down my spine. Jez had tried to join the Irregulars – could he identify Holmes?

The boy looked up from his ball playing, the picture of innocence. He was perhaps ten years old. No light of recognition. I felt a surge of relief.

Burton gestured for him to return my vesta. The child raised his eyebrows and shrugged. 'Who, me?'

Burton cleared his throat. The boy laughed and came toward me. I kept him at arms' length as I retrieved it from him. When I put it back in my pocket, I then noticed my cufflink was missing. 'My cufflink!' I cried.

Holmes and Burton laughed but Holmes stopped abruptly when the boy handed a small card to Burton. A sudden chill overtook me. I often carried my friend's calling card with me, and, by God, I had neglected to remove it from my pocket for our little charade today. Jez had taken it with my vesta.

Burton read it, looked at us both, then tossed it on the ground, where he placed his muddy boot upon it, grinding it into the dirt. Without any visible signal from him, we found three large Gypsies crowding in behind us.

Burton looked from Holmes to me and back to Holmes again, calculating. With a grunt he pointed to me, and the two nearest me were on me in the blink of an eye, one twisting my right arm behind my back, the other holding a knife to my throat. I could feel the blade nicking my skin.

All activity ceased and our little group became a frozen tableau.

Burton looked at us again, this time settling quickly on my friend. 'Sherlock Holmes!' said he, indicating the card. 'I know your name. And you have been well described in the papers. Well done. You are almost convincing as a scholar. Too bad your friend was careless with your calling card.' He smiled at me, and the knife dug a little deeper into my skin. It was all I could do not to flinch. 'Now tell me why you are here. Or this man who is so dear to you – oh yes, I can see this – may meet with a terrible accident.'

Holmes stayed calm but had grown pale. Burton had calculated correctly. My friendship with Holmes was sometimes a liability.

'It will go poorly for you if you hurt him, Mr Burton,' Holmes said carefully. 'The police know that we are here.'

'I doubt it. You despise the police,' said Burton. 'That much of your story is real. I can tell.'

'Not all of them. Inspector Lestrade of Scotland Yard knows. If we do not return, he and his men will be here within twenty minutes.'

The boy who pickpocketed me was now by Burton's side, whispering to him. The man grimaced, then turned back to stare at us a moment longer.

Holmes turned to the boy. 'Jez Burton?' he asked. 'Brother of Lash Burton? I believe he also used the name Lash Crowley?'

The boy looked startled.

'You know my name because you attempted to join the Irregulars,' said Holmes, 'like your brother.'

Burton barked out a question in Romani to the boy, who nodded sheepishly.

Holmes turned back to Burton. 'The Irregulars are a group of street urchins whom I employ to do jobs for me from time to time. They gather gossip, find people, run errands. A lucrative and very useful profession. Jez knows this. If so, he can confirm my friendship with Mr Gregory Lestrade of the Metropolitan Police.'

Burton reached out and grabbed Jez by the arm and squeezed so hard the boy winced. He said something harsh in Romani.

The boy quailed, then nodded. He replied in a low voice, also in Romani. Silence followed.

'All right. All this is true. You are lucky that Jez did not recognize your face. But you lied about this meeting. What do you want here?'

'I will admit the lie. I came here for two reasons, Mr Burton. It is true that I seek information on Neptune Bandini, whom I mentioned. He may be implicated in a case I am investigating. But more importantly, I seek any information which might lead me to find whoever struck Lash Burton a blow to the head and threw him into the Serpentine.'

Burton nodded and the man with the knife dropped it and retreated. But he did not move far.

'And why would you care about this? The boy, I mean.'

'Lash Burton briefly worked for me. I look after my Irregulars.'

Jez whispered something into the Gypsy leader's ear again.

'Jez tells me Lash was dismissed from your group.'

'Yes. Nevertheless, if any boy is hurt while in my employ—'

'*Was* he in your employ?'

'The head boy, Wiggins, thinks he might have been trying to get back in my good graces by following a suspicious character.' Holmes turned to Jez. 'Was he? Did you see anything?'

The boy hesitated.

'Tell him if you know anything, boy,' said Esau Burton sharply.

'There is a sovereign in it for you,' said Holmes. 'But only if you tell me the truth.' The coin appeared in his palm. The boy fixed on it, willing it to be his.

'A man,' said Jez.

'Go on.'

'Lash. He did a little job for a man.'

'What job?' asked Holmes.

'Er . . . to find the best tattoo artist in the city.'

It was all I could do to stifle an audible reaction. Holmes and I exchanged a look.

'And who was that?' Holmes knew of course – it was the visiting Yamamoto. Lash Burton had been remarkably resourceful. Heffie's instincts about him, and indeed my own, had been right.

'Some bloke at a fair. Some Oriental. I don't know.'

'What happened, then?'

'Lash, he was to meet up and tell the man the tattoo bloke's name, and then get paid, see. In Hyde Park. I told 'im not to go.'

'Why?'

The boy shrugged.

'*Why?*' Holmes repeated.

'Something about that man.'

'Dangerous?'

Jez nodded. One didn't survive a life of petty crime without developing instincts. Certainly not someone of Jez's diminutive size.

'Can you tell me anything more?'

'What if I can?'

'Then I may find that man,' said Holmes.

'No.'

'No?'

'We tried. 'E is not to be found.'

'Tell me what you saw. Was it a tall man – young, old?'

Jez hesitated. Calculating.

'Tell him,' Esau Burton ordered.

Jez smirked and held out his hand. 'More.'

Burton nodded at us. 'Give it to him.'

Holmes dug into his pocket and added two coins to the sovereign. The boy reached for them, but Holmes pulled away.

'Information first.'

'Do it,' said Burton to the boy.

'Medium. Not tall. Not short. Hat, so don't know about hair. Pulled low so didn't see 'is face. Moustache. Moved like a cat.'

'Smoothly?' asked Holmes.

'Strong. Graceful, like. Like you swells learn to do.'

'A gentleman, then?'

'Maybe. Maybe not.'

'Please elaborate.'

'Not 'is clothes. But the way 'e moved, yeah.'

'Would you take him for a mark?' asked Holmes.

The boy hesitated. 'No.'

'Why not, if he moved like a swell?'

'Somefing else.'

'What?'

''E was sure of hisself.'

'Confident, would you say?' said Holmes.

The boy hesitated again, then nodded.

'What do you mean?' I interjected. I felt the boy was being evasive.

No answer.

'Did you witness him throwing Lash into the Serpentine?' Holmes asked.

'No. Lash, 'e met 'im behind the guard's house. I stayed out of sight, watching. They left.'

'But you did not follow?'

Jez shifted uncomfortably. 'No.'

'Why not?'

''Cause jus' then I saw a mark. I went for it. Lady with a reticule on a bench beside 'er.' He grinned. 'I got five pounds off 'er.'

'Then what?'

'Went back. They was gone.'

'And then?'

'I went off to do more business. Figured Lash knew 'ow to take care of hisself.' The boy looked down. 'We didn't see 'im no more after that.'

'Your description gives me very little to go on,' said Holmes.

'S'why we couldn't find him neither. An' we are very good at findin' our own.'

Our interview ended as abruptly as it began. Holmes paid the boy. I took out my handkerchief and put it to my neck. Only a drop of blood.

The Gypsy leader rose and we were escorted to the edge of the camp and the trail by which we arrived. Before departing, Holmes turned back to Esau Burton.

'About the man Neptune. The Gypsy fiddler. Why is he "dead to you"?'

'You are going to look after the boy, Lash?'

'I will find his killer, that I promise you.'

The man considered. 'All right, then. The fiddler – your Neptune Bandini. His real name is Neptune Burton. My nephew. But he left us. Changed his name. His disloyalty poisons our family.'

'Why?'

'As you said – friends with a Wandley.'

'Then Neptune was with you when the fire took place? He must have been a child.'

Esau Burton did not like the question. But he gave us the answer anyway.

'Neptune's mother – my sister – and his own baby sister were killed. He left us a few years after.'

'Was he knowledgeable about snakes?'

'Neptune?' Esau Burton laughed bitterly. 'Oh, yes. He was the best.'

CHAPTER THIRTY-FOUR

It Was Beneath Us

fter taking our leave, we made our way out of the encampment. Our cab had not waited for us, as we'd instructed. The clouds lowered and rain seemed imminent. We trudged wearily nearly a mile back down the road, past deserted farmhouses and a couple of factories.

Holmes said little but my thoughts were filled with what we had just learned. 'I am sorry about that calling card, Holmes. But that boy, Jez—' I began.

'Wiggins made a serious mistake in rejecting his brother Lash for the Irregulars,' said Holmes. 'The boy found Yamamoto for our murderer. Think of it!' He smiled sadly at the thought. 'I must find a way to help that family.'

'Do you think it was our murderer who threw the boy in the Serpentine?' I asked.

'Might have been. Or it might have been someone employed by the villain.'

Just then the heavens opened and drenched us, but we soon arrived at a welcoming public house. The host, seeing our wet clothes, sat us by the fire. Someone sent for a cab, but we were warned it would take some time. Plied with whisky and after a fine chop and potatoes, we took a breath at last. This respite went a long way to restoring my spirits and, I dare say, Holmes's as well.

Finally, a cab arrived and we turned homewards. It was dark and much colder by the time we arrived back at Baker Street. The streets were deserted and a new frost had turned the edges of the road white and the pavement into a dangerous sheet of ice. Holmes paused as we entered, looking down at the chequered tile doorstep.

'Someone has been by recently,' he remarked.

'At this hour? Were you expecting anyone?' I asked.

'Someone heavy, this ice has cracked,' he murmured.

'A delivery, perhaps?'

'Let us ask Mrs Hudson.'

Holmes sometimes forgot that the rest of the world did not keep to his relentless schedule. Of course, the good lady was not in the kitchen downstairs at this hour. I was pleased, however, to note a meat pie on the sideboard. A note was attached.

'Niece with a sick infant in Clapham. Back tomorrow by noon – Mrs H.'

'I didn't know she had a niece in Clapham,' I said.

He shrugged and I followed him up the stairs. It was a

very lucky thing I did. The door to the sitting room was shut tight, and we both paused.

'You left that door open, did you not, Holmes?'

Mrs Hudson had recently had radiators installed throughout the building, much to our displeasure, as Holmes and I preferred a fire. But I knew that Mrs Hudson ran the downstairs radiator full-on in this weather and the rising heat grew too hot for my friend's comfort.

At these times he often left the door to the hall open, with the window on the landing cracked to let in the cool air without making the room draughty. But Mrs Hudson would close this window and close his door as soon as he was gone, and sometimes even open the radiator in his sitting room, arguing that his gaunt frame needed warmth.

It was a little dance they had developed, and one that irritated my friend. I surmised that Mrs Hudson hoped to reduce our use of the fire, which was a great deal of work for her.

These mundane thoughts foolishly occupied me as we paused at the door to our sitting room. But something troubled my friend. I started to speak, but he put his finger to his lips, motioning me to be quiet.

He sniffed, then sniffed again, and slowly shook his head from side to side, still frowning.

Holmes's senses were nearly that of a wild animal's. He often smelled or heard things that ordinary humans – or at least this ordinary human – could not. Whatever he took in at that moment was beyond my ken.

'Have you your pistol, Watson?' he whispered.

I swallowed and shook my head. 'You told me not to—'

'Shh!' With silent gestures, he indicated something was behind the door. We would rush in, then separate right and left, a tactic we had employed more than once. 'On three, then,' he mouthed, then signalled with his fingers. *One. Two. Three.*

We burst through the door and immediately stepped apart, making a split target for anyone who might be within.

But there was no one there.

Strangely, the radiator was on full blast and the room was like a steam-bath. And now I noticed the faint, strange odour that had troubled Holmes. Dank, almost fishy. But not quite. I had smelled it before, but where?

Holmes stepped carefully further to the left, and I to the right. It happened, then, that I saw the body first.

Two legs protruded from behind the couch. Smallish legs. Corduroy trousers and rough brown shoes. 'Holmes!'

Instantly at my side, he stared down at the feet. 'It is Callum,' he said. We moved gingerly around the couch to where we could see the body.

It was indeed the snake handler from London Zoo, the old expert with the eyepatch who had replaced the drunken amateur. But he was quite dead. On his face was an expression of fright and horror that I shall never forget. His hand was up at his throat and his one eye bulged from its socket, seeming to stare at the ceiling as though a band of goblins had just descended towards him.

'Dear God!' I exclaimed. 'What has happened here?'

'Watson!'

I looked up from the body to see Holmes pointing to one corner of the room. There was a box about two feet

311

by three in size, with holes in it. A kind of trapdoor on the top of the box was wide open.

'It is here,' said Holmes.

Before I could respond or even grasp at his meaning, there was a sudden loud sound, a strange noise like the growl of a large carnivore, yet metallic. It was like no animal sound I had ever heard. It came again, perhaps closer. I glanced about to determine the source.

Holmes cried out, 'Watson! Beneath you!'

I turned and followed his gaze down. The carpet near my feet had strangely come alive!

An enormous snake, some twelve or fifteen feet long, emerged from under the divan at great speed, its head rising swiftly from the floor to the height of my knees . . . and then higher, higher, to waist level.

It slithered between us. The creature was equidistant from us both. Its head swivelled, looking from Holmes to me.

We froze.

The snake hovered, undulating. It was dark olive in colour, its scales smooth. As we stared at it, aghast, the snake's head seemed to grow in size as it flared its hood.

A king cobra. One of the deadliest snakes on earth. A forked tongue flicked in and out of its mouth. Smelling the air. Smelling us.

Its head moved left to right, taking us in one after the other. That sound came again, a terrifying noise. The growl of a huge wild animal.

The head swivelled my way, and its eyes fixed on me. The pupils were round. The mouth seemed to be smiling.

It was a rictus, a horror, the stuff of nightmares. It opened and the growl sounded again.

Perhaps I should have stayed still, but I could not help it. My body had a mind of its own. I backed up clumsily.

'Watson, stay still!'

But my movement had drawn its attention and the beast followed – and suddenly lunged at me. I leapt to the side, knocking over a table. It missed and arched in the air, upending a stack of books. The head swivelled once again to face me.

I was on the floor, backing away like a maniac – but it arched over me, growling.

In an instant, Holmes stood next to it with a vial of clear liquid in his hands. 'Guard your eyes, Watson!' he cried, and without further hesitation dashed a clear liquid onto my chest. The acrid smell made me choke and cough.

'Good God, Holmes!' Looking up through watering eyes, I saw the snake rear back from me in revulsion. Of course! Ammonia from Holmes's chemistry table. Dr Flackett had told us of this deterrent.

But I had no time to think further. Holmes scrambled away from the snake, but it turned in a fury and slithered after him, cornering him near the door.

Looking about frantically, he grabbed an umbrella from the stand near the door and held it aloft, like a fencer beginning a match.

The snake reared up and was now at nearly the full height of my friend, neck level, and not three feet away. Holmes waved the umbrella gently in the air.

The snake began following the movements of the

umbrella. For the moment, Holmes was . . . charming the snake! Or at least distracting it.

This could not end well. I looked wildly about for a weapon. I searched for anything within reach. On the wall. Anything.

And then I spotted the *kukri*, the Ghurka's knife I'd brought back from my service days that hung on the wall to the right of the hearth, just to one side of where Holmes faced the terrible reptile. But of what use would this be, exactly?

I inched toward it, but at that moment a horrific sound came from the snake, and it lunged at Holmes. He dodged it like lightning, but he was pinned in the corner and it fastened on him, just below the collarbone near his shoulder. He fell with a cry, the head of the snake clinging to his chest. I leapt toward the *kukri* and ripped it from the wall.

I was at his side in an instant. Holmes writhed on the floor, his hands clawing at the snake, which had dug in and would not be dislodged. Its long, powerful body thrashed about, becoming entangled with Holmes's legs.

It was injecting its lethal venom as I watched.

I did not hesitate but plunged the sharp point of curved knife at the junction of the snake's head and its body. It stabbed into the snake but then glanced off its powerful muscles and nearly punctured Holmes. Both continued to writhe as I leapt upon the struggling forms.

The knife was sharp, a deadly weapon when used against a human. I slashed at the base of the snake's head and, finally gaining purchase, began to saw forcefully. The snake flipped and arched, and Holmes, who had not uttered even a cry, grasped it a foot away from the head, trying to still the body so that I could complete the task. He was unable to speak, his breath coming in ragged gasps.

The snake perceived its danger and thrashed further, nearly jerking free from my grasp. But I held it close and continued to slash away. With a sudden last thrust, I severed the head from its body.

The length of the snake dropped to the floor but for one long, horrible moment, the head stayed clamped to Holmes's shoulder. He struggled to unhook it, but the slanted fangs made escape nearly impossible.

But I put my hands on the head and together we freed him from the heinous jaws.

It fell to the floor and lay there, the tongue darting in and out twice, and the rest of the body still moving for a good three or four seconds longer.

All this was in my peripheral vision now because my attention was on Holmes. He lay on the floor in shock, one hand on the wound where the snake had bitten him. He gasped and shuddered.

'Holmes!'

Silence.

I knew that cutting the wound and sucking at the blood to remove the venom would do little. And precious time would be lost.

'Holmes, can you speak? I am running for a doctor.'

He tried to inhale but his breath caught short. He coughed. I knew that the cobra's venom paralyzed the muscles of the diaphragm. How much had he received? It would not be long before he could not breathe.

'Stay, Watson.' The voice was hoarse. 'See me out.'

But I leaped up and made for the door.

'Watson!' he cried.

But I didn't stay. For the second time in this horrific week, I didn't listen to him.

I ran.

CHAPTER THIRTY-FIVE

Saving Grace

plunged down the stairs, knowing that I might have left my friend to die alone. I hoped against hope that my instinct for action was the right choice.

I dashed out into the icy rain, and luck was with me. A four-wheeler had just discharged its passengers in the next building and I was able to attract the driver's attention. He promptly rolled up to me.

'Help, please! I am a doctor, I need to get a man to hospital. Now!' The driver leaped from the cab without hesitation and followed me upstairs.

I directed us to Middlesex Hospital. Though not the closest, I had read that outside of Brompton Hospital it held the most extensive respiratory setup in London. It was our only chance.

We arrived in minutes, and Holmes was placed on a

trolley and rushed into the operating theatre. There he was stripped of his outer clothing and surrounded by three medical men and two nurses.

The doctor in charge, an arrogant young man with all the bravado of youth and a recent degree, blocked me from Holmes. 'Stand back. I am Dr Mitchell, in charge here. He is in good hands, sir. Now if you would kindly—'

'Cobra bite! He's going into respiratory arrest!' I elbowed my way to Holmes's side. Someone attempted to push me away, thinking I was an overwrought family member. 'I'm a doctor!' I shouted.

Holmes's breath was coming in ragged gasps.

'Dr Kreibl! Is he here?' I cried. 'He has what we need!' The famous tuberculosis specialist was the reason I'd chosen Middlesex.

A nurse caught my eye, nodded, and dashed off.

'Don't be an idiot, this man doesn't have tuberculosis,' Mitchell cried, then called over his shoulder to another doctor. 'Prentiss! Suction the wound!'

The wound had been sprayed with carbolic acid and a suction cup was placed on it. I knew this would do nothing.

'The venom paralyzes the diaphragm! We need a pulmonologist. A bellows. A . . . some kind of ventilator. Now!' I cried. A second young doctor caught my eye. He had heard me and clearly understood. With a nod, he too dashed from the room as the nurse had done.

But Mitchell waved me away and at his signal, two orderlies converged to keep me from my friend. Mitchell bent over Holmes, applying suction to the wound.

Holmes's face was white and had gone slack, his eyes

half closed, unseeing. The venom worked from the top of the body down, and eyelid ptosis was the first sign.

'You see?' said the surgeon. 'He is still breathing. But look at his face. The poison is systemic, so we must flush his system. We will suction the wound, bleed him, and pump the stomach!'

Wrong! But there were few more dangerous than a misinformed doctor. This man, in his ignorance, could cost Holmes his life.

'No!' I cried.

'Calm yourself. We will stabilize him. And we have called in a poison expert.'

'He'll be dead by then! A pulmonologist is what we need. The diaphragm is being paralyzed while you waste time. We need a bellows, something!'

Holmes was failing. His breathing was laboured, shallow, and it was only with the greatest of effort that he could breathe at all. His lips were turning blue. We were going to lose him.

I knew that the bellows had been used with only limited success in maintaining breathing, but what I did not know was if the device was handy here, or if something better had been devised, Middlesex Hospital, leading in tuberculosis treatment, might have something—

It had.

What followed was little short of a medical miracle.

The doctor and the nurse who had heeded my words returned on a run with a tall, older man with a shock of wild, white hair.

It was Kreibl! How the famous pulmonologist happened

to still be at the hospital at this ungodly hour was nothing short of a miracle. I later learned the dedicated scientist kept a cot in his laboratory and often slept there.

But at that moment he thundered into the room, shouting instructions. In an instant, two orderlies ignored Mitchell, seized the trolley and wheeled Holmes out of the room at a run, followed by two young doctors.

'You are making a mistake,' cried Mitchell, but to no avail. As a group we tore through the corridors, Kreibl shouting instructions as we ran.

In less than two minutes we were in his laboratory. And there was the machine I had heard of, and on which I had bet Holmes's life. It was a kind of large, square metal contraption, almost coffin-like, connected to a bellows and with a padded circlet to go around the neck. In seconds, Holmes was bundled directly inside it, the collar then clamped down and fastened tight, with only his head protruding.

'Fire it up!' said Kreibl, and in a moment the strange thing plunged into action. It worked by artificially inducing respiration by changing air pressure inside the box to mechanically breathe for the patient.

It was controversial and in the early stages of development. But it was deemed too expensive, too bulky, and required too many trained personnel. The very concept had been challenged and ultimately derided by some of medicine's finest.

But what if – just if – it might work?

Various cheaper models which covered only the chest, or conversely enclosed the head in a heavily oxygenated container while someone manually manipulated the lungs, had proven disastrous. But this one version – Kreibl's invention – had seen limited success.

But were we in time? *And would it work now?*

Once in motion, it required two men to monitor and adjust the airflow, and make sure the box had no leaks. A third had to closely watch the patient. I stood nervously staring at Holmes's white face, resting on the pillow, so still, like a marble likeness. His lips were now a darker blue. It was possible he was already dead.

'Check the airway is clear!' ordered Kreibl, and a doctor moved between me and Holmes to work at this while Kreibl put a hand on my shoulder and led me from the room.

Now in the hallway, I felt my own breath release. I must have swayed, for the man caught me by the arm.

'Sit down,' he said.

I did so on a bench nearby, and he joined me.

'Will he live?' I asked.

He shrugged. 'I would give him a fifty percent chance,' he said. 'You are a doctor, I am told.'

'Yes. John Watson. This man's friend. Have you ever had success with a snake bite? With this kind of paralysis?'

'Not in London, but a colleague in India brought a fellow back from a cobra bite using this very thing.'

'There is one of these contraptions in India?'

'Yes. The doctor there is my co-inventor. His mission is to treat snake bites. My interest is in tubercular patients and also those paralyzed patients being studied by my colleague Karl Medin at Karolinska.'

'I have read of his work.' Medin was studying another

form of paralysis that stopped breathing, which we later learned to call polio.

'The machine is assisting him to breathe and we have given him oxygen. He has a good chance if the restart of respiration takes hold.

'Is he conscious?'

'He will be in and out. Do not worry, he is in good hands. But I will tell you one thing – the survival of a cobra bite is reliant on luck.'

'Luck?'

'They do not envenom consistently. Your friend may have received any amount of venom – from none at all, called a dry bite, or enough to kill ten men. We will keep an eye on him.'

I stood and tried to look past him into the laboratory, but one of the doctors blocked my view of Holmes.

'Sit down, Dr Watson. There is nothing more for you to do.'

I wavered. Then I sat, and there I waited through the night.

CHAPTER THIRTY-SIX

No Rest for the Wicked

cience and luck prevailed.

Some twenty-four hours later, both Holmes and I were back at 221B, he in bed with strict instructions for a week of bedrest. As for myself, I nervously attended as both doctor and nurse – which consisted primarily of attempting to make the recalcitrant patient keep to his bed.

I had, of course, arranged for the removal of the snake remains, not wishing for Mrs Hudson to be more traumatized than she was already. The zoo had been informed and Dr Flackett arrived, having been briefed about the entire incident by the police. Aghast at the death of his assistant, he recounted that Callum had received a request to help someone with their pet cobra in Hampstead. He frequently did small jobs for private collectors, so no alarm bells had been set off.

However surprised and saddened was he by the man's death – 'He knew how to protect himself, this is highly irregular' – Flackett was even more strongly affected when he discovered that the dead reptile was in fact one of the jewels in the zoo's collection. He departed quickly with the remains.

The removal of the human corpse went without incident. Callum's identification was confirmed by Dr Flackett, and the police deemed the death an unlucky accident caused by the perpetrator himself. They were incurious as to the motive and were happy to write it off as a malevolent act of sheer madness. This did not, of course, explain the condition of the dead serpent, but so eager were they to conclude matters, they challenged nothing.

As for me, the less I thought about that creature the better. I wondered briefly how Callum had been induced to this heinous act. Money, I presumed, and whoever was behind this case somehow had a long reach. But how did this expert with snakes make such a basic and fatal mistake? Distracted by his 'client', perhaps? We would never know.

News of the event had reached the Palace, and waiting for Holmes upon our return from hospital was a polite note on royal stationery thanking him for his efforts, declaring the case closed and that no further investigation by Holmes was needed. Mycroft arrived to confirm this decision and explained in his taciturn manner that it was to the Palace's advantage that everyone forget everything about this case as soon as possible.

Needless to say, this did not go down well with the invalid.

Frankly, I knew it would not deter Holmes. He would not rest until the mystery had been solved and the perpetrator identified. Indeed, the very next day, only forty-eight hours after the horrific event in our sitting room, he took advantage of my dozing on the sofa to dress fully and call for a cab. Had I not been awakened by some random shouting in the street, I would have missed entirely what transpired next.

Holmes was in his coat and headed for the door when I awoke, and when nothing I said had an effect, I grabbed my coat and followed him out onto Baker Street. Moments later, we were in a cab and hurtling back towards Chelsea and the residence of Clarence Wandley and the man known as Neptune Bandini.

'Madness, Holmes!' I said.

He did not reply but gazed thoughtfully out the window. He looked, I thought, like a man sorely in need of rest. Much more rest.

'You very nearly died, you know,' I said.

'Yet here I am,' he said, and managed a smile. 'All thanks to you and that remarkable invention, dear Watson.'

On the day before, I had recounted the entire hospital experience to Holmes, and he even asked to read the medical journal where I had first heard of Dr Kreibl's work. But his churning brain would not tolerate bedrest, not when there was still a vital mystery to solve. That, I reasoned, was the hidden flaw in his character, one which threatened frequently to bring him down.

And so here we were, against doctor's orders – *this* doctor, to be precise – heading for Chelsea and the home of the man I considered most likely to have caused this near disaster. I was convinced that Neptune, not Callum, was the perpetrator of this near fatal attack and pleaded with my friend, but he would not listen to reason.

'Watson, there are a number of details which do not add up. Why would Neptune, who knows how to handle snakes, have sent Callum to do his dirty work? It may not have been Neptune's doing. Or, if Neptune is our culprit, and he is out for revenge on the family, might not Clarence Wandley, too, be in danger?'

'But they are clearly good friends,' I said, 'and would have been children when the Gypsy camp was set aflame.'

'Consider the copied artwork. One or both of them may be playing a very long game. I need to speak to them . . .'

We arrived not long afterwards and the cold wind had grown even colder. Standing before the house, facing the bright yellow door, Holmes rapped loudly with the heavy brass knocker. Silence.

I became aware of an older woman standing in the adjacent front garden, wearing three coats as she attempted to tie up some optimistic daffodils which were being whipped about mercilessly in the winds. She was staring at us with undisguised curiosity.

'You came here before,' she remarked.

'Have you seen your neighbours recently?' Holmes asked.

'Have not seen the weird little fellow – apologies, but how else might one describe him? The tall, handsome one was at home yesterday.'

'Distract her, please, while I unlock this,' whispered Holmes. I approached the lady, placing myself between her and Holmes so as to block her view, and handed her one of Holmes's calling cards.

'Do you know them well?' I asked.

'Hardly at all. Not particularly friendly, those two,' said she, glancing at the card. 'What is this? Sherlock Holmes, is that you?'

'No, that is my colleague over there. He is working with the police on a case.'

'The police!' she exclaimed, but I heard a small noise behind me and turned to see Holmes going through the front door. He motioned me to follow.

'They have given us the key,' I told her. 'Good day, madam. Would you kindly send word to Mr Holmes at that address if you see anything unusual here?'

'Hmph. You would be hearing from me daily. Everything is unusual there,' said she, turning back to her daffodils.

Inside, the house was extremely cold, very unlike our last visit. There were no sounds, and the grey skies outside and the half-closed curtains contrived to give the place a gloomy and foreboding look. No one seemed to be about.

The radiators were completely cold to the touch.

Carefully, Holmes began his investigation. Working together, we moved from room to room, ascertaining that no one was at home. We passed quickly through the dining room, but I lingered, looking out at the garden. Something was not right.

Holmes had moved into the kitchen, and before I could discern what was different in the garden, I heard a shout. I rushed into the kitchen as he examined something on the floor near the sink.

It was a dead snake. I was not sure what kind. At least, I thought it was dead. I poked at it with my toe.

'Watson!'

The creature moved, but barely. I jumped. 'It's alive!'

'Too cold,' said he. 'Someone has turned off all the heat. Watch where you step.'

'Careful, Holmes, remember you have been recently quite ill. Come. There is something in the garden, I think.'

He joined me back in the dining room and spotted it immediately. The steam-heating pipes were awry, disconnected. And at the far end of the garden, at the large box enclosure where the odd duo had kept their venomous snakes – *the door was slightly ajar.* All the snakes must be loose! Six, they had said . . .

We both instinctively looked at our feet. Nothing.

'They have either escaped, Watson, or more likely were let out. But given the temperature, we are probably safe!'

My instinct was to leave at once, but to my horror Holmes opened the door, plunged into the garden, and moved rapidly towards the snake house.

'No!' I shouted, but he had already reached the structure and carefully pushed the door all the way open. He stuck his head inside. *What on earth?*

'Holmes?' I was half-way across the garden to him.

He backed out of the box and pulled me back into the house, closing the door behind us.

'All gone. I don't think our pair would have left these doors ajar, nor purposely harmed their pets. Yes, pets, Watson. Clarence and Neptune have fled – with most of their snakes, I warrant. Time to leave, my friend, there is nothing further for us here.'

'What if more than one of the snakes are still here? That one in the kitchen . . .'

'Good point. We should let Dr Flackett know. Perhaps he or someone can come and save that one and look for any others.'

He started for the door, but in his inimitable style he suddenly froze like a hunting dog, pointing at the fireplace. 'What's this?'

'Careful, Holmes!' I cried. A latently warm fireplace might harbour an active serpent, but he had spotted something and was on his knees and rummaging through the ashes unconcerned. He fished out a partially burned letter, glanced at it, and with a cry of triumph rose and dashed out of the door, with me right behind him.

The old lady next door stared at us in concern.

'Don't go in there,' I warned. 'There is a snake loose. Send for Dr Rupert Flackett, master herpetologist at the London Zoo. He will know what to do.'

'A snake? I thought something was strange there! My goodness! Is it in a cage or something?'

'No, it is loose in the house. And it is poisonous,' I said. At her baffled look, I added, 'Seriously, madam.'

A passing cab paused for us, and we leaped in.

'Good thinking, Watson. She might well have thought to investigate on her own.'

'Break into the house? Do you think, really – that nice little old lady?'

'Yes, Watson. Oh, yes, indeed!'

CHAPTER THIRTY-SEVEN

Snakes Run Loose

he cab rattled northward, and it began to rain. Holmes unfolded the letter he had retrieved from the fireplace. It had only been singed around the edges. He let out a sharp exclamation of surprise and handed it to me.

The letter was on expensive stationery with an elegantly embossed name of the writer at the top: '*Peter Fogg Oliver*'. It was addressed to Clarence Wandley, and read as follows:

My dear Master Clarence,

If I may be so informal – I am writing to advise you of an unfortunate development instigated by your father. As you are aware, his original will named all three of you children as equal beneficiaries in the estate upon his death. Naturally, with Jane's sad passing, that was revised to name you and Kate only. However, only yesterday he struck you entirely from the will for reasons I cannot fathom. I was present at the time with his solicitor as he did so.

I cannot offer any explanation, but I can say that it seemed sudden and somewhat offhand.

It is my suggestion that you return home urgently and take this up with your father. Come alone, as I think you may have a better response without your friend along. I cannot explain why, but I feel optimistic that you can convince him to change his mind.

Yours in friendship,

P. F. Oliver

'What do you notice, Watson? Whom does this implicate, do you think?'

'I don't know where to begin, Holmes. Neptune has reason to hate the Wandleys, we have learned. Perhaps his friendship with Clarence was false. Might Neptune have read this letter, and now that Clarence has been struck from the will, he is no longer of any use? And so he killed Clarence and now . . . I don't know . . . he may be en route to the family home to seek revenge on the rest of the family? He has reason, to be sure.'

'A theory with some little merit,' said Holmes. 'But do continue. Who else might be the villain?'

I struggled to come up with another idea . . . But of course! 'Perhaps the mastermind behind all this is Kate. Why has she suddenly been named the sole heir? And we know the sisters had a distinct animosity. Could this have been the plan all along?'

'Indeed, Watson.'

'She does have much to gain. And, I will admit, I have never liked Kate. But . . . this seems perhaps less likely,' I said.

'Does it, Watson? Perhaps. In the matter of Kate, where is she now, I wonder? We have been operating under the assumption that she is in jeopardy. But my reasoning tells me that another is presently in more imminent danger. We must make haste before our multiple murder case expands further.'

It was true. So many deaths were entangled into this case – Jane Wandley, the tattooist, the dry goods seller and his wife, Callum and Lash had all been killed. Perhaps the Gypsy mother and her child, too . . . even Lady Wandley. But Holmes was being cryptic.

'Who is in danger, if not Kate?' I asked.

'Sir James!'

'Why?'

'A sudden alteration in a wealthy man's will sets my teeth on edge. Could the beneficiary have forced this change and might now hurry events along? Or could the loser – in this case Clarence, or his friend Neptune – have confronted Sir James, then failing to sway him, done the deed? Watson, we cannot linger. Dash upstairs and retrieve your Webley. We will head out at once to the Wandley Estate.'

Within minutes, our four-wheeler took off at a gallop, heading north to exit London. Although the ride was nowhere near as smooth as those we had enjoyed recently in the royal carriages, we were lucky in that we had found ourselves in a sturdy carriage of recent vintage pulled by two fresh horses.

'Holmes, there's something you should see. Mrs Hudson just handed me this note from Heffie.' I held out a folded paper.

'Read it to me,' he said irritably. I did.

'Mr Holmes, Kate ain't nowhere in London but I think she might well have gone home to roost. I'm heading up to the Wandley Estate. I might learn more of her there. No worries. Be assured, I will be careful. Remember you told me to broaden my horizons, so I am. Heffie.'

'Ah, no!' Holmes looked aghast at the news. 'That rash young lady!'

'She's fearless, Holmes.'

'And that is the problem.'

'What are you expecting there?'

'I'm expecting to confront the instigator of Jane Wandley's demise. And, if we get there in time, to prevent the murder of Sir James as well.'

'The killer is all one and the same, do you think? Kate? Neptune? Or . . . ?'

A loud crack of thunder sounded as though it was nearly atop our carriage. The flash of lightning lit up Holmes's pale profile against the dark carriage wall, and his grim expression struck me with fear. 'We have no time to waste!' he said.

If Sherlock Holmes knew who the killer was, he would not say.

CHAPTER THIRTY-EIGHT

Name Your Venom

 e arrived at the Wandley Estate well after midnight. While most would be asleep, it was nevertheless strange that not a single light showed even faintly in any window in the building. The storm raged and flashes of lightning were intermittently reflected off the tall, black windows of the ground floor, turning them – for moments – into pillars of fire. We ran to the front door and rang, but there was no answer.

The rain pelted down around us. Thunder boomed. We tried several windows and finally found an unlocked door on the side of the building.

Where were the servants? Why was the place deserted?

The interior was shrouded in darkness. No lights anywhere. The modern electrical lighting we had noted on our first visit was not in evidence. I found a switch and pressed it. Nothing.

We made our way into the main reception room where we had first met with Peter Oliver. There, in the centre of the room, just visible in the darkness lay a still figure. We ran to it.

It was Sir James, prone on the carpet, with a pool of blood forming a black stain at the side of his head. I checked for a pulse. Nothing.

'Too late!' cried Holmes, aghast. I bent over the body to get a better look. In the dim moonlight, it looked like a savage blow had been struck to the forehead and his face was covered in blood. I glanced around me. The room was dark, but I could just make out that the furniture had all been covered in sheets. It was like being surrounded by pale, hulking ghosts.

A flash of light appeared in a doorway followed by a voice. 'You're here!'

Peter Oliver bounded into the room, carrying a lantern. 'Thank God!'

'What has happened here?' asked Holmes.

I noted that Oliver's head was wrapped in a bloodied scarf.

'You are hurt!' I said, approaching him.

He waved me off. 'Neptune! Clarence's friend from London,' cried the man. 'He's in the grounds. He killed Sir James and struck me, and . . .' He reeled, dizzy, and I reached out to steady him.

'Let me have a look at your head,' I said, but he pulled away.

'No time now!' he said. 'We have to find him and stop him. He murdered Sir James, and now he is after Kate!'

'She is here then?'

'Yes. She is safe. I have hidden her.'

'Good man. But where are all the servants? Why is the electricity off?' asked Holmes.

'Sir James sent them all up north to ready the summer house. He does this every year. He is last to leave. He and I were in the process of closing up the house.'

'Where is Neptune now?'

'He ran out . . . into the storm! He's on some kind of rampage.'

Another flash of lightning and thunder boomed, now closer.

'Because of the change in the will?' I asked.

Oliver nodded.

'I see,' said Holmes with a kind of preternatural calm. 'Kate is to inherit all. We read the letter. What prompted her father to change the will?'

Oliver whirled to face him. 'I am not sure. I think he believed Clarence was involved in the horrible fate of his favourite child.'

'Where is Kate?'

'Don't worry! He will never find her. She . . . she is safe.'

'Where?'

'In my office.'

'How is that safe?'

'Neptune does not know of it.'

'I shall find him.' Holmes glanced at me, then turned back to Peter Oliver. 'Are you armed?' asked Holmes.

'No . . . no!' said Oliver. 'I cannot find my gun. Neptune would be dead if I—'

'Understood,' said Holmes. 'Watson. Your Webley!' I withdrew it at once, thinking to follow him on the search or perhaps to loan it to Peter Oliver.

But to my surprise, Holmes turned to me and said, 'Come to me at the window, Watson.' I did so. He lowered his voice and whispered, 'Now listen to me carefully. Keep Mr Oliver here and don't let him step outside. Don't let him out of this room. I'm going to check on Kate.'

'Holmes! What?' Nevertheless, I trained my gun on Peter Oliver.

'What on earth?' cried the young man. 'You need me to help you – there is a madman out there!'

'I think not,' said Holmes. 'Watson, please do not fail me.'

I kept my gun on Oliver. I could not fathom why. With Neptune bent on revenge, we might very well need the man's help.

'Holmes—?'

'Hands in the air, Mr Oliver! And keep well back. Don't let him come near you, Watson. Not a step closer. This man will kill you if he gets the chance.'

Peter Oliver? Surely Holmes was wrong about this.

My friend dashed out into the storm.

I stood facing Oliver. He stood there, hands in the air. Holding the gun in front of me, I stared at the fellow. Could it be? It did not seem likely. Perhaps Holmes's thinking had been impaired from his recent ordeal.

'Dr Watson, please! I know you believe me. Mr Holmes has made a terrible mistake,' said the young man. A tear coursed down his face. 'Why would he think . . . how could I, of all people . . . ?'

I could think of nothing to say. If Sir James's will was as we had been told, this man was set for life and had nothing to gain by any of this. He had only ever been helpful. And so eminently sane.

What on earth could be his motive?

'We need to find Neptune. I tell you, that man will kill us all!' Oliver implored. 'He and Clarence must have been furious that the entire estate had been left to Kate. And, of course . . . Neptune lost his mother here long ago. Mr Holmes is in danger – Neptune is a formidable man!' He inched toward me.

I struggled with my thoughts. 'Stay back!'

There was a noise behind him, and suddenly Heffie O'Malley entered the room. She must have found her way in through the same door we had. She was drenched like a river rat, eyes shining and both hands balled into fists.

'Dr Watson, I found 'er. I found Kate Wandley. She's here! Where's Mr 'olmes?'

It was at this point she noticed the gun in my hand and followed my aim to Peter Oliver, who was standing quite near her.

'Heffie!' I cried. 'Move away from—'

But before I could warn her of the danger, Oliver turned like a cat . . . *like a very graceful cat* . . . and in a single move, he enveloped the diminutive girl in his arms and hooked one around her neck, pulling her off balance and neatly into a chokehold directly in front of him.

Heffie is a skilled street fighter and not easily bested, but somehow this man, in a very fast move, had gained the upper hand.

She let out a guttural sound, and then, as his arm tightened around her neck, strangled gasps. The girl could not breathe! He placed his other hand flat against her brow and pressed, hard, bending her head at an awkward angle, sideways.

'Drop the gun or I'll break her neck!' he shouted. As he said this, he yanked her backward, off her feet, and her head further tilted at a dangerous angle. Heffie's eyes bulged from their sockets as his arm tightened further.

I was wrong about Peter Oliver. I was stunned.

'Drop it and step away,' he commanded.

I did so.

The three of us stood there in a terrible tableau, near the dead body of Sir James. Another flash of lightning lit us up, and I now saw a very different young man. Oliver had turned into a gargoyle, a rictus of fury twisting his boyish features into a picture of evil.

My thoughts were a jumble. Holmes had been right. Why had I doubted him for a moment? *Peter Oliver!* But why? *Why?*

'Kick the gun over here,' he said. 'Do it now.'

I did, but in my fear I aimed awkwardly, and it slid along the carpet and landed four or five feet to his left. His eyes flashed down to it, then back up at me.

'Fool!' With a sudden move, he released Heffie from the chokehold, grabbed her by the hair and flung her down before him, jerking her head and arching her backward over his knee. She whimpered in pain, her hands grasping her hair, trying to unhook his grip.

He dragged her toward the gun until it was within his

reach. Then he struck Heffie a sharp blow in the face and cast her aside, where she fell limply onto the carpet, unconscious. Or perhaps dead.

'Heffie!' I cried, as the man swept up the gun and turned it on me.

'Move and I'll shoot you. Or, rather, I'll shoot you quicker. Your friend was right – I will kill you if I get the chance,' said Oliver with a grin. 'And I guess I do have the chance now, don't I?'

If I was to die in this place, at least I wanted to understand what was utterly incomprehensible to me.

'Why?' I stammered.

'Love,' said a voice behind me. It was Sherlock Holmes.

CHAPTER THIRTY-NINE

The Tells

ove, hubris, greed. All wrapped together. But mainly love.'

Holmes moved to stand off to one side of me about six feet away. Why, oh, why, did my friend so rarely carry a gun? 'Peter Oliver, you had us all fooled – nearly,' he said.

'Hands up!' commanded Oliver. 'Move over and stand closer to your friend.'

But Holmes stood fast, a small smile playing across his features. 'Dear me, Watson, that is your gun, I believe. But Mr Oliver, before you shoot us, perhaps you would like to hear what gave you away.'

But Peter Oliver did not take the bait. He waved the gun towards Heffie, lying still on the floor next to him. 'I see your game,' said he. 'Stand next to Dr Watson right now, or I'll shoot this little gutter rat.'

'We don't care about her,' said Holmes casually.

Oliver carefully aimed the gun at her head. 'I think you do.'

Holmes let out a breath. He nodded and moved to stand next to me.

'All right, we do.'

'That's better. And I warrant you did *not* know it was me. I gave nothing away. This is not a game of cards.'

'True enough. It is not a game. It is more like a complex chemical equation, worthy of a scientist such as yourself. It did take me some time, but eventually you revealed yourself to me in many little ways.'

'I doubt it.'

Holmes said nothing but smiled.

Oliver paused. 'What little ways?'

'Your taste in salacious recordings hinted at a less than savoury predilection, but it was not as obvious as Pierre Brouillard, Kate's fictitious lover, who exists nowhere in Paris. *Brouillard*, of course, is "fog" in French. Your middle name, Fogg.'

'Coincidence.'

'Hardly. Quite telling was your recounting of your observation of poor Jane Wandley's tattoo. "On her *head*," you said to me. When you visited Windsor Castle, only the facial tattoos had been discovered. So, how did you know to say . . . "head"?'

Peter Oliver shrugged. 'Slip of the tongue.'

'And then there was Jane Wandley's lovely gold mirror.'

'It was a gift Jane left me. Your explanation grows more preposterous.'

'You stole it; it was no gift. The *why* of this mirror and its connection to the ouroboros – although I did not divine it at first – was the key.'

Oliver shrugged. 'Even if you were to live past tonight, no one would believe this. You are a fantasist.'

'No, it is you who are the fantasist. What a complicated, bizarre crime! You kidnapped and drugged the woman you loved, arranged for the tattoo in a way that would implicate her brother, then killed all who took part. Then, with even more hubris, you risked discovery by bringing her back to Windsor Castle.'

'And why would I do that?'

'You planned to be on hand when she awoke from her ordeal and discovered her ghastly desecration. The horror, the humiliation, especially for a woman obsessed with beauty! But *you* would be the hero to save her, to spirit her away from ultimate shame, and take her back home.'

Peter Oliver said nothing.

Out of the corner of my eye, I thought I detected movement from Heffie, prone on the floor. Her hand perhaps? I glanced down quickly, not wishing to draw attention. Nothing.

'But why the ouroboros?' Holmes continued. 'Horrific. Creative. And relevant, as it would appear. As a chemist, you are of course familiar with Kekule's purported dream of an ouroboros that gave him insight into the structure of the benzene molecule? Ah, I see that you are. But the ouroboros has many meanings. One of the meanings of the snake swallowing its own tail is a *return to home.*'

Holmes's voice grew soft. 'You loved Jane, and you

wanted her for yourself. You found a way to bring her home. Confronted daily by her image reflected in that mirror, she would never leave.'

Oliver shrugged.

'A remarkably obtuse but brilliant plan. Yes, utterly brilliant,' said Holmes.

Peter Oliver struggled to keep the smile from his face, but his pleasure was evident. Even a madman wishes to be admired.

Holmes continued, 'But it all went wrong. Poor Jane awoke in the Palace while you were still placing the clues. She deduced your secret. Fought you. And so she had to die.'

'Jane killed herself. The police know this. Your theory would never hold water.'

'The knife wounds on her wrists tell a different story. Both cut in the same direction. Equally deep cuts. A murder, not suicide.'

'What a penchant for morbid details you have, Mr Holmes. You are correct. But Jane gave me no choice. It was for the best.'

The best? Dear God, the hubris of this fiend, I thought.

'What a terrible disappointment her discovery of you must have been! After all that careful planning, involving so many. And costly, no doubt. And then to be thwarted by the woman you loved. And, yes, I do think you loved her, in your unique and twisted way. I do have one question: I presume the snake at 221B was your doing? How did you entice Mr Callum to deliver it there . . . and how did that expert snake handler happen to die?'

Oliver laughed. 'Well, of course I wanted you and Dr Watson dead, and for the crime to look like a Gypsy gesture. Anyone or anything is for sale at the right price – even you, Mr Holmes, I warrant. I hired the grubby little man to accompany me and deliver a caged "gift", as I told him, to Baker Street. Once there, I set it free from its box, and as the old fool scrambled to retrieve it, I distracted him. The snake did the rest.'

'At considerable risk to yourself.'

'Needs must. And, shall we say, I left quickly.' Oliver smiled.

'Clever indeed,' said Holmes. 'And once Jane Wandley was dead, the estate was within reach . . . By the way, where is Kate Wandley now?'

'That harridan? It doesn't matter.'

'She is a challenge, to be sure. Of course it was you, disguised as a policeman, who "rescued" Kate at the cannery, saving her from a bomb – which you yourself placed – and brought her here?'

Holmes's words surprised me but made sense. Oliver's twisted smile was confirmation. Had the fiend transferred his affections to the younger sister?

'She is simply another element in your scheme,' continued my friend. 'Next, you forced Sir James to rewrite his will, then killed him. Both Kate and Clarence would be suspects: Kate, might have coerced her father, or Clarence might be out for revenge.'

Peter Oliver smiled. 'It's unfortunate that you will never have the opportunity to make your case. No one would have believed you, though – it is all entirely improbable.

How would I have located the tattoo artist, for example? A rare talent.'

'Lash Burton. An enterprising young boy known to find anything in London. And then you killed him, too.'

Oliver tried to cover his surprise. 'Was that the little pickpocket's name?'

'You were seen with him. And identified by his brother.'

The villain shrugged. 'A Gypsy boy. No policeman would believe him.'

He was right. I had seen evidence of this myself.

There was a sudden noise and we turned to see a tall figure holding a lantern, standing in the doorway. It was Neptune Burton – drenched, dripping, and lit with fury. He had no doubt just heard the Lash Burton story.

'Peter Oliver!' the man bellowed. 'Fiend! Lash Burton was my cousin. And . . . and you helped Lady Wandley set fire to our camp years ago.'

'Ah, yes,' said Holmes pleasantly. 'Esau Burton told us – the young man who "moved like a cat". Of course, it would not be easy for a woman in long skirts to enter a Gypsy camp unseen and set several wagons ablaze.'

Peter Oliver laughed. A strange, dry cough of a laugh. 'Well, yes. Helpful factotum, you know. But you will all die with the thought. Stand over there, next to these two,' he instructed, waving the weapon at Neptune.

Neptune did not move. 'I doubt it was easy to kill Lash,' he said. 'A smart lad.'

Oliver shrugged. 'Couldn't swim though, could he? Move! Do it now, or I'll shoot you in the stomach. A very slow and painful death. Cooperate and I may be merciful.'

Neptune moved slowly, silently, like a lumbering bear, capable of a sudden charge, I thought. But he now stood next to us. I glanced down at Heffie. No movement. I must have been mistaken. Was the girl dead? I longed to kneel and attend to her.

'Don't even think of it,' said Oliver, noticing my gaze.

'Before we all die, Mr Oliver, might we clear up a detail or two?' Holmes turned to Neptune. 'Why did you come here tonight, Mr Burton?' he asked.

The tall Gypsy hesitated. 'Clarence received a letter from Peter Oliver urging him to come and talk to his father, to get the old man to change his mind. I sensed it was a trap and came in his stead.'

'Where is Clarence now?' asked Oliver.

'With friends. You will never find him,' said Neptune.

'Ah, Mr Oliver,' said Holmes. 'Another clever ploy in a long list. My hat is off to you. But before you kill us, please satisfy me on one more point. What is your plan for Kate Wandley? Have you kidnapped her for the inheritance? Or are you "in love" again?'

Oliver hesitated. 'Well, since you are going to die, what does it matter? I have her hidden away. Similar plan, but with some variation. She is a poor substitute for her sister. I am still working out the details.'

'I know what they are,' said Heffie suddenly from the floor.

Oliver gave a start and turned to look at the girl. Holmes, Neptune and I instinctively took that moment to widen the gaps between us.

'Kate's tied up in some underground space out back

beneath a big buildin',' said Heffie. With difficulty, she sat up, rubbing the back of her head. 'And in a bit of a pickle.'

'Heffie, are you all right?' I cried.

'Stand closer together,' shouted Oliver, noticing our movement.

'What pickle, dear girl?' said Holmes, as we each took an arm and helped Heffie to her feet. She took in the group of us, immediately understanding the situation. She and Holmes exchanged a quick look.

'Stop moving! *Now!*' Peter Oliver's voice raised in pitch. He swung his gun back and forth between the four of us. He cocked it. We froze.

'It's fillin' up wi' water,' said Heffie. 'She'll drown if you don' get her outta there in pretty short order, I would say.' And indeed, the sound of a torrential downpour filtered into my consciousness.

'No one is going anywhere,' said Oliver, panic in his eyes. 'Move back, all of you. Against that wall. The girl will die first!'

'Ohhh!' moaned Heffie, flinging herself sideways as if fainting – and I lunged to catch her.

Oliver shouted, 'Stand still!'

Holmes and Neptune both seized that moment of inattention to leap on Peter Oliver. The three men crashed to the floor, and the lantern went out. For several awful seconds the men struggled in the darkness. Then a simultaneous flash of lightning and crash of thunder nearly obliterated the sound of a single gunshot.

The dark figures on the floor were suddenly still. Silence. I could not see what had happened in the gloom.

'Holmes?'

More silence. Dear God.

Then the familiar voice cut through. 'I'm all right, Watson.'

Holmes extricated himself from the tangle of bodies and slowly stood up. 'I managed to turn his gun on him. Shot in the heart, I think.'

'If he had one,' I said.

The dim moonlight coming in through the window glinted off Peter Oliver's dead eyes, staring sightless at the ceiling. But the Gypsy, too, lay unmoving.

'Neptune?' said Holmes.

A low keening sob erupted from the man as slowly he rose to his feet. 'I wanted to be the one,' said he. He glared at Holmes. 'The one to kill him.'

'Be satisfied the job is done,' said Holmes.

I helped Heffie once again from the floor.

'Heffie, where is Kate Wandley?' Holmes asked urgently.

'She's in trouble. We may be too late!' Heffie cried. She stood up, wobbly but indomitable. 'She's tied up, down in a little room under that building out the back. And it's fillin' up wi' water. Fast!'

'I knew he had a hidden space!' Holmes cried. 'The remains of the wine cellar under Peter Oliver's office. They had trouble with flooding, remember?'

All three of us dashed out into the storm.

CHAPTER FORTY

The Rising Damp

hrough the downpour we searched frantically all around the perimeter of Peter Oliver's office building, finally discovering an entrance to the former wine cellar, well concealed by vines. Down steep stairs we found Kate Wandley, bound and gagged, seated on the floor in four inches of standing water. As Holmes had surmised, it was clearly a part of the original wine cellar Oliver had shown us filled in with rocks and dirt, evidently concealing this hideaway. He had had plans for this secret room, even though it was obviously vulnerable to flooding.

As Heffie had said, it was filling with water. The water had risen up around the unfortunate Kate's ankles and was lapping at her hips. The woman, fully conscious, appeared to be bravely holding back a state of panic.

I removed her gag.

Her first words were, 'You certainly took your time. Were you planning to let me drown?'

Neptune and I knelt in the water on either side of Kate Wandley. Her bindings were complicated, running through a rack that used to hold wine bottles and was secured to the wall. We began to work to free her.

'Hurry up!' she cried. 'Where is that disgusting skilama-link, Peter Oliver? Mad as a hatter. I never liked him.'

Not *thank heavens*. Not *thank you*. But then, this was Kate Wandley, and she was true to form.

'Peter Oliver will not bother anyone again, Miss Wandley,' said Holmes. 'He is dead.'

'Well, something good came of this!' She glared at Neptune and me as we struggled to free her from the ropes binding her hands behind her. Her sharp eyes focused on the Gypsy, and a wave of recognition swept over her face. 'You again! This was Clarence's Gypsy friend when we were children,' she said to me. 'He started Clarence's snake obsession!'

I glanced up to see Holmes had moved to a nearby table on which was a lantern, burning brightly, and a collection of pots of ink, some alcohol, bandages and needles. With a quizzical expression, Holmes held up a bottle.

'Kate, it seems that Peter Oliver thought that tattooing you would keep you here,' he mused. 'That was his plan for Jane, after all.'

'Twisted maniac! My God! And that was his idea for me?' she said. 'When he brought me down here, he was somewhat incoherent. I thought he was just – I don't know – trying to claim ownership. A lunatic!'

Holmes looked down to where Neptune and I continued to work at the ropes. 'Certainly,' he said. 'Oliver pulled you away from the mob at the cannery, did he not?'

'How do you know that?'

'I have my methods.'

'Rescued, so I thought at the time,' said Kate. 'A bomb was found there, he told me.'

'He set the bomb,' said Holmes. 'Was Peter Oliver dressed as a policeman then? Moustache and all?'

'Why, yes, he was.'

'Did it not occur to you to question his disguise, his fortuitous rescue?'

'I did not have the chance. He chloroformed me right after, and I awoke here.'

I followed Holmes's look to the gold mirror which had been moved down to this room and positioned facing the young woman.

'I think by this point in his plan he was no longer in full possession of his wits,' said he.

'If that is your best observation, Mr Holmes, it's a wonder that you found me here at all,' she said. 'Come here, get me free!'

But everything changed in an instant. With a thud, a section of wall that had been leaking into this room suddenly gave way, and a flood of water began to gush through this new aperture. Kate screamed. The water rose to my knees and was rising fast. Peter Oliver, the mad engineer, had been right about the basement flood risk!

'My God, hurry!' cried the young woman.

But the bindings were still entangled in the wine rack,

and we struggled to free her. 'Hold this while I pull here,' Neptune instructed. I did, and the ropes suddenly whistled through my hands, painfully shredding skin across my partially healed burns as it did. 'Ouch!'

We were just in time. The water was above my knees and nearly to Kate's shoulders. We pulled the young woman free and got her to her feet. Had we not freed her the water would have been over her head in less than a minute. We struggled through the rising water towards the exit.

As we moved up the stone steps and out of this fearsome chamber, we encountered Heffie waiting at the top for us. She had found an enormous umbrella and had it opened. Standing under it herself, but already fully drenched, she was quite a sight.

'As if *that* will help,' Kate said to Heffie. She paused at the top of the steps, Neptune and I on either side, and turned back to glare at Holmes. Even after her dramatic rescue, this young woman still found it within her to be disagreeable.

'Not your finest hour, Mr Holmes. A very near miss. And, if I'm not mistaken, my father is dead. For all the good you did helping our family, you are little late to the party.' She turned to Heffie. 'Get that umbrella out of my face, girl!'

'Girl! You are an ungrateful reprobate,' said Heffie, her East End accent and scholarly vocabulary clashing beautifully. I could not help but laugh. 'Mr 'olmes and Dr Watson saved your sorry self.'

'Well, eventually, they did. Aren't you the little wastrel who joined Miss Ferndale's organization?'

'Yes, I'm that little wastrel 'oo also found you 'ere. And Mr Holmes and Dr Watson and this tall fellow got you out. Now 'oo's late to the party, Kate Wandley? You and . . . well . . . *you!*'

CHAPTER FORTY-ONE

Ye Spotted Snake

y word, doctor! What have you been into now?' exclaimed Dr Patrick Sheehan, examining the rope burns on the palm of my hand which had complicated my previous injury. It was late afternoon two days after the harrowing events at the Wandley Estate, and Holmes and I were recovering at 221B. Young Dr Sheehan, who had treated me in gaol, had been kind enough to respond to Holmes's summons and was in the process of redressing my hand.

'Watson, you really must take more care,' Holmes said. 'This last adventure was a near miss!' *Pot, kettle*, I thought. My friend looked utterly exhausted as he lounged on the divan, still in his dressing gown even at this hour. Having slept through yesterday entirely, I felt quite refreshed. Perhaps he would need more time to recover.

Heffie, equally fresh, and looking uncharacteristically

chic in a new frock of electric blue, lingered near our dining table, helping herself to tea and cakes which had been laid out on a silver tray. Dr Sheehan had attended her first, checking over the cut on her forehead inflicted by Peter Oliver. She was a hardy soul, clearly the daughter of a prize fighter, and was little the worse for wear.

Dr Sheehan busied himself rebandaging my hand.

Heffie glanced about her as she stuffed a large bite of cake into her mouth. 'Looks nice in 'ere,' she remarked. 'Wot happened?'

Holmes did not reply. After the deceased snake handler and the beheaded serpent had been removed earlier, Mrs Hudson had apparently taken it upon herself to further eradicate the sense of disorder. Holmes's usual clutter had been corralled into neat stacks, much to his annoyance. A vase of flowers uncharacteristically brightened the mantelpiece.

A member of the Palace staff had come and gone, conveying Her Majesty's gratitude for Holmes's discretion in solving the hideous crime with minimum impact on the staff. Along with this came thanks for the beautiful foal. Both the newborn and his dam had been welcomed into the royal stables with great enthusiasm and were doing well. But that was not the only good news. Holmes, as it turned out, had been busy yesterday while I slept.

'Mr 'olmes,' said Heffie, 'I wanted to thank you for what you done yesterday about Lash Burton.'

What was that, I wondered, and when had he ever had the time?

Heffie noticed my puzzlement. 'While you was asleep all

day, 'e rescued Lash's body from a pauper's grave – don' know how – and sent word and money to the Burtons for a proper service and burial. That crowd were ever so grateful.' I glanced at Holmes in surprise. Few realized the deep generosity hidden under his sharp exterior.

'And I'm grateful too,' Heffie went on. 'I 'ad taken a liking to that little fellow. 'E had real promise, 'e did. 'E might have been another me,' she said.

'Doubtful,' said Holmes, his eyes still closed. 'There's something for you over there, Watson,' he said, 'with a note.' He waved an arm towards a table next to the door. There sat a shiny new Remington typewriter, with a white envelope affixed to it.

'Read it to us, doctor,' said Holmes.

I crossed over to it and opened it. It was from Miss Emily Ferndale. I read:

'*Mr Holmes and Dr Watson,*

'*In addition to your payment, enclosed, I wish to give you this American typewriter, which I believe may benefit Dr Watson in recounting your tales. I have altered completely the approach I am taking to help the women of the factories, and that is to keep as many of them* out *of the factories as I can. I have funded an expansion of literacy programmes in the East End and opened four typing schools for women throughout London. It is but a drop in the ocean but may, I hope, grow.*

'*Thank you again.*

'*Sincerely—E. F.*'

Well, that was welcome news. I had no doubt that Miss Ferndale would be successful in her efforts. As for the typewriter, I preferred my pen but might give this machine a try some time in the future. Holmes rose to get a glass of water, and just then the bell sounded below. Moments later, Neptune Burton and young Clarence Wandley stood at the door to our sitting room.

The gelatinous Clarence, clothed today in sea-green velvet, took in the group of us. He slunk in and, weaving about, said in his softly sibilant voice, 'Good day, lovely gentlemen and lady. We are here to offer thanks.' Without invitation, he stretched out upon Holmes's settee, as though he owned the place. Neptune remained in the doorway, smiling awkwardly.

My temper flared. In the aftermath of our adventure, a burning question had come to mind. At the risk of destroying the bonhomie, I rose and challenged our visitor. 'Neptune Burton, answer me this! Was it not you and a friend who attacked us in the alley?'

'Oh, sit down, Watson. Of course it was,' said Holmes. 'He wanted to scare us off.' He turned to Neptune. 'Formidable fellow you brought along, Mr Burton.'

'My cousin is a professional wrestler.'

'I warrant you two could easily have killed us. But you needed to buy time to get Clarence out of the city and hide him away from all these malevolent forces.'

Neptune Burton nodded.

'Consider, Watson: based on Clarence's artwork, his arrest was imminent. And Mr Burton here had reason to believe that his friend, slight of build and with his uncommon appearance and way of expressing himself, might not survive incarceration. An opinion which I share, by the way.'

Clarence rose and took Neptune's arm affectionately. 'He sent me to Dorset to hide away with friends.'

Heffie and Dr Sheehan regarded all this with some confusion.

'And what happened to your pet snakes?' I asked.

'Safe with another friend,' said Neptune. 'The police would have killed them all. Except for little Ambrose – he got away from me as I attempted to gather them up. I don't know what happened to him.'

'With a name like that, he no doubt survived,' said Holmes. At the group's puzzlement, he added for their erudition, 'Ambrose means "immortal".'

'Enough of this, Neptune,' said Clarence impatiently. 'Let's do the deed. We have a ssss-surprise for you, Mr Holmes. A gift.'

Holmes and I exchanged a look of alarm. A *live* gift?

Neptune, on cue, stepped back into the hall and brought in an enormous oil painting of a giant cobra, hood open, fangs visible, ready to strike – all in bilious greens and golds. I recognized Clarence's inimitable style.

A stunned silence followed.

Neptune stood awkwardly holding the painting. Clarence Wandley cast his eyes around the sitting room walls. 'There, over the fireplace, I think,' he said. And before Holmes could respond, Neptune took down our framed etching of a Swiss waterfall, set it aside, and hung in its place the expertly rendered but utterly horrific image.

There was a pause as the artist looked from one to another, awaiting a reaction.

Heffie, Dr Sheehan and I said nothing.

'That is quite something,' Holmes said eventually. 'I shall treasure it always.'

Clarence had got what he came for and leaped from the settee. At the door, the young artist paused on the threshold. 'My sister Kate sends her regards. We have split the estate and are selling it. She has bought a tiny château in France. And I have bought the house next door to ours. Our neighbour decided suddenly to move.'

The daffodil lady, I thought.

'And now we shall build our own miniature château in Chelsea! Good day! And . . . enjoy!'

They left. Holmes strode to the fireplace and removed the snake painting. He thrust the monstrosity into the hall, face against the wall, and closed the door. I took up the original print and rehung it above the fireplace.

'What an interesting life you lead,' said Dr Sheehan. He frowned at me. 'But you have been entirely reckless with your hands, Dr Watson. It is a good thing you are not a surgeon,' said he, 'or a musician.' Noting Holmes's violin in a corner, he smiled. 'Who plays the violin here?'

''E does,' said Heffie, cheerfully, nodding towards my friend. 'Won't you play somethin', Mr 'olmes?'

'I am not a performing seal,' he said, crossly.

'Just a few notes?' said Heffie with a smile. 'Please.'

'I am a music lover, too,' said Dr Sheehan.

There was a pause. Heffie and the doctor sat down, side

by side on the divan, facing Holmes expectantly. How could he disappoint this audience?

'Oh, come on, Holmes.' I said. 'Grace us with a few notes.'

'All right. But afterwards, one of you must name the composer and the title.'

Holmes picked up his violin and began playing a lively air. It was unfamiliar to me, but quite pleasing. He set down his instrument and eyed the group.

Heffie smiled but shrugged her shoulders. 'I don' know,' she said to Holmes. 'But you can broaden my 'orizons.'

'It is . . . Mendelssohn, I think,' said Sheehan. 'Am I right?'

Holmes smiled and waved his bow at us. 'Very good, doctor. But which song?'

None of us knew the answer.

Holmes laughed. 'Isn't it obvious? It was "Ye Spotted Snake". From *A Midsummer Night's Dream*.'

We laughed along with him. 'Again, please, Mr 'olmes,' said Heffie.

As Holmes played the lilting tune again, I reflected on the lingering horror of this serpentine, twisted case. And while Kate Wandley may have put me in mind of Shakespeare's ass-headed faerie queen, she was no villain, and Holmes had, at least, rescued her.

But what shall remain vivid in my memory forever was the sheer number of murders Holmes had untangled. There were no fewer than ten! I reflected upon the gruesome list: first, the tragic Jane Wandley, the long-ago murder of

Neptune's mother and baby sister, the poisoning of the villainous Honora Wandley, the shopkeeper and his wife, the tattooist Yamamoto, Sir James, Callum, and poor Lash. And, though killed in self-defence and by Holmes himself, Peter Oliver brought the tally of violent deaths to eleven, making this perhaps the single deadliest investigation of Sherlock Holmes's career.

Later, sitting alone with Holmes before the fire, I mused that I would be happy never to encounter a snake again. 'The Speckled Band' some years ago, and 'The Serpent Under' just now, were more than enough reptilian adventures to last a lifetime.

THE END

For interesting facts and pictures pertaining
to the people and places in this book,
please visit the author's website
www.macbird.com

Acknowledgements

Thanks above all to my brilliant husband Alan Kay, unerringly kind, witty and supportive, even throughout his many trials. Thanks to my always delightful editor at HarperCollins, David Brawn. To my new and encouraging agents Charlie Campbell and Sam Edenborough, and to those who helped me batter this writing manuscript into submission – the very cool Dana Isaacson, but also the Oxnardians, and the Trans-Atlantic Scribes, Kieran Devaney, as well as my tough betas – Catherine, Charles, Sophia, Robert and Dennis.

Thanks to two literal knights, Professor Sir David Warrell, herpetologist extraordinaire, and to Sir Nicolas Black, medical historian, who weighed in on key research. Neither gentleman is to blame for the few liberties I took (though none to rival Sir Arthur's milk-drinking, trained serpent!) – see my annotations at www.macbird.com.

Thanks also to Patrick, Rosa, Ian and Tony, who keep the Kay/MacBird team upright, and to Gerber and Co. for minding the store. Thanks to Leunora and Natalie who keep us in line and supplied with cake, and to my new friends at the Hampstead Players, especially Matt Sargent, who unexpectedly lit up my life.

Special thanks to Ryan Johnson who made the last two years of work on this novel possible at all.

About the Author

Born in San Francisco, Bonnie MacBird now lives in London, just off Baker Street. She has degrees in music and film from Stanford and has been a passionate Holmes fan since the age of ten. Prior to writing novels, she spent thirty years in Hollywood as a development executive, screenwriter (original writer of *TRON*), Emmy winning producer, and actor.

MacBird is a Baker Street Irregular, on the Council of the Sherlock Holmes Society of London, and a member of many Sherlockian scions. Her first Holmes novel *Art in the Blood* was translated into seventeen languages and began her series, of which this novel is the sixth. They can be read in any order, and the author invites readers to check out her online annotations for a deeper dive into the facts behind the stories.

Visit her at www.macbird.com.